PRIZE STORIES 1967:
THE O. HENRY AWARDS

Prize Stories 1967:

THE O. HENRY AWARDS

Edited and with an Introduction by
WILLIAM ABRAHAMS

Doubleday & Company, Inc., Garden City, New York
1967

CONTENTS

PUBLISHER'S NOTE

The present volume is the forty-seventh in the O. Henry Memorial Award series. No collections appeared in 1952 and 1953, when the continuity of the series was interrupted by the death of Herschel Brickell, who had been the editor for ten years.

In 1918 the Society of Arts and Sciences met to vote upon a monument to the master of the short story, O. Henry. They decided that this memorial should be in the form of two prizes for the best short stories published by American authors in American magazines during the year 1919. From this beginning, the memorial developed into an annual anthology of outstanding short stories by American authors appearing in American magazines, published, with the exception of the years mentioned above, by Doubleday & Company, Inc. Blanche Colton Williams, one of the founders of the awards, was editor from 1919 to 1932; Harry Hansen from 1933 to 1940; Herschel Brickell from 1941 to 1951; Paul Engle from 1954 to 1959 with Hanson Martin co-editor in the years 1954 to 1956; Mary Stegner in 1960; Richard Poirier from 1961 to 1966, with assistance from and co-editorship with William Abrahams from 1964 to 1966. William Abrahams becomes editor of the series with the present volume.

Doubleday has also published First-Prize Stories from the O. Henry Memorial Awards 1919–1966.

The stories chosen for this volume were published in the period from the summer of 1965 to the summer of 1966. A list of the magazines consulted appears at the back of the book. The choice of stories and the selection of prize winners are exclusively the responsibility of the editor.

INTRODUCTION: PRIZE STORIES 1967

Here are sixteen short stories chosen from among the thousand or more published in American magazines this year. Six of the sixteen appeared in magazines of large circulation; ten in the so-called "little magazines." The disproportion, which I hasten to point out is not the result of prejudice or preconceptions on the part of the editor, is significant enough to deserve comment. At the least, it reminds us of the debt that dedicated readers and writers of short stories continue to owe the "little magazines." By dedicated readers I mean those who read stories out of preference, as others read articles, who actively like them and seek them out and care enough to discriminate between the good, bad, and merely mediocre. By dedicated writers I mean those who *must* write, "the addicts," as Doris Lessing has recently called them, for whom the form is not only congenial but a necessity. "Some writers I know," Mrs. Lessing observed, "have stopped writing short stories because as they say 'There is no market for them.' Others, like myself, the addicts, go on, and I suspect would go on even if there really wasn't any home for them but a private drawer." Yet there must be very few writers, however dedicated or addicted, who would not prefer to have their stories published. As homes go, the "little magazines" have a good deal to offer. Suppose, then, that they did not exist? Suppose that in one year they were all together to cease publication, having run afoul of creditors, having lost the good will of a foundation or a patron or a board of regents, or for whatever reason—the effect upon the American short story would be immediate and lamentable.

Unfortunately one needn't resort to fantasy to discover in the current state of short story publication cause for alarm. It is disheartening to contrast the great expectations of only a few years ago with the anti-climactic realities of the present. How bravely, for example, certain of the magazines of largest circulation—those designed to please an audience of millions with a variety of instructive "features"—declared themselves hospitable to "quality fiction," and went on to feature an occasional excellent story, and even continue to do so, although the interval between such occasions widens. But by now it is quite clear that while these magazines might speak of "quality fiction," what they really wanted were "quality writers," prestigious names to brighten a cover, however much or little their stories would brighten the actual contents of the magazine itself. This notion that "quality writers," rather than the slick, shallow entertainers of a more innocent age, are names worth dropping in public is very much a phenomenon of the 1960s. It is another aspect of that much-touted cultural explosion that has manifested itself everywhere, from the supermarkets to the highest places, so that it is permissible, for example, to confuse Robert Lowell with Matthew Arnold since both are known to be O.K. names even by those who patently haven't read them, and in any case it's the gesture that counts. Thus it came about that these success-oriented magazines, kitchen-centered for women and bedroom-centered for men, committed themselves to a monthly cultural gesture, only to discover that first-rate writers will always be in short supply, nor are they likely to produce first-rate stories on demand, month after month. The solution resorted to was characteristic of the culture explosion: to promote a large number of second-raters to more imposing status—on to the very cover—and to palm off their stories as the real thing. It is easier, though, to confer status than it is to discover merit where little or none exists, and so, for the past year or two, a literary equivalent of Gresham's Law has been in operation. The brief halcyon period of excellence is giving way to a soporific mediocrity, not made any the more tolerable by its air of knowingness in matters of sex. (The taboos are down everywhere, and as one reads yet another swinging story of making it and hating it or loving it, one rather wishes that they weren't.)

This reversion to type among the mammoth monthlies may be thought regrettable, but too much importance needn't be attached to it. Mediocre stories are always with us (even in the little magazines that profess the highest standards) for truly good stories aren't always easy to find, and at least it must be said in behalf of these mammoths that they are willing to *publish* short stories: for better or worse they serve as a market, and from time to time a story of genuine merit will appear in their pages. No, the serious cause for alarm lies in the indifference, or even the hostility, toward the short story that is evident in a number of magazines of large circulation (and in certain of the "little magazines" too) that used to publish fiction regularly, but now no longer do so.

Let us say that Editor "A" of Magazine "X" has a certain number
of pages to be filled each month. If he allots a minimum number of
those pages to fiction, and if the same meager allotment of space
regularly occurs, I think it is fair to say that Editor "A" and Magazine
"X" are hostile, or indifferent, to the short story. This is the prevail-
ing situation generally, and it explains why some of those writers of
whom Mrs. Lessing was speaking, the non-addicts, have stopped
writing short stories: there is no market for them. Editor "B" and
Magazine "Y" would agree that what's wanted now are articles, not
stories, articles of all sorts, shapes, and subjects, the more articles the
better, and by the same token, fewer stories.

We are living in the heyday of the article. At the present time
there's hardly a magazine, whatever its category—from the miniscule
to the mammoth—that doesn't offer its readers articles in abun-
dance. They are wanted, and in a way that stories are not. Perhaps
in an anxiety-ridden age like ours, when certainties aren't easily
come by—"this iron time of doubts, disputes, distractions, fears"—
there is a peculiar reassurance in the factuality of the article.

Consider the article: it describes brilliantly; it analyzes convinc-
ingly; it informs you, and at the same time never asks that you be
implicated in its situation; it makes no demand except to be read—
once. Reading an article is like looking through a pane of glass, never
into a mirror.

Obviously this is very different from what the short story does, and
demands of us, but it is not my purpose here to analyze, or compare
and contrast, or evaluate the story and the article, to the disadvan-
tage of the one and the glorification of the other. The two forms
are so different, their functions so different, that there ought to be a
place for both. But apparently this is not possible. In far too many
magazines, the blatantly popular, the anxiously middlebrow, and the
aggressively intellectual alike, the preponderance of space is given
to articles—the problem of Sophia Loren, the problem of Lyndon
Johnson, the problem of Marshall McLuhan. Meanwhile the number of stories such magazines publish grows fewer each year: one can
foresee a time when even the token gesture will no longer be made,
on the palpably false pretext that good stories aren't being written.
(Here I would single out an honorable and brilliant exception, *The
New Yorker,* which continues to publish vastly more short fiction
than any other magazine in this country or England, some of it
trivial and anecdotal, but a good deal more of it at a remarkably

high level of quality. Flogging *New Yorker* fiction has been a favorite sport for years, going back—I suspect—to the second week of the magazine's history, and much of the criticism is valid enough: that there are areas and styles of experience to which the editors are obdurately unresponsive, and others, such as memoirs of happy but eccentric childhoods, upon which they dote excessively. Yet all editors have their limitations, and I should think editors of certain other high-minded but less affluent magazines would welcome *The New Yorker's* lapses of judgment, for it makes available to them stories they would not otherwise have a chance to see.)

I repeat: the passion for articles has led to a stringent decrease in space allotted to fiction. And such space as there is—pitifully little —goes usually to writers of established reputation and performance. I would add, quite properly so—a man oughtn't to spend years mastering his craft and then be told there is no market for him. But it means that the opportunities in the magazines of large circulation for new or unknown writers have been drastically curtailed. (*The Atlantic* is the only national magazine that makes it a matter of publicly announced policy to publish stories of new writers, and does so each month.) It also means that much of the fiction that one reads in the larger magazines is more distinguished for competence than originality. Overfamiliar in style, predictable in content, it has been professionally crafted to "the mystical moment of dullness." A middle-aged writer of some prominence, who has yet to be represented in the O. Henry collection, complained not long ago that young writers were favored here—hence his omission. I can assure the gentleman that this is not the case, even though I discover that this year the first three prize-winners, Joyce Carol Oates, Donald Barthelme, and Jonathan Strong, are all under thirty-five, a fact to which no more and no less importance need be attached than that a few years ago the first prize was awarded to Katherine Anne Porter. All that is looked for is an authentic talent, and a willingness to work in territory of one's own.

But the vogue for the article has led certain gifted writers to abandon the territory of fiction altogether. Persuaded that there is no market for short stories, or perhaps having lost interest in them, they have begun to write articles themselves. The results are often impressive and sometimes quite odd. We are told that a new, hybrid form is being developed; that out of the fusion of a heightened literary sensibility and a scrupulous passion for fact will come the art of the future. Perhaps. Meanwhile, contemplating the situation as it is at present, let us praise, cherish, and encourage the addicts of the short story, those who write them, those who read them, and the magazines that publish them.

WILLIAM ABRAHAMS

PRIZE STORIES 1967:
THE O. HENRY AWARDS

JOYCE CAROL OATES is the author of two collections of short stories, *By the North Gate*, and *Upon the Sweeping Flood*, and her stories have appeared in many American magazines. Her first novel, *With Shuddering Fall* was published in 1964. The next will be *A Garden of Earthly Delights*. Previous stories by Mrs. Oates have been included in *The Best American Short Stories* and in *Prize Stories: The O. Henry Awards* for 1963, 1964 and 1965.

In the Region of Ice

S ISTER IRENE was a tall, deft woman in her early thirties. What one could see of her face made a striking impression—serious hard gray eyes, a long slender nose, a face waxen with thought. Seen at the right time, from the right angle, she was almost handsome; in her past teaching positions she had drawn a little upon the fact of her being young and brilliant and also a nun, but she was beginning to grow out of that.

This was a new university and an entirely new world. She had heard—of course it was true—that the Jesuit administration of this school had hired her at the last moment to save money and to head off the appointment of a man of dubious religious commitment. She had prayed for the necessary energy to get her through this first semester. She had no trouble with teaching itself; once she stood before a classroom she felt herself capable of anything. It was the world immediately outside the classroom that confused and alarmed her, though she let none of this show—the cynicism of her colleagues, the indifference of many of the students, and above all, the looks she got that told her nothing much would be expected of her because she was a nun. This took energy, strength. At times she had the idea that she was on trial and that the excuses she made to herself about her discomfort were only the common excuses made by guilty people. But in front of a class she had no time to worry about herself or the conflicts in her mind. She became, once and for all, a figure existing only for the benefit of others, an instrument by which facts were communicated.

About two weeks after the semester began, Sister Irene noticed a new student in her class. He was slight and fair-haired, and his face was blank, but not blank by accident, blank on purpose, suppressed and restricted into a dumbness that looked hysterical. She was prepared for him before he raised his hand, and when she saw his arm jerk, as if he had at last lost control of it, she nodded to him without hesitation.

"Sister, how can this be reconciled with Shakespeare's vision in *Hamlet?* How can these opposing views be in the same mind?"

Students glanced at him, mildly surprised. He did not belong in the class, and this was mysterious, but his manner was urgent and blind.

"There is no need to reconcile opposing views," Sister Irene said, leaning forward against the podium. "In one play Shakespeare suggests one vision, in another play another; the plays are not simultaneous creations, and even if they were, we never demand a logical—"

"We must demand a logical consistency," the young man said. "The idea of education itself is predicated upon consistency, order, sanity—"

He had interrupted her, and she hardened her face against him— for his sake, not her own, since she did not really care. But he noticed nothing. "Please see me after class," she said.

After class the young man hurried up to her.

"Sister Irene, I hope you didn't mind my visiting today. I'd heard some things, interesting things," he said. He stared at her, and something in her face allowed him to smile. "I—could we talk in your office? Do you have time?"

They walked down to her office. Sister Irene sat at her desk, and the young man sat facing her; for a moment they were self-conscious and silent.

"Well, I suppose you know—I'm a Jew," he said.

Sister Irene stared at him. "Yes?" she said.

"What am I doing at a Catholic university, huh?" He grinned. "That's what you want to know."

She made a vague movement of her hand to show that she had no thoughts on this, nothing at all, but he seemed not to catch it. He was sitting on the edge of the straight-backed chair. She saw that he was young but did not really look young. There were harsh lines on either side of his mouth, as if he had misused that youthful mouth somehow. His skin was almost as pale as hers, his eyes were dark and somehow not quite in focus. He looked at her and through her and around her, as his voice surrounded them both. His voice was a little shrill at times.

"Listen, I did the right thing today—visiting your class! God, what a lucky accident it was; some jerk mentioned you, said you were a good teacher—I thought, what a laugh! These people know about good teachers, here? But yes, listen, yes, I'm not kidding—you are good. I mean that."

Sister Irene frowned. "I don't quite understand what all this means."

He smiled and waved aside her formality, as if he knew better. "Listen, I got my B.A. at Columbia, then I came back here to this crappy city. I mean, I did it on purpose, I wanted to come back. I wanted to. I have my reasons for doing things. I'm on a three-thousand-dollar fellowship," he said, and waited for that to impress her. "You know, I could have gone almost anywhere with that fellowship, and I came back home here—my home's in the city—and enrolled here. This was last year. This is my second year. I'm working on a thesis, I mean I was, my master's thesis—but the hell with that. What I want to ask you is this: Can I enroll in your class, is it too late? We have to get special permission if we're late."

Sister Irene felt something nudging her, some uneasiness in him that was pleading with her not to be offended by his abrupt, familiar manner. He seemed to be promising another self, a better self, as if his fair, childish, almost cherubic face were doing tricks to distract her from what his words said.

"Are you in English studies?" she asked.

"I was in history. Listen," he said, and his mouth did something odd, drawing itself down into a smile that made the lines about it deepen like knives, "listen, they kicked me out."

He sat back, watching her. He crossed his legs. He took out a package of cigarettes and offered her one. Sister Irene shook her head, staring at his hands. They were small and stubby and might have belonged to a ten-year-old, and the nails were a strange near-violet color. It took him a while to extract a cigarette.

"Yeah, kicked me out. What do you think of that?"

"I don't understand."

"My master's thesis was coming along beautifully, and then this bastard—I mean, excuse me, this professor, I won't pollute your office with his name—he started making criticisms, he said some things were unacceptable, he—" The boy leaned forward and hunched his narrow shoulders in a parody of secrecy. "We had an argument. I told him some frank things, things only a broadminded person could hear about himself. That takes courage, right? He didn't have it! He kicked me out of the master's program, so now I'm coming into English. Literature is greater than history; European history is one big pile of garbage. Skyhigh. Filth and rotting corpses, right? Aristotle says that poetry is higher than history; he's right; in your class today I suddenly realized that this is my field, Shakespeare, only Shakespeare is—"

Sister Irene guessed that he was going to say that only Shakespeare was equal to him, and she caught the moment of recognition and hesitation, the half-raised arm, the keen, frowning forehead, the narrowed eyes; then he thought better of it and did not end the sentence. "The students in your class are mainly negligible, I can tell you that. You're new here, and I've been here a year—I would have finished my studies last year but my father got sick, he was hospitalized, I couldn't take exams and it was a mess—but I'll make it through English in one year or drop dead. I can do it, I can do anything. I'll take six courses at once—" He broke off, breathless. Sister Irene tried to smile. "All right then, it's settled? You'll let me in? Have I missed anything so far?"

He had no idea of the rudeness of his question. Sister Irene, feeling suddenly exhausted, said, "I'll give you a syllabus of the course."

"Fine! Wonderful!"

He got to his feet eagerly. He looked through the schedule, muttering to himself, making favorable noises. It struck Sister Irene that she was making a mistake to let him in. There were these moments when one had to make an intelligent decision . . . But she was sympathetic with him, yes. She was sympathetic with something about him.

She found out his name the next day: Allen Weinstein.

After this, she came to her Shakespeare class with a sense of excitement. It became clear to her at once that Weinstein was the most intelligent student in the class. Until he had enrolled, she had not understood what was lacking, a mind that could appreciate her own. Within a week his jagged, protean mind had alienated the other students, and though he sat in the center of the class, he seemed totally alone, encased by a miniature world of his own. When he spoke of the "frenetic humanism of the High Renaissance," Sister Irene dreaded the raised eyebrows and mocking smiles of the other students, who no longer bothered to look at Weinstein. She wanted to defend him, but she never did, because there was something rude and dismal about his knowledge; he used it like a weapon, talking passionately of Nietzsche and Goethe and Freud until Sister Irene would be forced to close discussion.

In meditation, alone, she often thought of him. When she tried to talk about him to a young nun, Sister Carlotta, everything sounded gross. "But no, he's an excellent student," she insisted. "I'm very grateful to have him in class. It's just that . . . he thinks ideas are real." Sister Carlotta, who loved literature also, had been forced to teach grade-school arithmetic for the last four years. That might have been why she said, a little sharply, "You don't think ideas are real?"

Sister Irene acquiesced with a smile, but of course she did not think so: only reality is real.

When Weinstein did not show up for class on the day the first paper was due, Sister Irene's heart sank, and the sensation was somehow a familiar one. She began her lecture and kept waiting for the door to open and for him to hurry noisily back to his seat, grinning an apology toward her—but nothing happened.

If she had been deceived by him, she made herself think angrily, it was as a teacher and not as a woman. He had promised her nothing.

Weinstein appeared the next day near the steps of the liberal arts building. She heard someone running behind her, a breathless exclamation: "Sister Irene!" She turned and saw him, panting and grinning in embarrassment. He wore a dark-blue suit with a necktie, and he looked, despite his childish face, like a little old man; there was something oddly precarious and fragile about him. "Sister Irene, I owe you an apology, right?" He raised his eyebrows and smiled a sad, forlorn, yet irritatingly conspiratorial smile. "The first paper—not in on time, and I know what your rules are . . . You won't accept late papers, I know—that's good discipline, I'll do that when I teach, too. But, unavoidably, I was unable to come to school yesterday. There are many—many—" He gulped for breath, and Sister Irene had the startling sense of seeing the real Weinstein stare out at her, a terrified prisoner behind the confident voice. "There are many complications in family life. Perhaps you are unaware—I mean—"

She did not like him, but she felt this sympathy, something tugging and nagging at her the way her parents had competed for her love, so many years ago. They had been whining, weak people, and out of their wet need for affection, the girl she had been (her name was Yvonne) had emerged stronger than either of them, contemptuous of tears because she had seen so many. But Weinstein was different; he was not simply weak, perhaps he was not weak at all, but his strength was confused and hysterical. She felt her customary rigidity as a teacher begin to falter. "You may turn your paper in today, if you have it," she said, frowning.

Weinstein's mouth jerked into an incredulous grin. "Wonderful! Marvelous!" he said. "You are very understanding, Sister Irene, I must say. I must say . . . I didn't expect, really . . ." He was fumbling in a shabby old briefcase for the paper. Sister Irene waited. She was prepared for another of his excuses, certain that he did not have the paper, when he suddenly straightened up and handed her something. "Here! I took the liberty of writing thirty pages instead of just fifteen," he said. He was obviously quite excited; his cheeks were mottled pink and white. "You may disagree violently with my interpretation—I expect you to, in fact I'm counting on it—but let me warn you, I have the exact proof, precise, specific proof, right here in the play itself!" He was thumping at a book, his voice growing louder and shriller. Sister Irene, startled, wanted to put her hand over his mouth and soothe him.

"Look," he said breathlessly, "may I talk with you? I have a class now I hate, I loathe, I can't bear to sit through! Can I talk with you instead?"

Because she was nervous, she stared at the title page of the paper: "Erotic Melodies in *Romeo and Juliet*" by Allen Weinstein, Jr.

"All right?" he said. "Can we walk around here? Is it all right? I've been anxious to talk with you about some things you said in class."

She was reluctant, but he seemed not to notice. They walked slowly along the shaded campus paths. Weinstein did all the talking, of course, and Sister Irene recognized nothing in his cascade of words that she had mentioned in class. "The humanist must be committed to the totality of life," he said passionately. "This is the failing one finds everywhere in the academic world! I found it in New York and I found it here and I'm no ingénu, I don't go around with my mouth hanging open—I'm experienced, look, I've been to Europe, I've lived in Rome! I went everywhere in Europe except Germany, I don't talk about Germany . . . Sister Irene, think of the significant men in the last century, the men who've changed the world! Jews, right? Marx, Freud, Einstein! Not that I believe Marx, Marx is a madman . . . and Freud, no, my sympathies are with spiritual humanism. I believe that the Jewish race is the exclusive . . . the exclusive, what's the word, the exclusive means by which humanism will be extended . . . Humanism begins by excluding the Jew, and now," he said, with a high, surprised laugh, "the Jew will perfect it. After the Nazis, only the Jew is authorized to understand humanism, its limitations and its possibilities. So, I say that the humanist is committed to life in its totality and not just to his profession! The religious person is totally religious, he *is* his religion! What else? I recognize in you a humanist and a religious person—"

But he did not seem to be talking to her, or even looking at her. "Here, read this," he said. "I wrote it last night." It was a long free-verse poem, typed on a typewriter whose ribbon was worn out. "There's this trouble with my father, a wonderful man, a lovely man, but his health—his strength is fading, do you see? What must it be to him to see his son growing up? I mean, I'm a man now, he's getting old, weak, his health is bad—it's hell, right? I sympathize with him. I'd do anything for him, I'd cut open my veins, anything for a father—right? That's why I wasn't in school yesterday," he said, and his voice dropped for the last sentence, as if he had been dragged back to earth by a fact.

Sister Irene tried to read the poem, then pretended to read it. A jumble of words dealing with "life" and "death" and "darkness" and "love." "What do you think?" Weinstein said nervously, trying to read it over her shoulder and crowding against her.

"It's very . . . passionate," Sister Irene said.

This was the right comment; he took the poem back from her in silence, his face flushed with excitement. "Here, at this school, I have few people to talk with. I haven't shown anyone else that poem." He looked at her with his dark, intense eyes, and Sister Irene felt them focus upon her. She was terrified at what he was trying to do—he was trying to force her into a human relationship.

"Thank you for your paper," she said, turning away.

When he came the next day, ten minutes late, he was haughty and disdainful. He had nothing to say and sat with his arms folded. Sister Irene took back with her to the convent a feeling of betrayal and confusion. She had been hurt. It was absurd, and yet— She spent too much time thinking about him, as if he were somehow a kind of crystallization of her own loneliness; but she had no right to think so much of him. She did not want to think of him or of her loneliness. But Weinstein did so much more than think of his predicament, he embodied it, he acted it out, and that was perhaps why he fascinated her. It was as if he were doing a dance for her, a dance of shame and agony and delight, and so long as he did it, she was safe. She felt embarrassment for him, but also anxiety; she wanted to protect him. When the dean of the graduate school questioned her about Weinstein's work, she insisted that he was an "excellent" student, though she knew the dean had not wanted to hear that.

She prayed for guidance, she spent hours on her devotions, she was closer to her vocation than she had been for some years. Life at the convent became tinged with unreality, a misty distortion that took its tone from the glowering skies of the city at night, identical smokestacks ranged against the clouds and giving to the sky the excrement of the populated and successful earth. This city was not her city, this world was not her world. She felt no pride in knowing this, it was a fact. The little convent was not like an island in the center of this noisy world, but rather a kind of hole or crevice the world did not bother with, something of no interest. The convent's rhythm of life had nothing to do with the world's rhythm, it did not violate or alarm it in any way. Sister Irene tried to draw together the fragments of her life and synthesize them somehow in her vocation as a nun: she was a nun, she was recognized as a nun and had given herself happily to that life, she had a name, a place, she had dedicated her superior intelligence to the Church, she worked without pay and without expecting gratitude, she had given up pride, she did not think of herself but only of her work and her vocation, she did not think of anything external to these, she saturated herself daily in the knowledge that she was involved in the mystery of Christianity. A daily terror attended this knowledge, however, for she sensed herself being drawn by that student, that Jewish boy, into a relationship she was not ready for. She wanted to cry out in fear that she was being forced into the role of a Christian, and what did that mean? What could her studies tell her? What could the other nuns tell her? She was alone, no one could help, he was making her into a Christian, and to her that was a mystery, a thing of terror, something others slipped on the way they slipped on their clothes, casually and thoughtlessly, but to her a magnificent and terrifying wonder.

For days she carried Weinstein's paper, marked A, around with her; he did not come to class. One day she checked with the graduate office and was told that Weinstein had called in to say his father was ill and he would not be able to attend classes for a while. "He's strange, I remember him," the secretary said. "He missed all his exams last spring and made a lot of trouble. He was in and out of here every day."

So there was no more of Weinstein for a while, and Sister Irene stopped expecting him to hurry into class. Then, one morning, she found a letter from him in her mailbox.

He had printed it in black ink, very carefully, as if he had not trusted handwriting. The return address was in bold letters that, like his voice, tried to grab onto her: Birchcrest Manor. Somewhere north of the city. "Dear Sister Irene," the block letters said, "I am doing well here and have time for reading and relaxing. The Manor is delightful. My doctor here is an excellent, intelligent man who has time for me unlike my former doctor. If you have time, you might drop in on my father, who worries about me too much, I think, and explain to him what my condition is. He doesn't seem to understand. I feel about this new life the way that boy, what's his name, in *Measure for Measure*, feels about the prospects of a different life; you remember what he says to his sister when she visits him in prison, how he is looking forward to an escape into another world. Perhaps you could *explain* this to my father and he would stop worrying." The letter ended with the father's name and address, in letters that were just a little too big. Sister Irene, walking slowly down the corridor as she read the letter, felt her eyes cloud over with tears. She was cold with fear, it was something she had never experienced before. She knew what Weinstein was trying to tell her, and the

desperation of his attempt made it all the more pathetic; he did not
deserve this, why did God allow him to suffer so?

She read through Claudio's speech to his sister, in *Measure for
Measure*:

> *Ay, but to die, and go we know not where;*
> *To lie in cold obstruction and to rot;*
> *This sensible warm motion to become*
> *A kneaded clod; and the delighted spirit*
> *To bathe in fiery floods, or to reside*
> *In thrilling region of thick-ribbèd ice,*
> *To be imprison'd in the viewless winds*
> *And blown with restless violence round about*
> *The pendent world; or to be worse than worst*
> *Of those that lawless and incertain thought*
> *Imagines howling! 'Tis too horrible!*
> *The weariest and most loathèd worldly life*
> *That age, ache, penury, and imprisonment*
> *Can lay on nature is a paradise*
> *To what we fear of death.*

Sister Irene called the father's number that day. "Allen Weinstein
residence, who may I say is calling?" a woman said, bored. "May I
speak to Mr. Weinstein? It's urgent—about his son," Sister Irene
said. There was a pause at the other end. "You want to talk to his
mother, maybe?" the woman said. "His mother? Yes, his mother,
then. Please. It's very important."

She talked with this strange, unsuspected woman, a disembodied
voice that suggested absolutely no face, and insisted upon going
over that afternoon. The woman was nervous, but Sister Irene, who
was a university professor after all, knew enough to hide her own
nervousness. She kept waiting for the woman to say, "Yes, Allen has
mentioned you . . ." but nothing happened.

She persuaded Sister Carlotta to ride over with her. This urgency
of hers was something they were all amazed by. They hadn't suspected that the set of her gray eyes could change to this blurred, dis-
tracted alarm, this sense of mission that seemed to have come to her
from nowhere. Sister Irene drove across the city in the late afternoon traffic, with the high whining noises from residential streets
where trees were being sawed down in pieces. She understood now

the secret, sweet wildness that Christ must have felt, giving himself for man, dying for the billions of men who would never know of him and never understand the sacrifice. For the first time she approached the realization of that great act. In her troubled mind the city traffic was jumbled and yet oddly coherent, an image of the world that was always out of joint with what was happening in it, its inner history struggling with its external spectacle. This sacrifice of Christ's, so mysterious and legendary now, almost lost in time—it was that by which Christ transcended both God and man at one moment, more than man because of his fate to do what no other man could do, and more than God because no god could suffer as he did. She felt a flicker of something close to madness.

She drove nervously, uncertainly, afraid of missing the street and afraid of finding it too, for while one part of her rushed forward to confront these people who had betrayed their son, another part of her would have liked nothing so much as to be waiting as usual for the summons to dinner, safe in her room . . . When she found the street and turned onto it, she was in a state of breathless excitement. Here, lawns were bright green and marred with only a few leaves, magically clean, and the houses were enormous and pompous, a mixture of styles: ranch houses, colonial houses, French country houses, white-bricked wonders with curving glass and clumps of birch trees somehow encircled by white concrete. Sister Irene stared as if she had blundered into another world. This was a kind of heaven, and she was too shabby for it.

The Weinstein's house was the strangest one of all: it looked like a small Alpine lodge, with an inverted-V-shaped front entrance. Sister Irene drove up the black-topped driveway and let the car slow to a stop; she told Sister Carlotta she would not be long.

At the door she was met by Weinstein's mother, a small nervous woman with hands like her son's. "Come in, come in," the woman said. She had once been beautiful, that was clear, but now in missing beauty she was not handsome or even attractive but looked ruined and perplexed, the misshapen swelling of her white-blond professionally set hair like a cap lifting up from her surprised face. "He'll be right in. Allen?" she called, "our visitor is here." They went into the living room. There was a grand piano at one end and an organ at the other. In between were scatterings of brilliant modern furniture, in conversational groups, and several puffed-up white rugs on the polished floor. Sister Irene could not stop shivering.

"Professor, it's so strange, but let me say when the phone rang I had a feeling—I had a feeling," the woman said, with damp eyes. Sister Irene sat, and the woman hovered about her. "Should I call you Professor? We don't—you know—we don't understand the technicalities that go with— Allen, my son, wanted to go here to the Catholic school; I told my husband why not? Why fight? It's the thing these days, they do anything they want for knowledge. And he had to come home, you know. He couldn't take care of himself in New York, that was the beginning of the trouble— Should I call you Professor?"

"You can call me Sister Irene."

"Sister Irene?" the woman said, touching her throat in awe, as if something intimate and unexpected had happened.

Then Weinstein's father appeared, hurrying. He took long impatient strides. Sister Irene stared at him and in that instant doubted everything—he was in his fifties, a tall, sharply handsome man, heavy but not fat, holding his shoulders back with what looked like an effort, but holding them back just the same. He wore a dark suit, and his face was flushed, as if he had run a long distance.

"Now," he said, coming to Sister Irene and with a precise wave of his hand motioning his wife off, "now let's straighten this out. A lot of confusion over that kid, eh?" He pulled a chair over, scraping it across a rug and pulling one corner over, so that its brown underside was exposed. "I came home early just for this, Libby phoned me. Sister, you got a letter from him, right?"

The wife looked at Sister Irene over her husband's shoulder as if trying somehow to coach her, knowing that this man was so loud and impatient that no one could remember anything in his presence.

"A letter—yes—today—"

"He says what in it? You got the letter, eh? Can I see it?"

She gave it to him and wanted to explain, but he silenced her with a flick of his hand. He read through the letter so quickly that Sister Irene thought perhaps he was trying to impress her with his skill at reading. "So?" he said, raising his eyes, smiling, "so what is this? He's happy out there, he says. He doesn't communicate with us anymore, but he writes to you and says he's happy—what's that? I mean, what the hell is that?"

"But he isn't happy. He wants to come home," Sister Irene said. It was so important that she make him understand that she could

not trust her voice; goaded by this man, it might suddenly turn
shrill, as his son's did. "Someone must read their letters before
they're mailed, so he tried to tell me something by making an allusion to—"

"What?"

"—an allusion to a play, so that I would know. He might be thinking of suicide, he must be very unhappy—"

She ran out of breath. Weinstein's mother had begun to cry, but
the father was shaking his head jerkily back and forth. "Forgive me,
Sister, but it's a lot of crap, he needs the hospital, he needs help—
right? It costs me fifty a day out there, and they've got the best place
in the state, I figure it's worth it. He needs help, that kid, what do I
care if he's unhappy? He's unbalanced!" he said angrily. "You want
us to get him out again? We argued with the judge for two hours to
get him in, an acquaintance of mine. Look, he can't control himself—he was smashing things here, he was hysterical, his room is like
an animal was in it. You ever seen anybody hysterical? They need
help, lady, and you do something about it fast! You do something!
We made up our minds to do something and we did it! This letter—
what the hell is this letter? He never talked like that to us!"

"But he means the opposite of what he says—"

"Then he *is* crazy! I'm the first to admit it." He was perspiring,
and his face had darkened. "I've got no pride left, this late. He's
a little bastard, you want to know? He calls me names, he's filthy,
got a filthy mouth—that's being smart, huh? They give him a big
scholarship for his filthy mouth? I went to college too, and I got out
and knew something, and I for Christ's sake did something with it;
my wife is an intelligent woman, a learned woman, would you guess
she does book reviews for the little newspaper out here? Intelligent
isn't crazy—crazy isn't intelligent—maybe for you at the school he
writes nice papers and gets an A, but out here, around the house, he
can't control himself, and we got him committed!"

"But—"

"We're fixing him up, don't worry about it!" He turned to his wife.
"Libby, get out of here, I mean it. I'm sorry, but get out of here,
you're making a fool of yourself, go stand in the kitchen or something, you and the goddamn maid can cry on each other's shoulders.
That one in the kitchen is nuts too, they're all nuts. Sister," he
said, his voice lowering, "I thank you immensely for coming out
here. This is wonderful, your interest in my son. And I see he

admires you—that letter there. But what about that letter? If he did want to get out, which I don't admit—he was willing to be committed, in the end he said OK himself—if he wanted out I wouldn't do it. Why? So what if he wants to come back? The next day he wants something else, what then? He's a sick kid, and I'm the first to admit it."

Sister Irene felt that sickness spread to her. She stood. The room was so big that it seemed it must be a public place; there had been nothing personal or private about their conversation. Weinstein's mother was standing by the fireplace, sobbing. The father jumped to his feet and wiped his forehead in a gesture that was meant to help Sister Irene on her way out. "God, what a day," he said, his eyes snatching at hers for understanding, "you know—one of those days all day long? Sister, I thank you a lot. A professor interested in him —he's a smart kid, eh? Yes, I thank you a lot. There should be more people in the world that care about others, like you. I mean that."

On the way back to the convent, the man's words returned to her, and she could not get control of them; she could not even feel anger. She had been pressed down, forced back, what could she do? Weinstein might have been watching her somehow from a barred window, and he surely would have understood. The strange idea she had had on the way over, something about understanding Christ, came back to her now and sickened her. But the sickness was small. It could be contained.

About a month after her visit to his father, Weinstein himself showed up. He was dressed in a suit as before, even the necktie was the same. He came right into her office as if he had been pushed and could not stop.

"Sister," he said, and shook her hand. He must have seen fear in her because he smiled ironically. "Look, I'm released. I'm let out of the nut house. Can I sit down?"

He sat. Sister Irene was breathing quickly, as if in the presence of an enemy who does not know that he is an enemy.

"So, they finally let me out. I heard what you did. You talked with him, that was all I wanted. You're the only one who gave a damn. Because you're a humanist and a religious person, you respect . . . the individual. Listen," he said, whispering, "it was hell out there! Hell! Birchcrest Manor! All fixed up with fancy chairs and

Life magazines lying around—and what do they do to you? They
locked me up, they gave me shock treatments! Shock treatments,
how do you like that, it's discredited by everybody now—they're
crazy out there themselves, sadists—they locked me up, they gave me
hypodermic shots, they didn't treat me like a human being! Do you
know what that is," Weinstein demanded savagely, "not to be
treated like a human being? They made me an animal—for fifty
dollars a day! Dirty filthy swine! Now I'm an outpatient because I
stopped swearing at them. I found somebody's bobby pin, and when
I wanted to scream I pressed it under my fingernail, and it stopped
me—the screaming went inside and not out—so they gave me good
reports, those sick bastards, now I'm an outpatient and I can walk
along the street and breathe in the same filthy exhaust from the
buses like all you normal people! Christ," he said, and threw himself
back against the chair.

Sister Irene stared at him. She wanted to take his hand, to make
some gesture that would close the aching distance between them.
"Mr. Weinstein—"

"Call me Allen!" he said sharply.

"I'm very sorry—I'm terribly sorry—"

"My own parents committed me, but of course they didn't know
what it was like. It was hell," he said, thickly, "and there isn't any
hell except what other people do to you. The psychiatrist out there,
the main shrink, he hates Jews, too, some of us were positive of that,
and he's got a bigger nose than I do, a real beak." He made a noise
of disgust. "A dirty bastard, a sick, dirty, pathetic bastard—all of
them— Anyway, I'm getting out of here, and I came to ask you a
favor."

"What do you mean?"

"I'm getting out. I'm leaving. I'm going up to Canada and lose
myself, I'll get a job, I'll forget everything, I'll kill myself maybe—
what's the difference? Look, can you lend me some money?"

"Money?"

"Just a little! I have to get to the border, I'm going to take a bus."

"But I don't have any money—"

"No money?" He stared at her. "You mean—you don't have
any? Sure you have some!"

She stared at him as if he had asked her to do something ob-
scene. Everything was splotched and uncertain before her eyes.
"You must . . . you must go back," she said, "you're making a—"

"I'll pay it back. Look, I'll pay it back, can you go to where you live or something and get it? I'm in a hurry. My friends are sons of bitches: one of them pretended he didn't see me yesterday—I stood right in the middle of the sidewalk and yelled at him, I called him some appropriate names! So he didn't see me, huh? You're the only one who understands me, you understand me like a poet, you—"

"I can't help you, I'm sorry—I—"

He looked to one side of her and then flashed his gaze back, as if he could not control it. He seemed to be trying to clear his vision. "You have the soul of a poet," he whispered, "you're the only one. Everybody else is rotten! Can't you lend me some money, ten dollars maybe? I have three thousand in the bank, and I can't touch it! They take everything away from me, they make me into an animal . . . You know I'm not an animal, don't you? Don't you?"

"Of course," Sister Irene whispered.

"You could get money. Help me. Give me your hand or something, touch me, help me—please—" He reached for her hand and she drew back. He stared at her and his face seemed about to crumble, like a child's. "I want something from you, but I don't know what—I want something!" he cried. "Something real! I want you to look at me like I was a human being, is that too much to ask? I have a brain, I'm alive, I'm suffering—what does that mean? Does that mean nothing? I want something real and not this phony Christian love garbage—it's all in the books, it isn't personal—I want something real—look—"

He tried to take her hand again, and this time she jerked away. She got to her feet. "Mr. Weinstein," she said, "please—"

"You! You—nun," he said scornfully, his mouth twisted into a mock grin. "You nun! There's nothing under that ugly outfit, right? And you're not particularly smart even though you think you are; my father has more brains in his foot than you—"

He got to his feet and kicked the chair.

"You bitch!" he cried.

She shrank back against her desk as if she thought he might hit her, but he only ran out of the office.

Weinstein: the name was to become disembodied from the figure, as time went on. The semester passed, the autumn drizzle turned into snow, Sister Irene rode to school in the morning and left in the afternoon, four days a week, anonymous in her black winter cloak, quiet and stunned. University teaching was an anonymous task, each day dissociated from the rest, with no necessary sense of unity among the teachers: they came and went separately and might for a year just miss a colleague who left his office five minutes before they arrived, and it did not matter.

She heard of Weinstein's death, his suicide by drowning, from the English department secretary, a handsome white-haired woman who kept a transistor radio on her desk. Sister Irene was not surprised; she had been thinking of him as dead for months. "They identified him by some special television way they have now," the secretary said. "They're shipping the body back. It was up in Quebec . . ."

Sister Irene could feel a part of herself drifting off, lured by the plains of white snow to the north, the quiet, the emptiness, the sweep of the Great Lakes up to the silence of Canada. But she called that part of herself back. She could only be one person in her lifetime. That was the ugly truth, she thought, that she could not really regret Weinstein's suffering and death; she had only one life and had already given it to someone else. He had come too late to her. Fifteen years ago, perhaps, but not now.

She was only one person, she thought, walking down the corridor in a dream. Was she safe in this single person, or was she trapped? She had only one identity. She could make only one choice. What she had done or hadn't done was the result of that choice, and how was she guilty? If she could have felt guilt, she thought, she might at least have been able to feel something.

DONALD BARTHELME was born in Philadelphia, grew up in Houston, and attended the University of Houston where he was the editor of the student newspaper. He has also worked as a magazine editor, a museum director, and served with the Army in Korea and Japan. His collection of stories, *Come Back, Dr. Caligari*, published in 1964, is available in an Anchor Books edition. He is currently working on a novel. Mr. Barthelme has been published in *Harper's*, *The Reporter*, *Contact*, *The New Yorker* and other magazines. His story "Margins" was included in *Prize Stories: The O. Henry Awards* for 1965.

See the Moon?

I KNOW you think I'm wasting my time. You've made that perfectly clear. But I'm conducting these very important lunar hostility studies. And it's not you who'll have to leave the warm safe capsule. And dip a toe into the threatening lunar surround.

I am still wearing my yellow flower which has lasted wonderfully.

My methods may seem a touch light-minded. Have to do chiefly with folded paper airplanes at present. But the paper must be folded *in the right way*. Lots of calculations and worrying about edges.

Show me a man who worries about edges and I'll show you a natural-born winner. Cardinal Y agrees. Columbus himself worried, the Admiral of the Ocean Sea. But he kept it quiet.

The sun so warm on this screened porch, it reminds me of my grandmother's place in Tampa. The same rusty creaky green glider and the same faded colored canvas cushions. And at night the moon graphed by the screen wire, if you squint. The Sea of Tranquillity occupying squares 47 through 108.

See the moon? It hates us.

My methods are homely but remember Newton and the apple. And when Rutherford started out he didn't even have a decently

heated laboratory. And then there's the matter of my security check
—I'm waiting for the government. Somebody told it I'm insecure.
That's true.

I suffer from a frightful illness of the mind, light-mindedness. It's
not catching. You needn't shrink.

You've noticed the wall? I pin things on it, souvenirs. There is
the red hat, there the book of instructions for the Ant Farm. And
this is a traffic ticket written on a saint's day (which saint? I don't
remember) in 1954 just outside a fat little town (which town? I don't
remember) in Ohio by a cop who asked me what I did. I said I
wrote poppycock for the president of a university, true then.

You can see how far I've come. Lunar hostility studies aren't
for everyone.

It's my hope that these . . . souvenirs . . . will someday merge,
blur—cohere is the word, maybe—into something meaningful. A
grand word, meaningful. What do I look for? A work of art, I'll
not accept anything less. Yes I know it's shatteringly ingenuous but
I wanted to be a painter. They get away with murder in my view;
Mr. X on the *Times* agrees with me. You don't know how I envy
them. They can pick up a Baby Ruth wrapper on the street, glue
it to the canvas (in the *right place*, of course, there's that), and lo!
people crowd about and cry, "A real Baby Ruth wrapper, by God,
what could be realer than that!" Fantastic metaphysical advantage.
You hate them, if you're ambitious.

The Ant Farm instructions are a souvenir of Sylvia. The red hat
came from Cardinal Y. We're friends, in a way.

I wanted to be one, when I was young, a painter. But I couldn't
stand stretching the canvas. Does things to the fingernails. And
that's the first place people look.

Fragments are the only forms I trust.

Light-minded or no, I'm . . . riotous with mental health. I measure myself against the Russians, that's fair. I have here a clipping
datelined Moscow, four young people apprehended strangling a
swan. *That's* boredom. The swan's name, Borka. The sentences as
follows: Tsarev, metalworker, served time previously for stealing public property, four years in a labor camp, strict regime. Roslavtsev,
electrician, jailed previously for taking a car on a joyride, three years
and four months in a labor camp, semi-strict regime. Tatyana
Voblikova (only nineteen and a Komsomol member too), technician,
one and a half years in a labor camp, degree of strictness unspecified.

Anna G. Kirushina, technical worker, fine of twenty per cent of salary for one year. Anna objected to the strangulation, but softly: she helped stuff the carcass in a bag.

The clipping is tacked up on my wall. I inspect it from time to time, drawing the moral. Strangling swans is wrong.

My brother who is a very distinguished pianist . . . has no finger-nails at all. Don't look it's horrible. He plays under another name. And tunes his piano peculiarly, some call it sour. And renders *ragas* he wrote himself. A night *raga* played at noon can cause darkness, did you know that? It's extraordinary.

He wanted to be an Untouchable, Paul did. That was his idea of a contemporary career. But then a girl walked up and touched him (slapped him, actually; it's a complicated story). And he joined us, here in the imbroglio.

My father on the other hand is perfectly comfortable, and that's not a criticism. He makes flags, banners, bunting (sometimes runs me up a shirt). There was never any question of letting my father drink from the public well. He was on the Well Committee, he decided who dipped and who didn't. That's not a criticism. Exercises his creativity, nowadays, courtesy the emerging nations. Green for the veldt that nourishes the gracile Grant's gazelle, white for the purity of our revolutionary aspirations. The red for blood is under-stood. That's not a criticism. It's what they all ask for.

A call tonight from Gregory, my son by my first wife. Seventeen and at M.I.T. already. Recently he's been asking questions. Sud-denly he's conscious of himself as a being with a history.

The telephone rings. Then, without a greeting: *Why did I have to take those little pills?* What little pills? *Little white pills with a "W" on them.* Oh. Oh yes. You had some kind of a nervous dis-order, for a while. *How old was I?* Eight. Eight or nine. *What was it? Was it epilepsy?* Good God no, nothing so fancy. We never found out what it was. It went away. *What did I do? Did I fall down?* No no. Your mouth trembled, that was all. You couldn't control it. *Oh. O.K. See you.*

The receiver clicks.

Or: *What did my great-grandfather do? For a living I mean?* He was a ballplayer, semi-pro ballplayer, for a while. Then went into the building business. *Who'd he play for?* A team called the St. Augustine Rowdies, I think it was. *Never heard of them.* Well . . . *Did he make any money? In the building business?* Quite a bit.

Did your father inherit it? No, it was tied up in a lawsuit. When the suit was over there wasn't anything left. *Oh. What was the lawsuit?* Great-grandfather diddled a man in a land deal. So the story goes. *Oh. When did he die?* Let's see, 1938 I think. *What of?* Heart attack. *Oh. O.K. See you.*

End of conversation.

Gregory, you didn't listen to my advice. I said try the Vernacular Isles. Where fish are two for a penny and women two for a fish. But you wanted M.I.T. and electron-spin-resonance spectroscopy. You didn't even crack a smile in your six-ply heather hopsacking.

Gregory, you're going to have a half brother now. You'll like that, won't you? Will you half like it?

We talked about the size of the baby, Ann and I. What could be deduced from the outside.

I said it doesn't look very big to me. She said it's big enough for *us*. I said we don't need such a great roaring big one after all. She said they cost the earth, those extra-large sizes. Our holdings in Johnson's Baby Powder to be considered too. We'd need acres and acres. I said we'll put it in a Skinner box maybe. She said no child of hers. Displayed under glass like a rump roast. I said you haven't wept lately. She said I keep getting bigger whether I laugh or cry.

Dear Ann. I don't think you've quite . . .

What you don't understand is, it's like somebody walks up to you and says, I have a battleship I can't use, would you like to have a battleship? And you say, yes yes, I've never had a battleship, I've always wanted one. And he says, it has four sixteen-inch guns forward, and a catapult for launching scout planes. And you say, I've always wanted to launch scout planes. And he says, *it's yours*, and then you have this battleship. And then you have to paint it, because it's rusting, and clean it, because it's dirty, and anchor it somewhere, because the Police Department wants you to get it off the streets. And the crew is crying, and there are silverfish in the chartroom and a funny knocking noise in Fire Control, water rising in the No. 2 hold, and the chaplain can't find the Palestrina tapes for the Sunday service. And you can't get anybody to sit with it. And finally you discover that what you have here is this great, big, pink-and-blue rockabye *battleship*.

Ann. I'm going to keep her ghostly. Just the odd bit of dialogue: "What is little Gog doing."

"Kicking."

I don't want her bursting in on us with the freshness and originality of her observations. What we need here is *perspective*. She's good with Gregory though. I think he half likes her.

Don't go. The greased-pig chase and balloon launchings come next.

I was promising once. After the Elgar, a *summa cum laude*. The university was proud of me. It was a bright shy white new university on the Gulf Coast. Gulls and oleanders and quick howling hurricanes. The teachers brown burly men with power boats and beer cans. The president a retired admiral who'd done beautiful things in the Coral Sea.

"You will be a credit to us, George," the admiral said. That's not my name. I'm protecting my identity, what there is of it.

Applause from the stands filled with mothers and brothers. Then following the mace in a long line back to the field house to ungown. Ready to take my place at the top.

But a pause at Pusan, and the toy train to the Chorwon Valley. Walking down a road wearing green clothes. Korea green and black and silent. The truce had been signed. I had a carbine to carry. My buddy Bo Tagliabue the bonus baby, for whom the Yanks had paid thirty thousand. We whitewashed rocks to enhance our area. Colonels came crowding to feel Bo's hurling arm. Mine the whitest rocks.

I lunched with Thais from Thailand, hot curry from great galvanized washtubs. Engineers banging down the road in six-by-sixes raising red dust. My friend Gib Mandell calling Elko, Nevada on his canvas-covered field telephone. "Operator I crave Elko, Nevada."

Then I was a sergeant with stripes, getting the troops out of the sun. Tagliabue a sergeant too. *Triste* in the Tennessee Tea Room in Tokyo, yakking it up in Yokohama. Then back to our little tent town on the side of a hill, boosting fifty-gallon drums of heating oil tentward in the snow.

Ozzie the jeep driver waking me in the middle of the night. "They got Julian in the Tango Tank." And up and alert as they taught us in Leadership School, over the hills to Tango, seventy miles away. Whizzing through Teapot, Tempest, Toreador, with the jeep's canvas top flapping. Pfc. Julian drunk and disorderly and

beaten up. The M.P. sergeant held out a receipt book. I signed
for the bawdy remains.

Back over the pearly Pacific in a great vessel decorated with
oranges. A trail of orange peel on the plangent surface. Sitting
in the bow fifty miles out of San Francisco, listening to the State-
side disc jockeys chattering cha cha cha. Ready to grab my spot at
the top.

My clothes looked old and wrong. The city looked new with tall
buildings raised while my back was turned. I rushed here and there
visiting friends. They were burning beef in their back yards, brown
burly men with beer cans. The beef black on the outside, red on
the inside. My friend Horace had fidelity. "Listen to that bass.
That's forty watts worth of bass, boy."

I spoke to my father. "How is business?" "If Alaska makes it,"
he said, "I can buy a Hasselblad. And we're keeping an eye on
Hawaii." Then he photographed my veteran face, f.6 at 300. My
father once a cheerleader at a great Eastern school. Jumping in the
air and making fierce angry down-the-field gestures at the top of
his leap.

That's not a criticism. We have to have cheerleaders.

I presented myself at the Placement Office. I was on file. My
percentile was the percentile of choice.

"How come you were headman of only one student organization, George?" the Placement Officer asked. Many hats for top folk
was the fashion then.

I said I was rounded, and showed him my slash. From the Fenc-
ing Club.

"But you served your country in an overseas post."

"And regard my career plan on neatly typed pages with wide
margins."

"Exemplary," the Placement Officer said. "You seem married, ma-
ture, malleable, how would you like to affiliate yourself with us here
at the old school? We have a spot for a poppycock man, to write
the admiral's speeches. Have you ever done poppycock?"

I said no but maybe I could fake it.

"Excellent, excellent," the Placement Officer said. "I see you have
grasp. And you can sup at the Faculty Club. And there is a ten-per-
cent discount on tickets for all home games."

The admiral shook my hand. "You will be a credit to us, George,"
he said. I wrote poppycock, sometimes cockypap. At four o'clock the

faculty hoisted the cocktail flag. We drank Daiquiris on each other's sterns. I had equipped myself—a fibre-glass runabout, some-place to think. In the stadia of friendly shy new universities we went down the field on Gulf Coast afternoons with gulls, or excit-ing nights under the tall toothpick lights. The crowd roared. Sylvia roared. Gregory grew.

There was no particular point at which I stopped being promising.

Moonstruck I was, after a fashion. Sitting on a bench by the practice field, where the jocks chanted secret signals in their under-wear behind tall canvas blinds. Layabout babies loafing on blankets, some staked out on twelve-foot dog chains. Brown mothers squat-ting knee to knee in shifts of scarlet and green. I stared at the moon's pale daytime presence. It seemed . . . inimical.

Moonstruck.

We're playing Flinch. You flinched.

The simplest things are the most difficult to explain, all authorities agree. Say I was tired of p***yc**k, if that pleases you. It's true enough.

Sylvia went up in a puff of smoke. She didn't like unsalaried life. And couldn't bear a male acquaintance moon-staring in the light of day. Decent people look at night.

We had trouble with Gregory: who would get which part. She settled for three-fifths, and got I think the worst of it, the dreaming raffish Romany part that thinks science will save us. I get matter-of-fact midnight telephone calls: *My E.E. instructor shot me down.* What happened? *I don't know, he's an ass anyhow.* Well that may be but still— *When's the baby due?* January, I told you. *Yeah, can I go to Mexico City for the holidays?* Ask your mother, you know she— *There's this guy, his old man has a villa.* . . . Well, we can talk about it. *Yeah, was grandmother a Communist?* Nothing so dis-tinguished, she— *You said she was kicked out of Germany.* Her family was anti-Nazi. *Adler means eagle in German.* That's true. There was something called the Weimar Republic, her father—*I read about it.*

We had trouble with Gregory, we wanted to be scientific. Toys from Procreative Playthings of Princeton. O Gregory, that Princeton crowd got you coming and going. Procreative Playthings at one end and the Educational Testing Service at the other. And that serious-minded co-op nursery, that was a mistake. "A growing understand-

ing between parent and child through shared group experience." I
still remember poor Henry Harding III. Under "Sibs" on the mem-
bership roll they listed his, by age:

> 26
> 25
> 23
> 20
> 19
> 15
> 10
> 9
> 8
> 6

O Mrs. Harding, haven't you heard? They have these little Christ-
mas-tree ornaments for the womb now, they work wonders.

Did we do "badly" by Gregory? Will we do "better" with Gog?
Such questions curl the hair. It's wiser not to ask.

I mentioned Cardinal Y (the red hat). He's a friend, in a way.
Or rather, the subject of one of my little projects.

I set out to study cardinals, about whom science knows nothing.
It seemed to me that cardinals could be known in the same way
we know fishes or roses, by classification and enumeration. A
doomed project, perhaps, but who else has embraced this point of
view? Difficult nowadays to find a point of view kinky enough to
call one's own, with Sade himself being carried through the streets
on the shoulders of sociologists, cheers and shouting, ticker tape un-
winding from high windows . . .

The why of Cardinal Y. You're entitled to an explanation.

The Cardinal rushed from the Residence waving in the air his
hands, gloved in yellow pigskin it appeared. I grasped a hand. "Yes,
yellow pigskin!" the Cardinal cried. I wrote in my book, *yellow
pigskin*.

Significant detail. The pectoral cross contains nine diamonds, the
scarlet soutane is laundered right on the premises.

I asked the Cardinal questions, we had a conversation.

"I am thinking of a happy island more beautiful than can be
imagined," I said.

"I am thinking of a golden mountain which does not exist," he said.

"Upon what does the world rest?" I asked.

"Upon an elephant," he said.

"Upon what does the elephant rest?"

"Upon a tortoise."

"Upon what does the tortoise rest?"

"Upon a red lawnmower."

I wrote in my book, *playful.*

"Is there any value that has value?" I asked.

"If there is any value that has value, then it must lie outside the whole sphere of what happens and is the case, for all that happens and is the case is accidental," he said. He was not serious. I wrote in my book, *knows the drill.*

(*Oh I had heard reports, how he slunk about in the snow telling children he was Santa Claus, how he disbursed funds in unauthorized disbursements to unshaven men who came to the kitchen door, how his housekeeper pointedly rolled his red socks together and black socks together hinting red with red and black with black, the Cardinal patiently unrolling a red ball to get a red sock and a black ball to get a black sock, which he then wore together. . . .*)

Cardinal Y. He's sly.

I was thorough. I popped the Cardinal on the patella with a little hammer, and looked into his eyes with a little light. I tested the Cardinal's stomach acidity using Universal Indicator Paper, a scale of one to ten, a spectrum of red to blue. The pH value was 1 indicating high acidity. I measured the Cardinal's ego strength using the Minnesota Multiphastic Muzzle Map, he had an M.M.M.M. of four over three. I sang to the Cardinal, the song was "Stella by Starlight." He did not react in any way. I calculated the number of gallons needed to fill the Cardinal's bath to a depth of ten inches (beyond which depth, the Cardinal said, he never ventured). I took the Cardinal to the ballet, the ballet was "The Conservatory." The Cardinal applauded at fifty-seven points. Afterward, backstage, the Cardinal danced with Plenosova, holding her at arm's length with a good will and an ill grace. The skirts of the scarlet soutane stood out to reveal high-button shoes, and the stagehands clapped.

I asked the Cardinal his views on the moon, he said they were the conventional ones, and that is how I know all I know about cardinals. Not enough perhaps to rear a science of cardinalogy upon, but enough perhaps to form a basis for the investigations of other investigators. My report is over there, in the blue binding, next to my copy of *La Géomancie et la Néomancie des Anciens* by the Seigneur of Salerno.

Cardinal Y. One can measure and measure and miss the most essential thing. I liked him. I still get the odd blessing in the mail now and then.

Too, maybe I was trying on the role. Not for myself. When a child is born, the locus of one's hopes . . . shifts, slightly. Not altogether, not all at once. But you feel it, this displacement. You speak up, strike attitudes, like the mother of a tiny Lollobrigida. Drunk with possibility once more.

I am still wearing my yellow flower which has lasted wonderfully.
"What is Gog doing."
"Sleeping."
You see, Gog of mine, Gog o' my heart, I'm just trying to give you a little briefing here. I don't want you unpleasantly surprised. I can't stand a startled look. Regard me as a sort of Distant Early Warning System. Here is the world and here are the knowledgeable knowers knowing. What can I tell you? What has been pieced together from the reports of travellers.

Fragments are the only forms I trust.

Look at my wall, it's all there. That's a leaf, Gog, stuck up with Scotch Tape. No no, the Scotch Tape is the shiny transparent stuff, the leaf the veined irregularly shaped . . .

There are several sides to this axe, Gog, consider the photostat, "Mr. W. B. Yeats Presenting Mr. George Moore to the Queen of the Fairies." That's a civilized gesture, I mean Beerbohm's. And when the sculptor Aristide Maillol went into the printing business he made the paper by *chewing the fibers himself*. That's dedication. And here is a Polaroid photo, shows your Aunt Sylvia and me putting an Ant Farm together. That's how close we were in those days. Just an Ant Farm apart.

See the moon? It hates us.

And now comes J. J. Sullivan's orange-and-blue Gulf Oil truck to throw kerosene into the space heater. Driver in green siren suit, red face, blond shaved head, the following rich verbal transaction:
"Beautiful day."
"Certainly is."

And now settling back in this green glider with a copy of *Man*. Dear Ann when I look at *Man* I don't want you. Unfolded Ursala Thigpen seems eversomuchmore desirable. A clean girl too and with interests, cooking, botany, pornographic novels. Someone new to show my slash to.

In another month Gog leaps fully armed from the womb. What can I do for him? I can get him into A.A., I have influence. And make sure no harsh moonlight falls on his new soft head.

Hello there Gog. We hope you'll be very happy here.

JONATHAN STRONG grew up in Winnetka, Illinois, and is now living in Cambridge, Massachusetts. He is twenty-two years old. "Supperburger" is his first published short story.

Supperburger

To have a town house in town, in the center of things, has been one of my desires, like the red brick town houses with black trim and iron balconies on the street that curves down the hill to the river. I think it would be nice to sit in a dark red Victorian chair in the afternoons, reading, looking at the balconies across the street as they catch the sunlight on their ironwork and the red of the bricks deepens. In fact that is how it is now, that is where I am sitting, but the house is not mine. I am on the second floor, in the living room. The first floor has a dining room in front and a kitchen in back. I caught sight of a bowl of peaches on the dining table when I was let in and sent directly upstairs. The back room on the second floor seems to be a study, or perhaps a music room. Arthur Supperburger owns the house, and he is a composer. I am just a boy, or a kid, as I like to say. Boy sounds round and soft, but kid is a little more straight up and down, a little harder, perhaps a little less likely to grow old. It includes an attitude, a free way of knowing people, a sense of unattachment. If I am a kid, I can come here for supper a couple of times, for a few weeks, and then go off for a while. It would be my privilege. If I am a boy, I have to report, I have to let them know what I am doing so they can watch over me. When I grow up, and I do not think I will have to for a while because people still mistake me for fifteen and I am already eighteen and I imagine it will go on like that for some time and perhaps when I am twenty-six they will think I am twenty, but when I do grow up I will have to come to supper only if I am prepared to make something of it, to keep being friends with the people who ask me, to bear the responsibilities and maybe ask them to supper sometime. The thought scares me because most people end up liking me much more than I like them, and all I can do is get up and leave and not be seen for a while and perhaps pretend not to see them if I pass them on the street. The street is the trouble, I suppose, the one that curves down the hill to the river. I pass many people there, especially now that I am out of school and see people who only come out during the day as well as the people I used to meet in the evenings. That means I meet a lot of ladies, the sort who live by themselves in old town houses. They all know each other and get together at the concerts on Friday afternoons and maybe other times, like at their reading clubs. I have come to like the concerts a lot because I go almost every Friday with one of the ladies or another. I meet most of them walking their dogs. I say something about the dog, and they say something about my hat or my boots, and then when they find out I am a nice kid and know how to talk to ladies they ask me for tea. So that way I get to know a lot of them during the day. My friends from school get out about four, and I run into them at the Doughnut Shop, and we sit around. It gets boring, but I like to catch up on what they are doing. Most of my friends are a year younger, so they are still in school. They usually go home in the evenings, and I am pretty much on my own after six, though I do have some friends my age on the hill. First I stop by my room, just a small one without any bathroom which I pay for by the week, and I change my clothes. During the day I usually wear my suede cowboy boots because they do not look so tough for the ladies. At night I wear the black ones, and I put on my faded jeans. I spend a lot of money on colored shirts, and I try to wear a different one every night. Then I have my old suede jacket and of course my hat, which is what the ladies usually like most even though I cannot wear it to the concerts. Then I go out to see who is around. That is when I meet men or at least older kids, kids from college. I do not usually like kids from college because, even though they are very nice to me and ask me to go places, they get across the idea that they think they are better than I am. But sometimes I do not mind them. I met Supperburger in the evening. I knew who he was because they played one of his compositions at a concert I went to and he had taken a bow. He walked past me and did not seem to notice me, but on an impulse I turned and ran up to him and asked if he was not Arthur Supperburger even though I knew he was. Then I told him I had heard his Symphony, which embarrassed me later because I looked at the program back in my room and it was not a Symphony but a Symphonic Suite, but he did not say anything except that he was glad I liked it. Then he walked on. I am used to talking to people on the street, and I am able to tell what they are thinking. Most people would think this composer fellow was simply not interested in talking to a kid, but I can tell when someone is a snob and when he wishes inside he could talk. I was pretty sure Supperburger wished he knew how to talk to me but was so embarrassed and surprised that he wanted to avoid the situation. I could tell because I noticed his eyes catch sight of the way my bright yellow shirt was unbuttoned a few buttons so my dark red T-shirt would show. The light was good then. We were standing by one of the gas lamps they have to make the street look more Victorian. He only looked for a second, but usually if a person looks only a little it means he likes me. I think it is strange how most people do not try to look good. If everyone did, it would be more interesting. I decided to see Supperburger again, though I did not run after him. That would make him even more uneasy, so I left him and went to look in a phone book for his address. The next night I stood across the street from his house, looking up at the window I am sitting inside now. I usually change my shirt, as I said, but I thought I would wear the same one again that night, so he would remember. He came out early in the evening and noticed me. Supperburger is a nice looking man, but he is in his forties and could have been my father. His hair is sandy gray, and he is rather tall. Once I tried to imagine him as a kid, but I do not think he was one for long, maybe only once one summer, and then it stopped when September came. It is hard to tell, but I have given it a lot of thought. It is September now, when I am sitting inside his house and most of my friends are back at school, so I am thinking of him with September colors in his face and hair, but it was early August when I met him, and I had a feeling he was remembering an August many years before. I am good at telling people's feelings, and I think I may talk to him about it tonight. Anyway, that night he came out of his own house and saw me standing across the street. While I had been waiting there I had seen the maid cleaning up in the dining room, and I had seen Supperburger standing at one of the living room windows with a woman beside him, looking out. I wondered if it was his wife or maybe his sister. But he came out alone, with a trench coat on because it was cool. He saw me immediately and must have recognized me because I was under a lamp, but he did a funny turn and went the opposite way up the street. I have been through this sort of thing before, but it can still seem funny to me. If people would be less afraid of looking at each other they would enjoy each other more. Just as Supperburger went off up the street a girl named Charles walked by. I know her from hanging around the Doughnut Shop. I think Charles is her last name. She likes me a lot, but she is a sad one because she is sort of dumpy and does not try to do much with her face. She laughed because she saw me standing under the lamp, and then she played at being a whore picking me up, but I just stood smiling. Then she got mad because I did not say much to her. She said she wanted to go to a party and no one would take her and of course I would not either, she said. She did most of the talking. Then she got a little sad and said how cute I looked and she did not care what I thought of her as long as she could look at me. I feel sorry for her, most of the time, but I cannot think of the right thing to say so I just keep quiet, and I know that hurts her. But soon she was on her way that night, off to the party by herself. There are a lot of parties on the hill in the summer. When she was gone I was about to track down Supperburger when I saw him coming down the street. He must have assumed I had gone and was returning to make his walk down the hill. When he saw me it was too late to turn around again, so he walked briskly by as if he had planned his roundabout route. I stepped right out and asked for the time, and he almost flinched but he told me, and then I knew I had been right all along because he asked if I was not the boy who had told him yesterday about hearing his Symphonic Suite. I smiled and got in stride with him, and we walked down to the river together. I introduced myself as Patrick Polo, which is my full name. He asked me what I did, and I said I was an art student, which is not really true though I do have two drawing classes a week. Then he asked if I was bored and lonely here, and that surprised me. I have met a lot of people on the street and never known them to ask something as personal as that right away. I was glad he had asked it, so I decided to tell him the truth, which I usually avoid on the subject of boredom and loneliness, and I said yes. From then on I felt I was friends with Supperburger.

Sitting by the window here and looking around the room I like to imagine the house is mine, or maybe my father's. Of course I would rearrange it exactly my way, but the feeling would be mostly

the same. I like the bookshelves being full. The shelf right next to
me has books by men I have never heard of: Dowson, Swinburne,
Henley, but of course I have heard of Kipling and there is a big set
of his books, and I know about Wilde. Rossetti sounds like he
would be Italian, but he is not because I took one volume out. I am
Italian, or at least I am on one side. The other side is mostly Irish.
They wonder where I get my blond hair. I just took down one of
the Swinburnes, and one poem called "The Triumph of Time" is all
underlined in red, by Supperburger I suppose. I like it, but it is sad.

> Before our lives divide forever,
> > While time is with us and hands are free
> (Time, swift to fasten and swift to sever
> > Hand from hand, as we stand by the sea),
> I will say no word that a man might say
> Whose whole life's love goes down in a day;
> For this could never have been, and never—
> > Though the gods and the years relent—shall be.

I used to write poems in school, but I have not since I left. I went
to the best high school in the city, even though I did not live near
it, because I was good in school. My father sent the extra money
because it cost a little, but then he decided he would not send me
any for college. I do not mind because, as I said, I usually do not
like college kids. I am supposed to have a job, actually, but my father
does send me some money and I get a lot of free meals, so I will
not have to work for a while. He does not live in this part of the
city and never comes here, so he does not know what I am doing.
He came to my graduation last June, but he had to stay incon-
spicuous, he said. He is the Italian side. That is where I get a name
like Polo, though it is no relation to Marco Polo as far as I know.
My nickname is Pony, but I did not tell Supperburger who calls me
Patrick. Some people call me Polo Pony and some call me Pony
Polo, which is silly, and some just call me Pony, like Charles. Some
of the older kids on the hill call me Polo in a sort of mean way. My
mother, being Irish by ancestry, calls me Pat, but she is the only one
who does. She lives in this part of the city, though not too near, and
so I go have suppers with her occasionally. Personally I like being
called Pony though I have often thought of introducing myself as
Rick instead, just to see what it would be like having someone call

me Rick. Anyway, it is Patrick with Supperburger. I imagine he is
composing right now. This is the fifth time he has asked me for
supper, and I usually come early because I do not mind waiting in
this room. Up above the Kiplings is a shelf of music books, mostly
operas I have never hear of, like *Lakmé* and *L'Africaine,* and then
The Tales of Hoffmann which I think I have heard of. I have never
seen an opera, but Mrs. Supperburger said they would take me. It
was his wife, you see, who was standing at the window with him
that night. I was surprised. I would not have thought so, but you
never know about people for certain. She usually does not say much,
which is the opposite of Charles and also of most of those ladies I
meet in the afternoons. She just makes tea and sits behind the tea
table which is always very pretty, with china and linen napkins and
silverware and usually tomato sandwiches, though once it was cinnamon toast. Then at the dining table she makes sure I have enough
without forcing it on me like my mother does. Mrs. Supperburger's
name is Ruth, and one night, when I was in the hall putting on my
suede jacket and my hat and Supperburger had not come downstairs
yet, she came up to me and said very sweetly that I should call her
Aunt Ruth if I liked. It surprised me because I did not think she
would ever say something as openly as that. So I call her Aunt Ruth,
even though I think of her as Mrs. Supperburger, just as I think of
him as Mr. Supperburger or just Supperburger as his name was on
the program. Mrs. Supperburger is the sweetest woman I have met,
and most of the ladies on the hill are sweet in one way or another.
But she is gentle besides and a little sad, without pitying herself like
so many ladies around here do. When she carries in the tray with
the tea it looks very natural and pretty. I drew her like that in one
of my classes. She is a dignified sort of woman, not short or dumpy
at all. Her hair is almost gray, but she seems pretty young still. Her
clothes are usually soft colors and flowery, which is nice on her. She
never really laughs, but she is always smiling. In a few minutes she
will be coming in here, and then Supperburger will come out of his
study. He and his wife look good together because he is strong
enough to make her feel taken care of but not too strong, not to
overpower her. I wonder if he is a great composer. I am no judge,
and I know the ladies on Friday afternoons are no judges. They
all applauded politely because he is a local celebrity of sorts, but the
music was strange. It is hard for me to describe it because I know

nothing about music and cannot even sing, though I can dance rock and roll pretty well. I often go to the Drum Guitar which is where they have live rock and roll bands. But I did like his piece. In fact it was not like any other piece I have heard, and I think it is beautiful when someone can do something like no one else has. The same goes for dressing. When I got my hat my mother did not like it because none of the other kids wore a hat like that. My mother is very scared that I might be different. There was one part of the Symphonic Suite I can still remember, though not exactly how it sounded. It was quiet, and two trumpets started playing melodies to each other, most of the time not fitting together very well and sort of twisting around, but that made the parts that did fit seem all the more lovely. Then one got farther and farther away, and I imagined one sailing boat slowly drifting out to sea and me standing on the land calling to it as it became more and more cloudy with mist.

I can hear Mrs. Supperburger coming upstairs with the tea.

P. Hi, Aunt Ruth.

Mrs. S. Good afternoon, Patrick. Matty said she let you in about half an hour ago. I hope you haven't been bored.

P. No, I was looking at the books.

Mrs. S. What is it? Oh, Swinburne. That's one of Arthur's favorites. I wonder how you happened to pick that. No one reads him anymore.

P. It was on the shelf right here. It's a little sad, but I like it.

Mrs. S. It seems so old-fashioned to me when I read it. I remember when I was a girl being told by my grandmother that Swinburne was not the sort of thing a girl should read. Imagine that now.

P. It didn't seem old-fashioned to me, really.

Mrs. S. Where's that one poem? "Laus Veneris." It was so shocking. My poor grandmother. There it is: ". . . for her neck, kissed over close, wears yet a purple speck wherein the pained blood falters and goes out."

It is funny to hear Mrs. Supperburger talking about things like that. Of course I know about them, hickeys the kids call them. That is why I wear turtlenecks a lot, so they will not show if I am going home for supper. It is especially hard in the summer when I am on the beach a lot not to be embarrassed by them. Mrs. Supperburger seems a little nervous. She is talking more than usual.

MRS. S. "Lips that cling hard till the kissed face has grown of one same fire and color with their own." It's so silly. Arthur loves it.

P. Aunt Ruth, you seem a little nervous today.

MRS. S. You're so funny, Patrick, the way you come right out and say things. Well, I'll tell you the reason. It's our anniversary, our twenty-fifth. Arthur and I were married on the twenty-first of September, 1941.

P. I really oughtn't to come to supper on your anniversary.

MRS. S. Why not?

P. I mean you probably would rather be alone.

MRS. S. Not at all. Arthur wanted you to come especially. It's a sort of party. Our nephew Louis is coming down from school. He goes to college in the East now. Do you want cinnamon toast?

P. Yes, please.

Now Mrs. Supperburger is getting silent again. She is leafing through the Swinburne with a sweet smile. I am drinking the tea and picking out the most buttery cinnamon toasts. I am afraid their nephew Louis is going to be one of those college kids, especially if he is not from around here. I wonder if he is ever called Louie. I usually do not like people who are always called by their full name. If the three of them start talking about intellectual things I might get bored. I like intellectual things, but people usually talk about them as if they were things everyone knew about already. Some of the college kids come into the Doughnut Shop and talk about things like Kierkegaard as if they invented them. If you want to say something I think you should say it on your own and not go quoting people. That is one nice thing about the ladies on Friday afternoons, they never quote anything. I suppose it is because they never read except at their reading clubs where one of them reads and the others are supposed to listen but do not. I went once, and it was very boring. Supperburger reads a lot, but I have never heard him quote. Everything he says comes from his own head. I wish he would come in. I get to feeling awkward when I am alone with Mrs. Supperburger very long. She is looking a little wistful, reading one of the pages in Swinburne. Her eyes are even a little wet. If she cries I will not know what to say. It is just like with Charles, although Charles is a self-pitier. I am afraid of saying nothing. The sunlight is coming in the windows at quite a slant now. All the dust on the round table by the couch shows.

MRS. S. Do you like the way I keep the house, Patrick?

P. You know it's my favorite house on the hill, Aunt Ruth, and I've been in most of them.

I said that with a laugh. I am beginning to feel very funny. I have never heard her say these sorts of things.

Mrs. S. I wasn't sure about having everything so Victorian at first. Arthur wanted it, so we did. I've kept it just as he liked all these years.

She is talking as though she was one of the old ladies. But she is only forty-five, I think. I might say she is almost being a little self-pitying.

Mrs. S. Does it seem old-fashioned, Patrick? Arthur says the reaction against Victorian things is over and they are coming back in fashion. I think he's right. The way you dress. That hat's out of Dickens. And your boots, not the cowboy ones but the others. You're like a street urchin. Do you suppose there will be street urchins again, like gypsies?

P. There always have been, I imagine.

Mrs. S. I never noticed them till now. They're all over the hill. Kids like you all decked out in bright colors. Every afternoon they're swarming up and down. I see them dancing in the windows. In the summer they're down by the river singing with their guitars. It's hats and boots, I think, and lots of hair and colors. When I was your age, in the thirties, everyone was so much more drab. At least the boys were.

P. There are lots of kids these days.

Mrs. S. I never saw them for so many years. All so lovely.

I like the word lovely. I know kids do not usually say words like that. Old ladies use it a lot. I wonder if Mrs. Supperburger is turning into an old lady. That means Supperburger is old too, though men usually do not get old as soon. They die sooner though. That is why there are a lot of old ladies living by themselves on the hill. I often think I will give it all up when I find I cannot keep my stomach flat anymore. I wonder if I will have much hair on my stomach. A lot of blond people do not, but then Italians do. I think Supperburger has German ancestry. He used to be blond, and he does not have much hair on his stomach. The knob on the music room door just turned. He has finished composing, I guess, and he is coming in.

S. Good afternoon, Patrick. Ruth . . . Patrick . . . I have finished my Ninth Symphony.

Now it is after dinner, and we are sitting around the table with coffee cups and peaches and special fruit-peeling knives to peel them. The announcement about the Ninth Symphony was very exciting and got us all celebrating. Mrs. Supperburger carried out the tea and came back with a bottle of champagne, and we all made toasts. That was when Louis came up, shown in by Matty, the maid. Supperburger welcomed him in a fatherly sort of way and introduced me as Patrick Polo, but I cannot remember what he said Louis's last name was. Supperburger is very good at making people feel easy and at home right away. Maybe it is because he is a little shy himself but not so shy as not to know what to say or not to keep saying things when everyone else is awkwardly pausing. It is a good thing because Louis does not seem to say much. So far he has only said hello and a few other things like yes and no and that he likes college a lot. In a way it is nice to hear a college kid not talk so much. Mrs. Supperburger told Louis right away about the Symphony and gave him a glass of champagne, though I noticed he did not drink it all. Then Supperburger said how it was a four-way celebration, not just because there were four people but because firstly it was the anniversary, secondly it was the day he finished the Ninth Symphony, thirdly it was Louis's first visit, and fourthly it was the first time Louis and I had met. That last thing was a little awkward. I felt funny because it is hard to be told you are going to be great friends with someone, but I did not mind because Louis is very nice. He has absolutely black hair, so he must be from Mrs. Supperburger's side which is not German and which would explain the last name I did not remember. He is about my size, medium, and has just as long hair coming down to his eyebrows. The funny thing is that while I have dark brown eyes, which is strange for a blond kid, he has shiny blue eyes, which is what I ought to have and he ought to have mine. Anyway, they look nice, and I was also glad he was not wearing the sort of things college kids usually wear, like Madras, but just a regular colored shirt with a T-shirt and jeans, except his were white jeans instead of blue. After Supperburger caused an awkward moment with his fourth reason, he quickly added that there was a fifth reason to make this day special but that was a secret. So we all wondered about that, looking forward to some surprise, and then I asked Louis if they ever call him Louie and he said no, so I said I would and told him he could call me Rick for short. I have always wanted to do that. The bad thing is that when Matty was serving lamb chops she said, "Pony, do you want two?" because she hears the kids calling me Pony when she waits for her bus outside the Doughnut Shop. So then Louie thought that was funny. In fact it was the only time he really relaxed, and he started calling me Pony. I think the champagne has calmed Mrs. Supperburger down. She had three glasses, which is more than the rest of us put together. She talked a lot during the meal, in a relaxed and pleasant way, telling us how she and Supperburger had met at the beginning of the summer in 1941 at a beach on the Cape. He was just out of college, where he had studied art it turns out and not composing, and he had a little cottage on the beach because he had decided to try to write music. That was when he started the Symphonic Suite I heard. She said they had played it in honor of their twenty-fifth anniversary. It sounds as though she had a beautiful time on the beach that summer, and they had decided to get married in the fall. She had to spend the month of August with her family on some cruise, and when she came back he had just finished the second movement. I remembered that was the one with the trumpets. She said he wrote the third movement as a sort of wedding march, and they were married on the first day of fall. I started wondering what the last two movements were supposed to be. Maybe the fourth was their wedding night. The fifth was short and came to a very funny end, and I could not imagine what it was. Anyway, it was nice to hear Mrs. Supperburger remembering things so happily. Maybe I will want to get married some day after all if it can still be so nice after twenty-five years. My parents never see each other anymore, though they are supposed to be married still because we are Catholics. I am not really a Catholic. I know one girl on the hill who drinks a lot and sort of sleeps around. She goes to two confessionals. In one she says she ate meat on Friday or something small like that, and in the other she says that she lied once! I do not go at all anymore. I would not have time to get it all in, and I do not think it matters anyway. Of course my mother assumes I go, and whenever I do see my father he says something about going to church which is funny coming from him. I have been thinking about my father off and on through dinner. Just as we were starting, the door bell rang, and it was Charles. She figured I might be here. She apologized for butting in, which is unusual for her, and said a man who said he was Patrick Polo's father had been around tonight asking the kids where I was. She said he seemed in a state, so she did not tell him anything. She seemed scared. I did not want to think about it. Charles was sort of playing up the drama of the situation, and you can never be sure with her how serious things are. She left right away saying she just wanted to clue me in. I forgot about it immediately, because I wanted to, but it keeps coming back to my mind, like now when I think about my father and church. I do not think the Supperburgers ever go to church. Mrs. Supperburger talked all through the main course, and now that it is dessert she is still talking but is getting a little vague. It reminds me of the night she asked me to call her Aunt Ruth. She was fuzzy and vague then too. Louie is not saying anything, though he keeps looking at me. Supperburger seems to be collecting his thoughts, just like me. I really like Mrs. Supperburger better when she keeps quiet and sweet.

Mrs. S. I really don't know why we have to have a maid, Arthur. I used to do most of it myself. It seems wrong for Matty to devote her life to keeping someone else's house and making someone else's food. Everyone should be doing his best to keep his own house. It's hard enough keeping your own things straight. Keeping a house should be private, not like a business. You should live only within the limits of your own powers to make yourselves comfortable. But no one tells us these things, and we go on thinking we should have a maid. A woman has to spend her waking hours making the house comfortable, but that's the way it's meant to be. A woman's supposed to be the servant of the house. And the mother of the children. That is what she wants. The balance is slipping. There aren't the lines between husbands and wives anymore. These career women! My grandmother may have said Swinburne was not for little girls, but she knew what a little girl was, God knows, and I don't anymore. Louis, you're smart. You're at college. Do people know the difference anymore? I don't think there is one now. These children on the hill, they're roaming around all evening. They don't know the difference.

S. I don't mean to interrupt the sociological discussion, but there is something I want to show Patrick upstairs. Louis . . . Ruth . . . you'll excuse us?

That came as a relief, though it seemed a little cold of him, just when Mrs. Supperburger was getting nervous again. As we leave she starts to talk about family things with Louie, aunts and uncles and people on her side, and Matty is clearing off the table.

I stopped on the second floor because Supperburger told me to run in and get the Swinburnes. I am a little uneasy about being alone upstairs with him again. But maybe it is just the secret fifth reason for the champagne he wants to talk to me about. I am also beginning to worry about my father again. Supperburger is already on the third floor, in the front bedroom.

It is a comfortable room and looks like a man's room. All of Mrs. Supperburger's things are in the back bedroom, and I think she sleeps in there sometimes too. He is in the big leather chair under the painting of a boat. I give him the Swinburnes and sit down on the edge of the bed. I think someday I may end up looking like Supperburger, except for his gray eyes. Of course he is taller and his teeth are all perfectly straight, but his coloring is like mine and he also looks younger than he is. He wears very dignified clothes, usually gray or sandy colored suits, but they do not make him look old or stuffy. In fact they set off how young he is inside them. He is built pretty well. His face is strong too, and though his skin is sort of rough, his gray eyes make him seem sweet-natured.

S. This is the day I have to say good-bye to you, Patrick.

P. What? Can't I come here anymore?

S. Were you planning to, really?

P. I wasn't planning not to.

S. You'll be going soon anyway. I know. So I would rather have it be good-bye on a recognized basis. Don't you think?

P. But you're not going anywhere?

S. No. But people come and go, don't they? You're coming and going most of the time and will be for a number of years. Eighteen, and you look younger. That makes a difference on the hill. You'll be here for another ten years. Maybe . . .

P. Don't you want me to come back?

S. Yes, Patrick. You can come whenever you want. I am just saying good-bye now.

I am feeling scared, but I do not think I am showing it.

P. I wonder what my father wants me for?

S. Perhaps he's found out about your life, here.

P. That shouldn't really bother him.

S. Many things bother people that no one else is aware of.

P. He doesn't care, and it really isn't his business anymore.

S. Patrick, how do you plan to keep from loneliness, in your life?

P. Well, everyone has to face that, don't they? I'll find other people who are lonely.

S. For supper, now and then?

P. No, I know I'll grow out of that. I'll want to settle down more.

S. But there will always be new people, up and down the street all day and in the evenings.

P. Do you think you are a great composer?

S. No.

P. But a good one?

S. No.

P. But I never heard anything like your Symphonic Suite. I think it is beautiful when someone does something different.

S. My music has been just like the other music being written today.

P. I never heard anything like it.

S. But you haven't been to many concerts, have you?

P. I've been to all three so far this year.

S. Well, I just follow the current style, rearrange it a little from someone else.

P. But you never quote! I have never heard you quote. You always say things of your own.

S. With you, Patrick, I don't need to quote. You have only seen me with you, or taking a bow from the audience, applauded by the little ladies.

P. I've seen you with Louie. He goes to college.

S. Do you like Louis?

P. Yes. He's very quiet.

S. Patrick . . . In saying good-bye, please forget the first night you came. All right?

P. All right.

S. Until you know someone, you do not know what you should do, or what they expect you to do, or what they want you to do, or even what you really want to do yourself. You were right then.

P. All right.

S. So, you like my music. I hope you will like my Ninth Symphony. I had Matty put two packages in the hall, one for you and one for Louis. They are manuscripts of the Ninth. It is dedicated to both of you. The manuscripts won't mean much, just a lot of notes, but one is for you. Make sure Louis gets his.

P. Thank you. Mr. Supperburger . . .

S. Maybe they will perform it soon on a Friday.

P. I'll be there.

S. I know.

P. Mr. Supperburger, is it at all like the second movement of your Suite?

He suddenly stood up, so quickly, almost with a leap. His eyes are watery, and I have never seen a look like his now, in his gray eyes.

S. Patrick . . . You understand people very well.

P. I meet a lot.

S. You have felt it. You have seen the connection. Oh but then, what good is that! My meanings indulge my own feelings. The music is still there, meaningless. A lot of notes, no objectivity, no architecture, just copy and my indulgences. But anyway, you have felt it. You hope the Ninth will be like that second movement?

P. I liked that part best.

Now he is sitting down again, under the painting, and his eyes are really tearful. I am surprised at myself because I do not feel funny about moving over and putting my arm on his shoulder and trying to make him feel better, though I do not keep it there long. After a while he looks up and starts to tell me a story.

S. You noticed the painting? I did it twenty-five years ago. You heard my wife talking about our summer together and how she left with her family in August. On the fifth of August, I was relaxing from my Suite by painting a motor yacht anchored out beyond my beach that day. A dark-haired boy came walking along the sand. He liked the painting, which so far was very brightly colored and not as misty as it has turned out, and he said it was his father's boat. Furthermore, his family was on shore then and had given him the yacht to use by himself for a month. His name was Paul, but I have forgotten his last name. Well, to put it shortly, I went with him, and we sailed free . . . up and down the coast, in the cockpit with the wind blowing, drifting in the sun a lot, out of sight of land, for a month. Then on a misty night, on the pier at the resort town where his parents stayed, they rejoined the ship. And I went ashore. I stood on the pier as servants carried trunks and boxes aboard. Paul helped. He was eighteen. Imagine the freedom of a boy at eighteen, already competent enough to sail off into the Atlantic alone, or not really alone, but his parents thought he was. He had been sailing boats since he was small. His parents, two of their elegant friends, and his

little brother, and a maid, they all went on board, and finally Paul,
after saying good-bye. I never saw him after that, just a boy standing on the deck of his father's yacht, blowing a trumpet maybe as
my musical indulgence told it, while the boat became more and
more cloudy with mist and I blew one back to him.

Now my eyes are watery too, and that is strange for me.

I hear the door opening and quickly get back all the way on the
bed and wipe my eyes, but Supperburger does not change his attitude at all. It is his wife, and she is holding a cocktail glass which
she puts on the dresser. Now everything is wrong. I am beginning
to feel so uneasy with these older people. I want to go talk to
Louie.

S. I was showing Patrick my painting.

Mrs. S. Oh, but he's been in here before.

S. I told him the story about it.

Mrs. S. What did you make of that, Patrick?

She is sounding like my mother does sometimes, sort of menacing.
I cannot talk. My mouth is trembling. I think she knows about
everything. What if my father knows? Maybe he has some people
out looking for me now. Or what if Charles lets out where I am
because I have not been very nice to her lately, I have not talked
to her much. Mrs. Supperburger takes a sip of her drink, and now
she does not look as angry, just worried instead and very sweet.

Mrs. S. Patrick . . . Think what you are supposed to be. I'm a
nice woman. I was watched over when I was little, but when I
grew up I found I was able to take the world as it is. I'm willing
to accept things. But where is love? What will happen to that little
girl who rang the bell at dinner, without you? Arthur reads Swinburne. Well, that's fine. But that's sex. Where is love? That's beauty
and color, and sound—music, you see, sensual things, dancing, colors
and hair, that boat. That couldn't stay, Patrick, do you see? Because
that depended on two people being exactly the same and wanting
the same, and staying the same. They can't. And you'll walk up
and down this street, Patrick. You're only eighteen. You have to
draw, to do something, not just be beautiful, not just draw beautifully but draw strongly. If you had a family . . . who can teach
you this?

I am too scared. In a moment I am going to have to get up
and leave, run out of here.

The front room on the fourth floor is a guest room. Louie is unpacking his things because he will be staying over the weekend. I did not know this was his room, but I am glad to be here. He says, "Hello, Pony," when I come in, but then he does not know what else to say and keeps busy with his unpacking. I do not want to talk anyway. I sit down on the bed. He is looking at me again. Suddenly I am starting to cry and he is beside me saying things will be all right.

Now it is later, and very dark. We hear someone in the hall. It is both Mr. and Mrs. Supperburger, and they have coats on. They say it is a lovely night and to come up on the roof and watch the stars. Being kids we do not need our coats, because it is really not that cool yet. Fall is just beginning. The stairs are in the hall closet and twist around till you come out on a big flat roof. It is higher than the others on the block, and there are two chairs and some flower pots. I am scared of heights, and there is not much of a rail around the edge. But the sky is beautiful, absolutely black with every star showing. And you can see all the rooftops on this side of the hill and look down the street to the river which is gray and flat in the distance. The gas lamps and the lights in rooms and houses are shining. Most windows are open, and I can hear rock and roll coming from every direction, up the hill and down it. Someone is playing "Good Lovin'" by the Young Rascals, which is my favorite song. I wish I was wearing my hat and my boots right now. I feel a little like the king of the hill. There is Louie, shivering a little. Even now he has not said much. I wonder what he will be like. This may be one of the last party nights before it gets cold. Charles is probably looking for someone to take her to one. It is only ten o'clock. I do not think Louie is much of a party-goer. Maybe that is better. Parties get boring. I wonder what he does at college.

Mrs. S. The sky is lovely late at night.

P. It's only ten.

Mrs. S. It's almost the time of year for Orion. I wish he was out on a night like this. That would be a glorious sight.

S. Stars . . . Stella. Do you know *The Tales of Hoffman*, Louis?

L. Yes. I love it.

S. Stella . . . his one perfect love, told through his stories.

Mrs. S. What are you talking about, Arthur?

S. Patrick knows. The stories I have told myself in my nine symphonies! And told no one else. Nine symphonies. If I could have written one great fugue, one tiny two-part invention even, worthy of a great composer, but . . . nine symphonies. I pore over the scores in the afternoons, and they eat me away. Nine manuscripts are out in the world, two for this last one. The manuscript for the first went down on a flaming battleship, in the war. I didn't even dare call that one a Symphony. It was a Suite, something simple. But as music? They were entirely in the fashion. If I could have written in the Nineteenth Century, I could have done it better. Today's styles don't suit my feelings. But what can you do? Revamp Massenet? Raff? At least, most people don't know that I'm copying, yet. My ladies applaud. But my wife knows. She always knew, and she loves me still. She keeps my name, Supperburger. That's a very silly name, but everyone gets used to it and forgets how silly it is. It's German. Nonsense. She had her own lovely name, LePays. We're French and German. Patrick, you must be Irish, or Italian. What are we doing here? This is North America, some Indian land across the sea . . . Lakmé, Selika the African . . . What are we doing speaking English? None of us are English. What's Matty speaking English for? She's African. The music they're playing on the hill tonight, is that African? It is sung in English. How did it get here? In this land . . . I wish I were out of sight of land.

He is standing by the edge. I think he wants to sail out, over it, to fall down to the gray circle around the gas lamp in front of the house. I am scared of heights. Luckily Mrs. Supperburger has his hand.

S. They're eating me away, my nine. I can't spend my time poring over them anymore. Soon they'll lose themselves in libraries. Stars . . . shooting stars only.

We are all looking up at the sky. When you look up you forget about the roof. You might be at sea or on a beach, except for all the music and the sound of cars, but I forget about them. We are standing quietly for a long time. Louie looks cold. I had almost forgotten about him while Supperburger was talking. So I give him a smile now. There is some noise in the alley behind the house. Someone is calling "Pony!" It is Charles. I just heard the kitchen window slam. Matty is yelling, "You come back here, young lady!" What is she doing? "Pony!" she keeps yelling. She sounds sort of hysterical, but that is not unusual with Charles. I think she is climbing the fire escape. We all go over to the back edge of the roof, and here comes that silly, dumpy girl stumbling up.

C. Pony! Pony! I saw you up there from the party across the street. You've got to go! Your dad found out you were here. I didn't tell him. I promise! He's mad. I had to come warn you. I didn't want you to think it was me that told him.

Now everything inside me is uneasy. A car horn sounds in the street. I am scared. Supperburger is walking to the front of the roof. I can hear my father's voice below.

MR. P. My son's up there! You get him out here! Patrick Polo! I want him out here!

He is almost barking, the way he talks. Louie must be confused. He does not know about any of this. I want to talk to him about it. But now, I must decide to go to the front of the roof.

P. Here I am.

MR. P. Kid, you get down here now!

P. I won't.

MR. P. You're pretty well known here, aren't you! Making a reputation already! Who's that?

S. Mr. and Mrs. Arthur Supperburger.

MR. P. I'm telling you, if I ever find my son here again, you've got trouble. What are you doing! Passing it on to the coming generation? Turning my son into a freak? I give it to you once more, kid: you're coming down here!

P. No.

MR. P. All right. That's the last of my money you'll get! Probably don't need it, earning a good wage on the street!

I am shaking. It is all lies. He does not know. How can he know people, being what he is. I do not want him. I do not want money. Charles and Louie are holding me on either side.

S. We have done nothing to your son, Mr. Polo. He has had dinner with my wife and me this evening. He is a fine boy and a credit to you.

MR. P. Christ have mercy!

He has stepped back into his car, with his two men. They drive up the street, screeching the wheels. Now everyone is here. Aunt Ruth and even Matty, who must have followed Charles up the fire escape. Supperburger is still standing, and I can hear him talking to himself, but out loud. I notice he is holding one of the Swinburnes.

S. I have done something to his son. I have not built a solid house for him but made him dwell on being young and beautiful, where he cannot stay. I have not learned but have grown old with the same song. If I had not been turned away the first time . . . If it had held on, and changed as one.

We are all listening now, but it is hard to understand him, Supperburger.

S. This is the day I have to say good-bye. People are afraid of being the same. It is too threatening. But to be different, truly, is very hard too. We should all try to be truly different and alone, some day. If you have written a Symphony, you may still be just a child. The greatest, with me, could never have been.

He is standing on the edge, holding Swinburne out, over the street. In this starlight, from behind, he looks almost like a boy. In this month I have not known him at all. He is very far from me. The book falls.

Mrs. S. Arthur!

Five stories. She is pulling him back from the edge, he is in her arms, he says to her, "My only love."

Now it is very late. We have been walking and telling each other things for hours. He is easy to talk to now. We said good-night to the Supperburgers, and to Matty, and we got rid of Charles pretty easily, though I am grateful to her for coming to warn me. I think most of the parties are over now, and everyone is in bed on the hill, except us, walking down the street, under the gas lamps, to the river. I may soon get tired of this street. I have never had anyone my age as interesting to talk to as Louie. Maybe I can get a job at his college, in the kitchen or something. I could live there and try writing poems again. Or take drawing classes. All sorts of plans are going through my head. If I only had money. I will have to work, that is only fair. I am eighteen. The funny thing is I do not really know Louis LePays. Maybe he will like me more than I like him. I have to learn to get used to people. Maybe I will become completely different. If life really is stretching out, and I am only eighteen . . . it is a long time.

JESSE HILL FORD, a native Southerner, has lived in West Tennessee for the past nine years. He is the author of two novels, *Mountains of Gilead* and *The Liberation of Lord Byron Jones*. Previous stories have appeared in *Prize Stories: The O. Henry Awards* for 1961 and 1966.

The Bitter Bread

IT WAS after Christmas, towards the end of December. There had come a sudden thaw. The roads got soft—the Devil was baking his bread, as the saying is, getting ready to pass out the hard luck for the New Year.

"Yes, yes," said the midwife, coming behind Robert in the narrow lane, toting her black suitcase. "It happen this way every year."

Maybe, thought Robert, maybe not. The damp cold tugged at his hands. Tonight the roads would freeze again. He looked back. "Can't you walk no faster?" he said.

"The first chile always slow," she replied.

"She alone by herself though," Robert said. "Lemme tote that bag—"

"Don't nobody tote this bag but me."

He waited up until she came alongside him and then, reluctantly, he matched his pace with her own. A hawk went hunting rabbits above the dun-colored fields to the left, patiently tracing back and forth, hovering along the shaggy fence rows. Woods already dark with the cold shadows of winter lay to the right of the lane.

He smelled woodsmoke. His dog, a little brown fice, yapped three times, nervously, like a fox, and ran under the house.

"He won't bite," Robert said leading the way across the porch and entering the little room ahead of the midwife. On the bed beside the fireplace, Jeannie had not raised up.

"It's just me," said the midwife. Jeannie stirred. "How old is she?"

"She seventeen," Robert said. He squatted down and set two

hickory logs into the fire. The logs hissed. Flame flickered from the red and yellow embers. It fluttered above the logs in the smoke. "How you feeling, Jeannie?" He asked without looking at the bed.

"No, no, *no*," said the midwife. Robert stood up. He looked around. The midwife had opened her suitcase. "We must take her to the hospital. Wrap her up warm. See how drowsy she is? Feel her?"

"Yes'm."

"Fever," said the midwife. "You ain't got a truck?"

"No."

"Wagon?"

"No."

"Then we have to tote her. Down to the main road we can flag somebody." The midwife leaned over the bed. "We got to get you to town, understand me? Can you hear me? You too drowsy—hear?"

"Yes," Jeannie said. She did not open her eyes.

"How you feel?" Robert said.

"I hurt some," Jeannie said in a sleepy voice.

Robert got her shoes from the hearth.

"Don't bother with that. We'll wrap her up like a baby, see here? Now, lift her," said the midwife. "That's the time."

"She feel hot," Robert said.

The midwife was ahead of him, out the door and across the bare yard. "Makase," she said, going ahead of him almost at a trot now. Carrying Jeannie held close against his chest, his powerful arms under her knees and her shoulders, Robert followed the midwife down the lane. The mud was already beginning to freeze crisp. Sunset made a dark red glow in the sky beyond soft fields of dead grass. Ahead and above him he saw the stars of evening.

Dark had come swiftly down by the time they reached the embankment to the highway. The midwife took off her scarf and waved at the first approaching headlights. A pickup truck stopped. The midwife opened the door. "This girl need to go to the hospital. . . ."

"Get in," said the white man.

Robert climbed into the warm cab, holding Jeannie on his lap like a child. The midwife closed the door and waved good-bye. The truck moved down the highway.

"Has she got anything catching?" said the white man.

"She having a baby."

"Oh." The white man turned the heater up and stepped harder on the gas pedal. Robert's feet began to tingle and get warm. The lights of Somerton appeared. At the Negro entrance to the hospital, down a narrow drive at the rear of the flat wooden building, the white man stopped the truck. He climbed out and came around to Robert's side. He opened the door.

"How much I owe you?" Robert said, climbing down with Jeannie in his arms.

"Nothing," the man said. "I was coming in town anyhow." He walked ahead and opened the door to the hospital.

"I'm much obliged to you," Robert said.

"You're welcome," said the man. "Good luck." And he was gone.

In one corner of the waiting room there was a statue of Lord Jesus, standing on a pedestal. Beside the Coca-Cola machine in the hall stood another statue, Mary, dressed in blue robes. "Yes, can I help you?" The white nurse came from behind a counter.

"We need the white doctor," Robert said.

"What's her trouble?"

"Baby," said Robert.

The nurse turned and walked up the corridor. She came back rolling a narrow hospital cart.

Now it's going to be all right, Robert thought. He put Jeannie on the cart.

"Straight down that hall to the front office. You'll see a window. The sign says 'Hospital Admissions.'"

"What about the doctor, please ma'am?"

"After she's admitted to the hospital we'll call the doctor. Meanwhile she can lie here in the hall. She seems to be resting."

"Yes'm," Robert said.

He went down the strange corridor. The woman behind the admissions window was a Sister in black robes. Robert answered her questions one after the other while she filled in a white form.

"Fifty dollars," the Sister said.

"Yes'm. Put it on the book. I'll pay it."

"Cash, now," she said.

He reached into the pocket of his denim jacket and brought out the bills and the change, six dollars and forty-seven cents. He laid it out for her. "I can put this here down."

"Didn't you hear me just explain to you a while ago? We have rules. Your wife can't be admitted until you've paid fifty dollars cash in advance."

"Fifty dollars," Robert said.

"Fifty dollars," the Sister said. "I didn't make the rule."

"She need the white doctor," Robert said.

"I'm sure she does, and we'll call the doctor as soon as we can get her into a hospital bed. The doctor can't deliver babies out in the hall. I'll hold these papers while you go for the money."

"Yes'm. I don't have it."

"Then you'll have to borrow it, won't you?"

"Yes'm."

She turned away in the bright, silent room beyond the glass, bent about other business. Robert went out the front door and walked quickly down the road. For the first time he knew he had been sweating in the warm corridor because the cold came through his clothes. The sweat combined with it to chill him. He pushed his hands into the pockets of his coat and set off walking. Fear caught at him then. He began suddenly to run down the side of the road. He turned and waved at the lights of a car. It passed him slowly by, its exhaust making a steamy white plume in the air that was freezing him. He began running again. He ran down towards the intersection, past a row of neat white houses. Dogs rushed down the lawns and leaped the ditch, barking. He walked then. The dogs backed nervously away, whining at the strange smell of him.

At the corner he stopped. There was a filling station on his right, well lit, and painted blue and red. Inside the station two white men warmed themselves beside a kerosene heater. He crossed the street. A sidewalk took up on the other side and he began running again. He had a glimpse of white faces peering at him from the passing cars. He ran doggedly on, sweating again, breathing through his mouth, and tasting the bite of the cold air. By now, he thought, the land would be frozen—nearly hard as this sidewalk, by now.

He passed the last houses in the white section of town. He saw the cotton gin and the railroad crossing. He stopped running and walked long enough for his heart to stop pounding so, long enough for the ache inside to ease a bit. Beyond the rail crossing and up a side street he saw Joe-Thell's barbecue stand and the beer hall.

Robert had passed some time in the place on Saturday evenings at strawberry harvest and during cotton season. He ran up the street and pushed through the flimsy door. Joe-Thell looked up, frightened. "What's wrong?" he said. "Say, Robert?" There were no customers in the place.

"I need to borrow fifty dollars," Robert said.

"That quick," said Joe-Thell. He was an old man, wise in the ways of the world and never at a loss for words. He listened as Robert explained, nodding to let Robert know he had heard the same story six dozen times before. Joe-Thell nodded, sadly amused. He struck a kitchen match and lit his cigarette. He wiped his hands on his apron.

"*This* time of year though," said Joe-Thell, "peoples ain't got any work. Peoples ain't got any money, and you got nothing to hock."

"If it was another time of year I wouldn't need to borrow," Robert said. "I can pay back."

"If I had it you could have it," said Joe-Thell. "But I don't have it. Here it is already after dark."

"Then who does have it?" Robert said. "Jeannie up there laying in the hall."

"You got to have a lender, Robert. Mama Lavorn about the only one I know that might go that high with you this time of the year."

"Mama Lavorn?"

"Sure," Joe-Thell said. "Over to the Cafe and Tourist. Don't you know the Cafe and Tourist?" Joe-Thell was smiling a weary smile. "Look here, Robert. Go back to the crossing and then follow the dirt street by the tracks, that's south on a dirt street that angles and slants off. Mama Lavorn got a red light that winks on and off above her front entrance. It's up that road on the right-hand side."

"Mama Lavorn," Robert said.

"Tell her I sent you. Say to her Joe-Thell said she might go that high."

Robert was already backing away to the door. He turned suddenly out into the cold again, running back the way he had come, crossing the railroad and running; running then up the dark dirt side street. He suddenly sprawled. He fell, crashing through thin ice into a puddle of freezing water. He leaped up, the front of him wet through. He was stung by the cold water. Almost without knowing it he was running again, but carefully now, watching for the pale gleam of the frozen puddles. His thin clothes began to stiffen in front where the puddle had wet them. His hands burned.

He crossed the porch beneath the blinking red light bulb and opened the front door. He saw Mama Lavorn smiling at him. She sat in a high chair behind the cash register. She was a fat, dark woman in a purple dress. She wore earbobs that glittered like ice when she moved her head.

"Lord, look here!" said Mama Lavorn. "I mean *somebody's* in a hurry!"

Her smile disappeared as he began talking. "So you need fifty dollars," she said. "You know anyplace else you can get it?" She didn't wait for him to say no, but went on: "Because if you do I'm going to give you good advice. Go there and get it. I'm a lender. If you get it here it's going to cost you money—*if* you get it."

"Please . . ." he said.

"The interest on a dollar for one week is two bits—twenty-five cents," she said. "In a week this fifty dollars gonna come to sixty-two fifty. Put it another way, you can bring me twelve and a half dollars every Saturday to take care of the interest and keep the fifty dollars until strawberry season if you have to."

Robert nodded. "Sign here, on this line." She pushed him a check on the Farmers and Merchants Bank. She handed him her fountain pen. He signed the check. "If you come up and don't pay, or if you miss a payment, all I have to do is take this check to court and they'll come after you. It means jail then, don't you know?"

"Yes'm."

She counted the money out of the cash drawer and into his big hand. "How come you so wet?"

"I fell," he said. Clutching the money, he made himself walk out the door. Then he ran.

Now, he was thinking, it *will* be all right. Running was easier now. The way back seemed shorter. The sidewalk started again. Almost before he knew it he saw the blue-and-red filling station, then the two white men, standing inside as before, beside the heater. Again the dogs rushed down at him but he hardly minded them. They drew back as though astonished and let him pass. Lightly he bounded over the dead short grass on the hospital lawn and took his time then, opening the front door and approaching the admissions window. He laid the five bills on the black marble shelf.

Silently the Sister took the money, counted it, and pushed him a receipt. "Take this to the nurse."

"The doctor?"

"The doctor will be called."

He went down to the Negro waiting room. The nurse took the receipt. "Do you have a regular doctor?"

"No," he said. "No, ma'am."

The nurse picked up the phone. Robert walked around the corner and into the hall to the cart. The hallway was dim. It didn't seem proper to touch his wife, not here.

"What took me so long," he said softly, "I had to go after the money."

Jeannie made no answer. Resting, he thought.

He walked back to the waiting room. It was deserted. Only Christ and Mary looked at him from pale, hard eyes. The red eye in the cold-drink machine said "Nickels Only." The doctor came briskly up the hall, nodded in Robert's direction, and muttered something to the nurse.

The two of them went into the dim hallway. Presently they came back.

"Should have called me at once!" the doctor said. "How long ago did you bring her in?"

"I think. . . ."

"You *think?*" The doctor came slowly from behind the counter. "Robert?" The doctor's white face had a smooth powdered look. His eyes were soft and blue.

"Sir?"

"Your wife's dead. She's been dead maybe half an hour. Sister will refund your fifty dollars. There'll be no fee for my services. There's the body to be taken care of—I usually call the L. B. Jones Funeral Parlor for Colored."

"And they bury her?"

"Well, they fix her and arrange a burial for her, yes. You have a burial policy?"

"I don't have one," Robert said.

"Doctor?" It was the nurse. The doctor went to the counter. He took out his fountain pen. In a moment he returned, holding a slip of paper. He handed the paper to Robert.

"That's the death certificate. However you decide about handling the burial will be all right. Whoever does it will need this."

"Thank you, sir," Robert said. He sat down on the yellow patterned sofa. The doctor went away.

Presently a priest appeared. "I'm sorry about your wife, my son. She's in the arms of God now. She's with God. Are you a Catholic?"

"No, sir."

"We always ask. Not many Negroes are Catholics. We've a few converts among the Negro personnel who work here at the hospital."

"Yes, sir."

"Can I help you in any way? With arrangements?"

The nurse handed something to the priest, who then handed it to Robert—the fifty dollars. Robert put the bills in the damp, cold pocket of his cloth jacket. He carefully folded the death certificate then. The embarrassment of grief had begun to blind him a little— to make him dizzy. He stood up and pushed the slip of white paper into the watch pocket of his overalls.

A big man, taller than the white people, he felt better standing up.

"We can't keep the body here," the nurse was saying.

Robert walked down the hall to the cart. He pulled the white sheet away. Then he wrapped Jeannie carefully in her quilt. He lifted her in his arms.

"If I can help in any way," the priest was saying. "If there's anyone I can call. . . ."

"Just open the door, please sir," Robert said.

The priest looked at the nurse. "Oh, this happens, it happens," the nurse said. "Wait till you've been here long as I have."

The priest opened the door. "God love you," he said.

Robert stepped into the cold. He walked slowly at first, until he reached the road, then he shifted his burden to his shoulder. It rested lightly. He walked at a quick steady pace and was soon out of town, beyond the last yellow street lamp. He chose the longer way, by the old road, a hard, narrow winding road that soon played out to gravel wending between the frozen fields.

At last he crossed the highway, climbed down the embankment, and entered the lane. His shoulder was numb. His side had begun to ache. As he had known it would be, the earth in the lane was frozen hard. The ground everywhere would be hard this night. Like a taste of sudden sickness, grief welled up inside him again, bone-hard and hard as the frozen ground, yet after the first few strokes of the pick the crust finally would give way. He knew the spade would bite and bite again, deeper and deeper still.

MARVIN MUDRICK is Professor of English at the University of California, Santa Barbara. He is the author of *Jane Austen*, the editor of *Conrad: A Collection of Critical Essays*, and has contributed criticism and fiction to many literary journals.

Cleopatra

No doubt we first interested each other because we were both transplanted New York Jews, restless with the energies that had once been expended in the blood-feuds and class-hatreds of the metropolis. Now, in the bland alien air of southern California, she enrolled in a class of mine at the college where I was already shrouded with rank and dignity. I read from the IBM cards at the first session, and a gleam of recognition like a secret handclasp passed between us: Leah; she had glossy abundant black hair, high cheekbones, large dark eyes, large nose; very handsome, a light-skinned Pocahontas; a tall girl with a figure not comfortably ancestral but trimmed and trained for Hollywood. That same day after class, in my office where she followed me and flopped with a beauty's privileged gracelessness into a chair, I was not surprised to learn that she had Hollywood ambitions, was already a veteran of the Las Vegas summer chorus line, modeled for local painters and photographers, maintained "contacts" in Hollywood which was only an hour's drive away, and meanwhile majored in dramatic arts. "I get straight A's," she volunteered, staring at me belligerently. Close up her face had a pale and hollow look, to which the fire-engine red of her big discontented mouth called excited attention.

Why was she doing me the honor? "Dwight had your novel class," she said. "Dwight thinks you're just wonderful. Dwight says I daren't graduate before hearing you on David Herbert Lawrence."

"Who is Dwight?"

"Dwight Cantrell is my husband." And so her puzzling surname —it couldn't be some mutation from a Jewish original? Cantor, per-

haps?—I connected at last with the nearly effaced image of a very
nice and literate young man in the Contemporary Fiction class of
two semesters back, who asked useful questions, wrote exams that
got A's, and had a hobby—flying, that was it. He came to my office
often to talk to me about it, it was the only thing he seemed really
enthusiastic about. "You can get killed," I suggested. He was a lean
crewcut Westerner in hipless denims as stylish as a new motorcycle.
"Statistics prove," he said, "that ninety-nine per cent of all plane
accidents are due to pilot failure." "And ninety-nine per cent of all
plane accidents result in death." "If you stay off the booze," he
persisted with his boyish grin, "it's much safer in a plane than in a
car." He actually asked me to let him teach me to fly: there was a
private flying club, to which he belonged, at the local airport. I was
reminded of my childhood vacations in Atlantic City, where one of
my daredevil dreams had been to take the half-hour ride in the
rackety "hydroplane" that skimmed up from the inner harbor and
roared and rattled above the beaches. Flying had seemed the defini-
tive heroism, but I never took the ride, and airliners many years later
were as heroic as a Greyhound bus. When Dwight Cantrell talked
about flying, he meant little planes, himself at the controls, cold
sober, checking the instruments. A drama of statistics, an actuarial
romance, starring the hero who would live forever; and I envied
him his wooden confidence. Now, a year later, I was envying him
this body that must have warmed and coiled with his on occasions
numerous enough.

Her lips moved easily and broadly as she spoke, not a prissy thin
line; rarely they opened wide in a welcoming smile over movie-star
teeth. She stopped once, in the middle of a statement about her
plans, to tap a painstakingly manicured long fingernail against her
front teeth: "Braces and the most expensive dentists," she said, "or
I'd look like the Wife of Bath."

"You're a product of modern science."

"I'm a product that's going to sell. You wait and see."

She was a bright student, not unlike her husband. She worked
hard, read carefully, wrote careful papers, talked freely in class, came
frequently to my office and in fact talked about her reading. She
was diligent and—well, "bewildered" is a rather misleading word
here, but her very downright mind was impatient with anything it
could construe as subtlety. She had brusque notions about masculine
cant, and was on the lookout for evidences of it in what she read

and heard: much of Lawrence annoyed her for this reason. She thought *Women in Love* should have been titled *Men in Love* or even—I had mentioned Lawrence's volume of poems—*Pansies*; and when an unlucky young man in the class discoursed on "the phallic principle," she sniffed with loud disdain.

"Mrs. Cantrell," I said, "would like to say a few words."

"I'm just jealous," she snapped angrily at me, "that's all. It must feel great to stick up for a principle."

She invited my wife and me to her apartment for several parties, mostly students with two or three couples from the younger faculty. She and Ellen disliked each other on sight: she was dressed in Chinese silk lounging pajamas in a room full of lavish blotchy paintings, beaded curtains, dolls, wedding photos on the TV set; after the briefest grudging inquiries she took no interest in any of the women. Or in Dwight, who served drinks and passed cheese and salami.

"You and your classroom crushes," said Ellen. "It's too bad you don't have the nerve to give her a try."

"Maybe I will, let me think about it."

"You wouldn't last a round with her."

"You see," I said, "I've always told you, you hate me."

"She'd take you apart just for kicks," concluded Ellen vindictively; and then, in gray afterthought, added: "She's a good-looking girl."

"So are you," I said with accurate gallantry.

"But not like that. She looks as if she owns the world."

"She intends to."

That semester she played Cleopatra in the college's annual Shakespeare performance. "Come see me, I'm really very good," she said. And she was. Her appearance—costume, makeup, bearing—was perfect: majestic and sensual, her face with its bold prominences alive to the mellowing distances of the theater. Astonishingly, she sounded right too, her throaty voice ranged from tender to raging and passionate as she carried the other players through on the power of her ambition. It was a triumph. We saw her at the cast party afterward. She glowed like a queen; she must have felt that nothing could hold her back now, and indeed, at the moment, so it seemed to me.

Once I allowed Dwight to persuade Ellen and me to go on an overnight camping trip with them. Dwight was of course an outdoor man. At the campsite in hot barren hill country, he seemed to have put up the army-surplus tent during the time it took Leah to

light her first cigarette. Ellen grew interested, and began to help with
the supplies and cooking arrangements.

"Ellen and I will go foraging for wood," said jaunty Dwight, "and
you tenderfeet can sit and talk."

"Look at them," sulked Leah as they walked off springily. "Pure-
hearted Gentiles, on the best of terms with Mother Nature. Dwight
has taught me to recognize a redwood, so big and *solemn*, but all
the rest are trees to me, and I can't tell one bird from another. And
I hate the outdoors, it gives me sunburn and freckles, and the mosquitoes eat me down to my toenail polish." She stretched and
yawned. "Otherwise I'm glad to be here alone with you, because
you talk so pretty."

I talked to her while she sat on the gravelly ground in the shadow
of the tent, till the others came back laden with dead branches for
the cooking fire. The next morning Ellen and I took a walk after
breakfast.

"What were you doing while we were gone?" Ellen demanded.

"What were *you* doing with the grandson of Gary Cooper?"

"Probably the same thing you were doing—feeling old." Ellen
laughed doubtfully. "You're a lazy man. You'll settle for a warm
bed, you coward."

Leah and Dwight graduated in June. Dwight had been a physics
major, and he started in immediately on a job with an aeronautical
electronics firm in Los Angeles. He was on the road most of the
time however, and Leah decided to stay in town for the summer to
work with a repertory theater. She was very lonely and out of sorts,
phoned me several times to complain about everything from men
to the weather, finally asked me to drop by her apartment one afternoon. I did, and, not having told Ellen, felt like a dangerous phi-
landerer.

"Talk to me," she said, squeezing my hand, sitting in her silk pajamas in that startling room, like a set designer's idea of a Singapore
whorehouse. "I'm so low I could die."

I gave her my standard pitch for gloomy students: You're very
young, all your life is before you, Joseph Conrad didn't speak a
word of English till he was twenty-one and look what happened to
him, spiced with faculty gossip and some roguish joshing about her
manifest attributes which she oughtn't to undervalue.

She sighed contentedly, expanding her remarkable chest. "You're

a dream, you're the bullshit artist of the world, you make a girl truly
tingle. Sweetie, let's run away together."

"Don't say it."

"I mean it, sweetie," she said, but her eyes were alert and amused.

"You treat Dwight like a comfort station. He keeps you respectable. Nobody else would put up with you."

"He's a bore, a fucking bore and an unfucking bore."

"Do you talk dirty with *him?*"

"Poor Dwight? Oh my God, he gets a hard-on if I say damn. Girls
who talk dirty rouse his instincts such as they are. Around him I
talk like Jane Austen."

"Why do you run him down?"

"Why not?" she shouted. "Am I more than tits and ass to him?
That all-American shnook, with his hobbies. I could invent him."

"Why the hell did you marry him?"

"When you're a girl some day, you'll understand. He nosed
around for three years, so wistful, like a puppy with an erection, he
begged and begged, and I didn't see anything better. I didn't even
see anything different—till you came along, you fathead!"

By the time I left she didn't bother to stand up, gave a curt nod
as I opened the door, and was filing her nails when I closed it behind me. I expected never to see her again; she was moving to Los
Angeles at the end of the month.

At Christmas I received a hand-painted card from her, in the style
of those abominable paintings; so it was she who had done them.
Shortly afterward came a rambling letter, addressed to me at the
campus. "Sweetie," it began, and she poured out her troubles. She
was attending an acting school to keep up her "contacts," trying to
seduce casting directors for a job in TV or the movies, had just
missed a fantastic break that she must see me to tell me about. I
must come to see her very soon; Dwight was traveling for the company every Wednesday through Saturday; I must come next Wednesday; she would stay at home next Wednesday to wait for me; she
was up at eleven so I mustn't come before eleven. She remembered
that I had always kept Wednesday free of classes and committees;
I liked it free for my writing. My memory of her had dimmed almost
to extinction, she was one of those people whose presence is like a
blow and whose absence is cancellation. The sight of that round
childish script in green ink stimulated nothing like lust or strong
curiosity. Nevertheless I was curious, and the image of her silk pa-

jamas nipped suddenly at the trailing edges of my imagination, which was always ready for a bit of irresponsible concupiscence. Occasionally I would spend a Wednesday at a university library at Los Angeles, and that was what I told Ellen I was going to do.

Leah's address was on one of the canyon roads in the Santa Monica Mountains. As I drove up the driveway, I saw her wave to me from the deck of the pool in front of the house, as if I were coming home for dinner like a reliable husband. She was wearing a bikini in the sunlight that glittered off the concrete and the water; she was still a knockout, with a midriff and navel that the Song of Solomon might have done justice to.

"My baby," she said cheerfully, as I shook her hand and ventured to kiss her on the cheek. "Would you like to take a dip?" In her letter she had said nothing about a pool.

"I didn't bring any trunks."

"Use Dwight's."

"I could have used Dwight's when I was fourteen. Haven't you noticed?"

She patted me on the stomach briskly. "I never look at a man," she said, "I just listen to him. It's a bad habit you confirmed me in."

It was hot, and I proposed that we go inside. The interior of the house—at least the living room—was an improvement on the apartment, airier and less cluttered, though some of the familiar paintings were on display.

"I'll change," she said, and disappeared down the hall. She came back in a wildly flowered dressing gown, and caught me examining a table stacked with recent copies of women's and movie magazines. "I can't read books anymore," she said. "When you're not there to tell me what they're all about, they depress me terribly. I tried Dostoevsky and Chekhov. But they're so *sad*." Then abruptly: "Are you hungry? Would you like some lunch?"

"Sure," I said, fascinated again by that generous and invulnerable face.

She got very busy like an obedient, rather inept little housewife, and managed to put together a huge tuna salad. Her appetite wasn't girlish, she took big mouthfuls, chattering away.

"How do you keep your figure?" I asked with exasperation.

"Oh?" She held up her fork for a moment. "I work out at the gym, I swim here. If I begin to grow a gut, I fast for a couple of days. I've got to protect the property." This time it was her own midsection that she patted.

She ate another mouthful. "Oh!" she cried. "My almost break! Let me tell you." It turned out that a casting director had sent her on a hurry call to the set of a prestige movie whose ingenue had been fired because of an unscheduled (and unsanctified) pregnancy. The producer had accepted her!—a chance in a million!—but the aging male star showed up next day and said no thanks because she was too many inches taller than he. Later *he* was replaced by a six-foot-four cowboy star, and the girl who got the rôle she missed had virtually the same measurements as Leah. "Except," said Leah dolefully, "that she's three inches smaller in the bust. They made a sample dress for me that first day, and she wore it in the movie—padded like a mattress."

"What do you do with all your time?"

"What do you think? I still do some modeling, bareass, and I spend hours fighting off the photographers with tooth and claw. It's not easy to be a woman. I follow the horses at Hollywood Park. One of the photographers bets for me. Have you ever kissed a jockey? No, you wouldn't. It's like kissing a little boy and all of a sudden discovering his tongue between your teeth. Quite a shock."

Visions of Gomorrah if not of Sodom tumbled like falling castles through my head. I knew she liked to unsettle me, and I never learned the trick of telling when she was lying. I decided the right way for me to feel was old and out of it.

"Stay for dinner," she said, looking at me with what I took to be mockery.

"No, I can't."

"Stay overnight, and I'll let you use my bathroom."

No, she must just be talking tough, she wanted me there and she wanted me away; more away than there, though; and I turned the talk back into channels shallow enough for me to splash in like the joker I used to be with her.

At length she sighed as in the past, pleasantly. "You know I love you," she said. "You're the only man for me."

"If I ever marry, I'll keep you in mind."

"How are your kids?" I think it was the first time she had asked about my children. She had seen them once, at a picnic.

"They're fine."

"They're cute, they look like your wife. When I'm thirty-five I'll have a kid. Imagine having Dwight Cantrell's kid! Maybe I'll let one of the jockeys knock me up and have an itsy bitsy kid, like a kitten."

"Have you ever thought of letting Dwight off the hook?"

"What hook? He thinks he's in paradise. As it is, I scarcely know I'm married to him. You said it, you know: he keeps me respectable. Some day maybe I'll be important enough to get a divorce."

I left earlier than I had expected to. She looked dreary, and as I opened the door of the car she put her arms round my neck. She shoved her body against mine hard enough to reclose the door and, with as much pressure as she could manage, kissed me on the mouth. "Remember me," she said. She waved while I drove away, and that face danced above the highway all the way home and didn't begin to fade till I parked the car in the garage and went in to dinner.

It kept on fading into oblivion again, by the odd law she exemplified: when that configuration of capricious energies was out of sight, it was as if it had never been at all, as if unlike her luckless husband she was so far from being inventable that unless I saw her in her marvelous flesh I could not believe she existed. When a letter came two years later, postmarked with the name of a San Francisco suburb, I had forgotten her again, and the round script in green ink did not bring her back. It was another long complaint, but more mournful, wearier I thought. Dwight had been transferred to the San Francisco office; he still spent most of his time on the road. She had never quite latched on in Hollywood; now she was concentrating on the little theaters in San Francisco. Meanwhile to stay busy she had taken a job in the chorus line at a night club. I ought to come see her, at home and in the show, and she named the days when she was at home and Dwight wasn't.

I didn't write her, and I didn't go. Months passed, without another letter. One week during the summer, an article I was working on was going badly, and I wanted to get away. I sometimes visited a friend in Berkeley, and that was where I told Ellen I was going. It was in fact where I really intended to go. I made it a kind of game: I wouldn't write Leah, or phone her, or do anything but drop in at her address at a time she had said she would be there; if she was and would talk, I'd spend a few hours, and then I'd go on up to Berkeley for my visit; if she wasn't, I would never seek her out again.

I rang the doorbell to her apartment at eleven-fifteen in the morning, and there she was at the door: the same phenomenon, in a different flowery dressing gown.

"You bastard," she said. "I thought you were out of my life for good." She kissed me a wet lipsticky smack on the mouth, rubbed against me so that I could feel her nipples, and jabbed a gentle fist into my ribs.

"Quite a reception," I was able to say.

"I've saved it for you because I'm sure you've got six or seven more kids by this time and never any attention from the lady of the house."

"There are no more kids, and the lady of the house is a whirl-wind in bed."

"You're a liar, but I'm accustomed to polite husbands."

Since I had started from home at six A.M. after toast and coffee, and had come up all the way at seventy without stopping, I let her make a skillet-sized omelet that served for her breakfast and my lunch.

"It's like old times," she said fondly, pouring my coffee.

"Old times were never like this."

"You've never seen me dance. Tonight you'll see me dance. You'll drive me in, watch the show from a ringside table, and take me home. You'll meet Arturo, the boss. He's a pimp and a slave-driver and won't take baths, and I can't find a kind word to say about him."

I had stumbled into a recoverable past, it felt like a honeymoon on the Nile, the purity and gold of vice that will redeem this ashy world. On the walls her awful paintings hung like pledges of her mortality: she will grow old and die. But till then she sat across from me with her elbows on the table, chewing away like a healthy horse, telling me all the gossip about the girls in the chorus, listening to me with heartbreaking delight while I acknowledged her as queen of the world, sovereign of heartbreak and delight, of inexhaustible bounties.

"You beautiful dumb Jew," she said, "why did you have to go and marry a *shiksa?*"

"You sound like everybody's Jewish mother."

"When I was old enough to look like a woman my father, who was very pious and prayed all day and was always wrapping and unwrapping those damned leather straps up and down his arm, told me that all the Jewish boys would lust after *shiksas* and all the

girls after *shagitzes*, and little by little the Jews would be assimilated
to the dusty promises of the false Messiah and vanish from the
earth. But I said, Pop, maybe you're wrong, maybe it'll be the other
way round and little by little the Jews will take over the world by
the strength of their sinful desires. He laughed and pinched my
cheek; he was a good man, even if he *was* religious."

"Leah, the kitchen philosopher."

"Professor X, the phallic principle without a foreskin."

"Leah, the dish that's never been had."

"I've been had, every way."

In my terror of the exaltation I was steeped in, I said: "By Arturo
the boss?"

She stared at me with the old mean look that, though I was at
last able to understand it as the general defense against men, chilled
me like death. "Yes," she said, "by Arturo, who stinks. By the comic
of the show, who tells dumb dirty jokes in his sleep. By every peep-
show photographer with a couch in his studio. By faggots who
wanted to reform. By girls, you mutt. Upside down and backwards.
In triples and squares. Inside out and hanging from the chandelier.
I'm a battlefield where nothing grows. Any other questions?"

"Yes," I said. "Will you let me spend the night?"

"I would have. I would have done even that for you because
you're the only man in the world and I love you. But now I won't."

"Why not?"

"Because I'm no good at it. Don't smile, don't be bitter, you big
baby. I'm a lousy lay, and that's one way I'm not going to dis-
appoint you."

"I don't care."

"Now you don't care, but later you would, you poet. Suffer."
She was angry, finished, very cold and deliberate.

Sitting there opposite her I began to tremble, slightly and then
worse and worse. She stared at me without alarm, she wanted to
make sure I wasn't faking; I wasn't, and my teeth started clattering
like bones. So she almost lifted me out of the chair, led me into
the bedroom, slid naked out of her gown, lay down beside me on
the bed, and gripped me tightly against her till I stopped trembling and began to have other notions again.

"Are you all right?" she said. "Say, that's a good trick."

"I feel like a millionaire."

"In just a minute you'll feel like five bucks and thank you ma'am.

Go ahead then; just once, you dreamer, so you'll know you haven't missed a thing. No, take your clothes off and crawl in. Between the sheets, I mean. It's laundry day today, anyhow."

So I was safe in gorgeous territory, and she stroked my head affectionately while I took my time enjoying the scenery.

"Do you love me?" she asked, brushing the sweat off my upper lip with an enameled fingertip as she leaned on an elbow over me where I lay resting like a happy tourist.

"I love you."

"And will you forget me when you leave?"

I pondered that for a moment, debating whether to tell the truth which for the moment I myself could scarcely credit. "Yes," I said.

"That's good. Stay the afternoon, and take me to dinner and then to the club, and leave me there. Don't come in, and don't pick me up. Go away, and don't come back. I like to keep you in a separate part of my head. You're my only child, and I'll love you forever."

When I drove up to the club, she put my hand on her breast and kissed me.

"Remember me," she said.

"I'll try not to."

"All right, forget me." She laughed, she might have been the promise of everything, she looked as easy to forget as life.

"Write me," I said as she got out.

"Sometime," she said over her shoulder, and was gone.

MIRIAM GOLDMAN lives in Lexington, Massachusetts, where she is at work on a novel and a two-act play. "Fireflies" and other short stories by her have appeared in *The Massachusetts Review*.

Fireflies

THE OTHER DAY I read a chapter called "The Firefly Hunt" by the Japanese writer, Tanizaki Junichirō. Reading, I stumbled on my own thirteenth summer. And though I know our memories return to us at once both maimed and magnified, it seemed to me those weeks were given back intact, an object not only lost and found, but darkened and gleaming with the special radiance that surrounds a green tract of childhood suddenly recovered.

My mother and I were spending the summer in Hightstown, New Jersey, farm country as flat as the palm of one's hand. We were staying with old school chums of my mother's, two childless couples, who migrated from Trenton to Hightstown every June until September. I see their house, white clapboard and small as a postage stamp, with a tiny porch tacked onto half of the front of it, like an unimportant second thought. After a late supper, when the three women had finished washing up, we all sat there, crowded together as in a theatre box, to watch the summer night come down; and when the last rim of light had finally faded away below the horizon and it grew too dark to see the fields, we went for a long and leisurely walk before sleep.

The grown-ups, even the women, had talked themselves out. Now they sang. I followed a short distance behind, catching fireflies. Above the open fields the sky hung brilliant and close, but on either side of the narrow road, at eye level and lower down, trains of sparks meandered and curved, star-particles one could reach out for and hold. They gleamed by the dozens in the tall dusty grass, and I could hear, more with my nerves than with my ears, the faint continuous swish they made as they flickered past. Not only were the fireflies magical, the adults too, as if under their spell, behaved miraculously, identifiably human. For once, I was able not only to understand their occupation but even to approve it. They sang. And since they were singing they must be happy, and since they were happy could be happily dismissed.

One of the men, Emanuel Speer, was a cantor, with a flexible, unnaturally powerful *heldentenor*. He lived his secret life passionately waiting to be discovered by the Metropolitan, a second Richard Tucker. Just by closing its eyes during the High Holiday services, his congregation was able to imagine itself at the opera, while a contrary process stained every aria he sang with the fast unalterable color of woe. Now, walking along under cover of darkness, he indulged his frustrated dreams to the hilt; denied his ambition, he gave of himself in our nightly walks without stinting—threw back his head, opened his arms, and assaulted the night. *Quell' amor ch'e palpito . . . dell' universo intero . . . misterioso altero . . .* he lamented, with the rhythmic thrust of a courante or gigue. In his pauses, my mother's soprano rose lightly, singing the songs of her girlhood in three-quarter time. I caught fireflies, held them enclosed in my hands to tire them, then set them on my blouse and in my hair to sparkle and gleam. Urged, I too sang.

> *Hold the wind, hold the wind,*
> *Hold the wind, don't let it blow.*
> *Hold the wind, hold the wind,*
> *Hold the wind, don't let it blow.*
> *My soul got lost in the midnight dew,*
> *Hold the wind, don't let it blow.*
> *The Morning Star was a witness too,*
> *Hold the wind, don't let it blow.*

No, my soul wasn't lost that summer, though the fireflies did lend themselves to that conceit; metaphysical insects, they glowed without fire or heat—off and on—between the darkness and the light. Holding them in my hands, I sometimes forgot what I was holding, and asked myself whether these could be the flickering souls of the dead, those who had been both mild and good in life. Still, I caught them nightly, dropped them into a milk bottle stuffed with grass, and carried them back to the narrow bare room my mother and I shared.

Happy nights . . . because my childhood was corroded by an

insane terror of the dark, these were my first happy nights. For me the darkness was a swamp, inhabited by murderers, maniacs, stealthy gray ravening wolves, and the rotting dead. If I was lucky, I saw my assassins, screamed, and was saved. But mostly, lying rigid in the ticking darkness, wiping my wet palms on the woolen blanket, I just knew that they were there. Now here was my mother within arm's reach; she slept restlessly too, as if contriving how best to soothe me, turning and turning to try and find a more comfortable position. She coughed softly. She sighed. All night long I could hear her breathe. Beside me on a stool, my night light, a milk bottle stuffed with fireflies and grass. One night we accidentally knocked the bottle over and stayed awake for a long while watching the fireflies dim and glow in the room; stayed awake so long, we heard the cry of a bird that we had never heard before whose name we didn't know: its call, a three times repeated descending trill, furry, mournful and strangely near. "How sad it sounds," my mother whispered, unable to stifle her sighs. Perhaps I sighed, but if I did, it was only to keep her company and from a welling up of joy.

That summer I was allowed to sleep as late as I liked and woke often close to noon. I ate my breakfast standing barefoot in my nightgown with my hair unbrushed, in one hand, a thick black buttered slice of bread sticky with honey, and in the other, a ripe and dripping peach. Still dazed from sleep, I wandered from the overheated kitchen where the women were preparing a hot midday meal, on out to the tiny porch where both men sat in the sun reading their newspapers, or doing what they called their "paper work." Neither hearing nor answering when spoken to, I remained unmolested, for I had learned early how to protect myself: spinning secret webs, I appeared weighed down with worries, but alert. Dreaming, eating, frowning, I planned the pleasures of the day; my few chores completed, and lunch for two in a brown paper bag, I ran half a mile down the track that cut through the corn to the farm where my summer friend lived.

We shared the same first name and believed this set a seal on our friendship as mystical as a blood-pact would have between us. And we shared, as well, the purest form of happiness—hour after hour of summer idleness, acres of idleness, untainted by guilt or evil pangs of conscience.

We swam in a pond ringed by tall grass and low growing sumac and starred over all its surface with water lilies. The bottom, as

in all such ponds, was oozingly slimy and a tangle of rubbery smooth
stems. When we stripped in our rowboat and jumped in, we looked
modestly away—just one good hard stare, then backs chastely turned.
My friend was a year older than I, but names aside, we were very
much alike, both blue-eyed, with skin darker from the summer than
our light streaked hair. She was sturdier, steadier, and sunnier than
I, of Polish descent, with their characteristic tilt of the cheekbones
and the eyes. Today I no longer remember her last name.

Once while we were swimming, we watched a strange man walk
half way round the pond and disappear. We held him in sight for
a long minute, standing in the water up to our noses. The sun
burned down; the boat drifted imperceptibly with the current; a
twig snapped under his foot; the dragon flies flashed as they pierced
and stitched the surface of the pond. Then how we roared, took a
few strokes and threw ourselves gasping into the boat convulsed
with laughter. A man—a man and we naked!—and we laughed until
we had to sit doubled over with our knees drawn up to our chins
to relieve the strain on our aching bellies. Then fell to thinking
about love.

At thirteen, I was still in my heroic age, dreaming not so much
about love itself but more how I could prove my worth. My lover
was featureless, a silhouette cast for the role of He Who Is Saved.
Saint without a halo, I sat nursing him, day and night, without
food or sleep, a wan spectre of tenderness; carrying my burden, I
ran out of flaming buildings, held raging mobs at bay, from how
many bridges crazily leaped! My motto: brave as a lion, strong as
a horse. And when we swam again that day after our hysterical
laughter, what a rescue I made then, down down down to the very
bottom of the shallow pond. That afternoon, I anticipated Lawrence Durrell and his "Clea" as did many another such adventurer
before me. Hacking away and hacking away, I twisted, turned, persisted, until lungs bursting I burst through the surface of the pond,
and laid my water lilies gently down on the bottom of the boat, in-
haling with pleasure their honeyed licorice scent. After such a triumph, I was content to wait and see, alas, whether love would
venture anything half so glorious for me. Letting the boat drift,
we lay back and gazed through half-closed eyes at the summer sky.
It arched over us hazily in the distance, like our future, but unlike
the future, we were able to make the clouds take on any shape we
wished. We remembered lunch when it was time to go home for

supper, and though we were suddenly ravenous, we forced ourselves to eat slowly in order to stretch our few remaining minutes together.

We saw each other at night once, after my father had come to take my mother and me home. I spilled my bottle of fireflies above her head; we were sentimental and tried to cry. Arms around each other's neck, we walked together part way down the road, promised very much, and kissed. Running the rest of the way alone in the dark, I forgot to listen for padding footsteps and to watch out for escaped lunatics crouching in the corn. I was already shaping the phrases of my first letter, and for the coming months, my every thought and sensation existed only to be stripped bare and shared in ink. And the next morning, all the long ride home from New Jersey to Boston over the ugly highway, I was composing a letter describing the long ride home over the ugly highway. When absentmindedly I happened to look up, I saw my mother's face contorted with silent weeping.

My father had just finished telling her that an old and beloved friend had been murdered—robbed and shot in his drugstore as he was getting ready to go home for the night.

"But why did you have to tell her now?" I demanded. "Couldn't you wait until we got back?"

"And what about me?" my father retorted. "Or don't you think I'm human, is that it? Still, that's what it means to be a duchess! Do you think you were left on the doorstep? Well, we didn't find you there, I can tell you that for certain. But now I'd like you to tell me something. Will I ever live to see the day when you think of anyone except yourself?"

Not very logical, my father, but along the way he often hit it and this time too he happened to be right. It wasn't my poor mother I was worrying about. As always, it was myself. I couldn't bear to think of the visit of condolence I knew I should be forced to make. What could I say? Where would I look?

"Well I won't go," I said, bringing their fury down on me.

But I did go and I remember that house of mourning: the living room rug rolled up and the furniture shoved back against the walls for some mysterious reason, as if for a dancing party; while through the curtainless windows, the late afternoon end-of-August sun blazed on the varnished floor scattered with cookies and toys and a soiled baby's diaper that saturated the air with its smell of ammonia and heated iron. And Mrs. Walther, whom I liked so much, her boney freckled face as grief-stricken as I had imagined a face of grief should be, but with an ecstatic light in her eyes, disquieting to preconceived notions—like a horse about to bolt. Her face, white, yes, as I had known it would be, yet not so much drained bloodless from prolonged weeping, as it was pale and luminous, polished by her tears.

JOSEPHINE JACOBSEN has begun only recently to publish fiction; "On the Island" is her third published short story. Her poetry and criticism appear widely in magazines and she is poetry critic for the *Baltimore Evening Sun*. Mrs. Jacobsen's fourth volume of poetry, *The Animal Inside*, was published in 1966 and she is co-author, with William Mueller, of *The Testament of Samuel Beckett*.

On the Island

AFTER DINNER the Driscolls sat for awhile with Mr. Soo, by the big windows looking out and down over the bay. There was nothing to close: they were just great oblong unscreened openings, with all that fantasy of beauty spread straight before them. Mary had not learned to believe in it, any more than she had learned to believe that the shadowy, bamboo-furnished, candlelit room behind them wouldn't be invaded by insects—even perhaps bats, or one of the host of hummingbirds. For storms, there were heavy shutters. But nothing ever seemed to come in; only the air stirred, faintly sweet, against their faces and their flaccid fingers; it grew spicier and more confused with scent as the dark strengthened.

Mr. Soo, in his impassive and formidable way, seemed glad to have them; or perhaps he was only acquiescent, in his momentary solitude. The inn was completely empty except for themselves, Mr. Soo, and the servants. This was rare, she gathered, even in the off-season she and Henry had chosen—and, indeed, their room had been occupied, only the day before yesterday, by another couple. A party of six would arrive after the weekend. Being here alone was part of their extraordinary luck. It had held for the whole trip: in Port of Spain they had got, after all, the room facing the Savanna; on Tobago they had seen the green fish come in, the ones that were bright as fire in the different green of the water; they had even seen, far off, on the trip to Bird of Paradise Island, a pair of birds of paradise, dim and quick through a great many distant leaves, but unmistakable in their sumptuous, trailing plumage.

This still, small place was their final stop before the plane home, and, just as they had planned it, it was beginning as it would end, hot and green, unpeopled, radiantly vacant. "It's the closest we'll get to real jungle," Henry said eagerly. And the jungle was no way away. The inn sheltered in cocoa bushes, shaded by their immortelles: Mr. Soo's plantation was a shallow fringe stretching for acres and acres, with the true jungle less than half a mile behind it. Mr. Soo, she felt sure, had never read one of Henry's books, but obviously was aware of his name, and this perhaps had led him to offer them brandy and sit by them in one of the gleaming, cushioned chairs, as they stared out to the disappearing sea. He did not look to Mary like a man whose pleasure lay in fraternizing with guests. Pleasure? His hair, in short, shining bristles, clasped his head tightly, giving the effect of pulling his eyes nearly shut by its grip. His face was the agreeable color of very pale copper; the mouth straight and thin, the nose fleshy. She and Henry had secretly discussed his age: thirty-eight? forty-four? thirty-seven? In the exhausted light he appeared now almost as though he had been decapitated and then had his head with its impassive face set, very skilfully, back upon his shoulders.

Mr. Soo had been born in Trinidad, but had come here to the island almost fifteen years ago, to raise cocoa. Mary was sure that the friends who had told them about the tiny inn had spoken of a Mrs. Soo, but she was not here and there was no reference to her. Arthur, the major-domo, had said only, "No Mrs. Soo," in response to an inquiry if she were away. Dead? Divorced? A figment of friends' imagination?

"Yes," Henry was saying, " 'like it' is too mild; they can't wait to come again. They're very bird-minded."

Mr. Soo looked at him in astonishment. "Your *friends?*"

"Yes. Very. Why?"

"They seemed to me," said Mr. Soo, obviously shocked, "very nice people. Intelligent. Not bird-minded."

Henry now gaped, baffled.

"Bird-*minded*, Mr. Soo," Mary said nervously. "I think you're thinking of how we sometimes say bird-*brained*. Bird-*minded*. It means thinking a lot about birds. Anxious to see new ones, you know."

Mr. Soo still had an offended air. "Very intelligent people," he said.

"*Very!*" said Henry and Mary simultaneously.

A rush of wings veered past the window, in the new darkness. "Very few here on the island, intelligent people," said Mr. Soo. "Just natives. Blacks."

There was a short pause. A faint yattering, like the rapid clack of unskilled castanets, came dimly from the upper reaches of an invisible tree.

"Haven't you any Chinese or Indian neighbors?" asked Henry, noncommittally.

"Fifteen miles," said Mr. Soo, "is the nearest. I do not like Indians," he added. "But they are civilized. They come from civilized country. On Trinidad, all the shops, the taxis, all mostly Indians. They have an old civilization. Very few criminals. Except when they are drunk. The criminal classes are the blacks. Every week, choppings."

Oh, God, thought Mary, here goes our jungle holiday. Well, she decided immediately, we don't *have* to talk to him; we can go to our room in a minute. She caught Henry's glance, flicked to his wrist.

"Good heavens, it's after 10.00!" he announced like an amateur actor. "If we're going to get up early for the birds . . ."

Mr. Soo said quickly, "Lots of birds. Even at night. Pygmy owls. They fool the other birds," he explained. "That honey-creeper, green honey-creeper. The pygmy owl fools him. Like this." He suddenly puckered his lips and gave a tremulant, dying whistle; afterward, he smiled at them for the first time. "And you see cornbirds. Tody-tyrants, too. And mot-mots, with long tails . . ." He sketched one with a quick hand on which the candlelight caught jade. "They pull out their own tailfeathers. And the kiskadee. That's French, corrupted French. *Qu'est-ce qu'il dit?* Means, what's that he says. Over and over. The kiskadee."

The Driscolls rose, smiling. Are the birds part of the inn, like the sour-sop drinks and the coconut milk and the arum lilies?—or does he like them? It seemed to Mary that he did.

"There was a bird this morning," she said, "on the piles . . ."

"A pelican," interrupted Mr. Soo.

"No," said Mary rather shortly. "I know pelicans." (For heaven's sake!) "A little boy told me what it was. But I can't remember. Like 'baby' . . ."

Henry and Mr. Soo said simultaneously and respectively, "A *booby!* That's what it was, a booby!" and, "A little boy?"

"The *nicest* little boy," said Mary, answering Mr. Soo. "He showed me the fiddler-crab holes and all the live things growing on the big rock, on the sea side."

"What was his name?" asked Mr. Soo unexpectedly. He had risen, too.

"I haven't an idea," Mary replied, surprised. "No, wait a minute . . ."

"A black boy," said Mr. Soo. "With a pink scar on his cheek."

Mary was not sure why the words she was about to say—"*Victor*, I'm sure he told me"—seemed suddenly inappropriate. In the little silence, Mr. Soo surprisingly bowed. "I am sorry," he said with obvious sincerity. "He is, *of course*, not allowed there. He has been told. This will be the last," he said quickly. "I am *so* sorry."

"Good heavens," said Henry, rather irritably, "he was fine—we enjoyed him. Very much. He was a bright boy, very friendly. He showed us how he would fight a shark—imaginary knife and all, you know."

"He was in the *water?*" said Mr. Soo with a little hiss.

During this contretemps, Arthur had approached; his dark face, lustrous in the candlelight, was turned inquiringly toward them over the brandy decanter.

"No, really, thanks," said Mary. She managed to smile at Mr. Soo as she turned away, hearing Henry say, "We'll be back for breakfast about 8.00," and then his footstep behind her across the lustrous straw roses of the rug.

Later in the night she woke up. Theirs was the only bedroom in the main building except for Mr. Soo's apartment. Earlier, massed poinsettia, oleander, and exora had blazed just beyond their casement windows in the unnatural brilliance of the raw bulb fastened outside—now, by a round gold moon that was getting on for full, blue and purplish hues had taken over. The bunches of blossom were perfectly still.

She could see Henry's dark head on his pillow; he was spread-eagled with one foot quite out of bed. Very soon, familiar pressure would swallow them. Henry, even here, was immersed in his plots, manipulating shadowy figures, catching echoes of shifting dialogue. It had nothing to do with happiness, or satisfaction, but she knew that increasingly Henry's mind veered from hers, turning in patterns whose skill she admired. Henry believed in his plots. His cause and effect, lovely as graph lines and as clear, operated below all things. This island, which seemed to her full of hints flying like spray, yielded itself to him in information of tensions, feathers, blossoms, crops. More and more, like a god let loose on clay, he shaped and limited. She loved him for this, too: for his earnestness and the perfection of his sincerity; but sometimes now, she knew, her mind seemed to him disorderly and inconsequential, with its stubborn respect for surprises.

A breeze had begun to stir. The blanched crests of blossoms nodded beyond the broad sill and there was a faint rattle of palm fronds. Also, something moved in the thatch.

I will go to sleep if I think of the right things, she said to herself, and she set about remembering the misty horses, galloping easily over the Savanna track in the Trinidad dawn; she'd stood in her nightgown on the balcony to see their lovely, silent sweep. And the fern banks on Grenada: hills of fern higher than towers, deep springing hills of fronded green. And the surf, the terrifying surf, when they'd launched the little boat off Tobago for the trip to Bird of Paradise Island. The turquoise water had broken in a storm of white over the shining dark bodies and laughing faces of the launchers, the boat tipping and rocking, flung crazily upward and then seized again by dripping hands. She'd felt both frightened and happy; Henry had hauled her in and they'd plunged up and down until finally they reached deep water and saw ahead of them, beginning to shape up in the distance, the trees which perhaps sheltered the marvelous birds. "Nothing is known of the breeding-habits of Birds of Paradise," her *Birds of the Caribbean* said. She repeated this, silently, sleepily. Nothing is known of the breeding-habits of Birds of Paradise. How nice.

Suddenly, she heard water, a seeping sound—though, on her elbow, she could see it wasn't raining. She swung her feet over the bed, but not to the floor. Luck had been good here, but in the dark she wouldn't walk barefoot and her slippers she kept under the sheet. She felt her way cautiously to the bathroom door. Inside, she lighted a candle—the generator went off at 11.00. The bathroom was immaculate, but water shone by her feet and seeped toward the depression which served as a shower-floor. The toilet was unobtrusively overflowing in a small trickle. Eventually the floor would be covered and water would ooze under the door. What on earth could they do about it tonight, though? Move in with Mr. Soo? She began to giggle faintly. But it was a bother, too; in remote spots things took forever to get themselves fixed. She put Henry's sandals on the window-ledge, blew out the candle, and closed the door softly behind her. Henry hadn't stirred. She got back in bed, thinking: It's a good thing I saw those sandals—they were *in* the water! The words set off an echo: but, as she remembered what it was, she fell asleep.

By morning, the water was in their room, reaching fingers in several directions; the heavy straw of the rugs was brown and dank. When they came out into the pale, fragrant sunlight of the big room, Arthur was throwing away yesterday's flowers from the two big blue vases on the low tables. Henry, dropping his binocular-strap over his head, stopped long enough to report their problem. Arthur looked at them with an expression of courteous anguish and ritual surprise and said that he would tell Mr. Soo.

When they returned two hours later, hungry and already hot, Mr. Soo had come and gone. His small table, with its yellow porcelain bowl filled each morning with arum lilies, was being cleared by Arthur, who brought them a platter of fruit and told them that after breakfast he would transfer them to Mr. Soo's room. They were astounded and horrified in equal proportions. "That's absolutely impossible," said Henry. "We can't inconvenience him like that. Why can't we go down to one of the beach cottages? Or up on the hill?"

Arthur, who at the moment represented all help except the invisible cook, did not say: Because I can't run back and forth and still do everything here. He said instead, "Mr. Soo did tell me to move you after breakfast."

Henry was anxious to talk to Arthur. Wherever they went, he absorbed gestures, words, inflections, as a lock-keeper receives water, with the earnest knowledge of its future use. He was very quick at the most fugitive nuance; later it would be fitted into place, all the more impressive for its subtlety.

Arthur had poured their second cups of coffee. Now he reappeared from behind the red lacquer screen, carrying one of the big blue vases. It was filled high with yellow hibiscus and he set it gently on one of the teakwood stands.

Henry said, in his inviting way, "You do a bit of everything."

Immediately, Aruthur came to the table. "Only I am here now," he said. "And the cook. Two boys gone." He held up two fingers. "Chauffeur is gone."

On short acquaintance, Mary did not particularly like Arthur. He had a confidential air which, she noticed, pivoted like a fan. At present it was blowing ingratiatingly on Henry. "Mr. Soo had a lot of trouble with help," said Arthur. Mary saw with a rather malign amusement the guest's breeding struggle with the writer's cupidity. The victory was tentative.

"Now *we're* upsetting things," said Henry, not altogether abandoning the subject. "It's ridiculous for him to move out of his room for us."

"Won't upset Mr. Soo," said Arthur soothingly. "He can shut he apartment off, sitting room, library. Another bath, too, on the other side. Used to be Mrs. Soo."

Mary could see the waves of curiosity emanating from Henry, but he gallantly maintained silence. "There is a sleep-couch in the sitting room," Arthur went on. "Mr. Soo does want you to be comfortable, and so." He pivoted slightly to include Mary in his range. His eyeballs had crimson veins and he smelled of a fine toilet water. "Mr. Soo is very angry with that boy," said Arthur. "Mr. Soo does tell he: Stay away from my beach, ever since that boy come here."

In spite of herself, Mary said irascibly, "But that's ridiculous. He wasn't bothering anyone."

"Bother Mr. Soo," said Arthur. "Mr. Soo is so angry he went last night to go to see he grandmother. Told he grandmother, that boy does come here again, he beat him."

"May I have some hot coffee, please?" asked Mary.

Arthur did not move. He swept his veined eyes from one to the other. "Mr. Soo does not own that beach," said Arthur. "Can't no mahn own a beach here. Mr. Soo's beachhouse, Mr. Soo's boat, Mr. Soo's wharf. But not he beach. But he don't let no mahn there, only guests."

"Why does he like this beach so much?" said Mary, for it was small and coarse, with plenty of sharp rocks. "The boy, I mean."

"Only beach for five miles," Arthur told her. "That boy, Vic-tor, come with he brother, come to he grandmother. They live topside. Just rocks, down their hill. Very bad currents. Sea-pussy, too. Can't no mahn swim there."

"May I have some hot coffee?" Mary said again.

Arthur stood looking at her. At this moment a considerable clamor broke out in the kitchen behind them. Voices, a man's and a woman's, raised in dispute, then in anger. The woman called, "Arthur! You come here, Arthur!"

Arthur continued to look at them for about two seconds; then, without haste, he went away, walking around the screen toward the kitchen.

"All right, all right," said Henry, answering a look. "But you know perfectly well we can't come here for five days and tell Mr. Soo who he must have on his beach."

"It isn't his beach."

"It isn't ours, either."

Something smashed in the kitchen. A door banged viciously. Outside the window went running easily a tall, big boy. His dark, furious, handsome face glared past them into the room. He dived down the wooden steps past the glade of arum lilies. His tight, faded blue-jeans disappeared among the bushes.

"What was *that* in aid of?" said Henry, fascinated.

Arthur appeared. He carried the faintly steaming enamel pot of coffee, and, coming up to them, poured a rich stream into Mary's cup. Then he said: "The big brother of Vic-tor, he's a bad bad boy. Daniel. Same name as the man fought the lion." He bowed slightly, thus reminding Mary of Mr. Soo, turned to the other teakwood stand, lifted the empty blue vase, and went off with it behind the screen.

"'*Fought* the lion'?" said Mary, inquiringly, to Henry.

"Well," said Henry, "I suppose Arthur places him in the lion's den, and then improvises."

That was the last of the excitement. They were transferred quickly and easily from their moist quarters; the toilet was now turned off and not functioning at all. Mr. Soo's room lacked all traces of its owner, unless a second bed could be viewed as a trace. It had a finer view than their abandoned room, looking all the way down the series of low terraces to the small, bright, rocky beach.

Greenness took over; the greenness of the shallows of the bay before it deepened to turquoise, of the wet, thick leaves of the arum lilies, soaked each morning by an indefatigable Arthur, of the glittering high palms, and the hot tangled jungle behind the cocoa bushes shaded by their immortelles. Mary had—unexpectedly to herself—wanted to leave before their time was up. She had even suggested it to Henry right after breakfast on that second morning. But Henry wanted to stay.

"It *isn't* Mr. Soo," she said, trying to explain. "It hasn't anything to do with that. It's something else. There're too many vines. Everything's looped up and tangled. The palms rattle against the tin and give me dreams."

"Don't be fey," said Henry rather shortly. "We'll be away from palms soon enough."

Mr. Soo continued cordial in his immobile fashion; he talked to them from his small table when, at dinner, their hours coincided. Once, he had Arthur make them each a sour-sop, cold and lovely as nectar, when they came in brown and sweaty from the beach rocks. But by some obscure mutual assent, there were no more brandies. After dinner, the Driscolls sat on their tiny terrace, watching the moon swelling toward fullness, and drank crème de cacao in tiny gourd cups provided by Arthur. They knew they were destined to share their final hours on, and their first off, the island with Mr. Soo. He too would be on the biweekly plane to Trinidad. Mr. Soo said he was going to Port of Spain to procure plumbing fixtures. Arthur said Mr. Soo was going to procure a number two boy and a chauffeur. Where on earth did Mr. Soo wish to be driven, over the narrow, pitted, gullied roads that circled the island? Through and through his plantation, perhaps. Arthur took no note of coldness in relation to his comments on Mr. Soo; also, Mary felt, the most ardent questioning would have led him to reveal no more than he had originally determined. His confidences went by some iron and totally mysterious auto-decision. She had absolutely no idea how his sentiments stood in regard to his employer.

On their last afternoon, the Driscolls went for a walk. Just before dusk, they decided to go deep along the jungle path. This was the hour for birds; all over the little island they were suddenly in motion. Almost none, except the hummingbirds with which the island fairly vibrated, flew in the golden hot midday, but at dusk the air was full of calls and wings.

Mary and Henry went along the middle ledge, above the arum lilies. Down on the beach, the fiddler crabs would be veering, flattening themselves, then rearing to run sideways, diving down holes into which fell after them a few trembling grains of sand. From here, the Driscolls could only see the white waves, leaping like hounds up at the rocks. They went along slowly, musingly, in the fading heat, up the steep path back of the garden sheds, below the giant saman, the great airy tree with its fringed, unstirring, pendant parasite world. With its colony of toe-hold survivors, it was like the huge rock on the beach, half in the tides, to whose surface clung and grew motionless breathers.

They turned up the small, dusty road toward the solid wave of tree-crests towering ahead. They had been this way twice before; they remembered a goat tethered up the bank at eye-level, a small scrubby cow standing uncertainly in the ditch. They would pass a cabin, half up the slope, with its back to the bay far below, its straw roof smothered under rose-colored masses of coralita. They walked in intimate silence. The road was daubed with the fallen blossoms of immortelles and their winged pods. Once, two laborers passed them, stepping quietly on their tough bare feet, the shadows of leaves mottling their dark erect bodies and bright blue ripped trousers, their machetes in worn scabbards swinging gently from their heavy belts.

Around a curve, they came on a dead, long snake, savagely slashed. Just before their path struck off the road there was a jingle and faint creaking, and around a tangle of scarlet blackthorn rode two native policemen, their caps tilted against the sunset, their holsters jogging their elbows. They pulled their small horses, stained with sweat, into single file; one raised his hand easily in a half-salute and both smiled. These were the first horses the Driscolls had seen on the island, and the first police. Of course, there had to be police, but it was strange how out of place they seemed. When the hushed fall of the hoofs in the dust died away it was as though horses and riders had melted.

Later, sitting on a fallen tree in the bush, Mary thought idly about the snake, the laborers, the policemen. Henry had gone further in, but she had felt suddenly that she couldn't walk another step. She sat on ridged strong bark coursed by ants and thought about the policemen, their faces, their small dusty horses, on that peaceful, hot patrol. Surely there must be almost nothing for them to do. And yet the idea of violence, she realized, had come to be the air she breathed. Not violence as she knew it in Henry's books, or in the newspapers at home—riot, rape, murder, burglary. This violence seemed a quality of growth—the grip of the mollusks on the wave-dashed rock, the tentacles of the air plants flowering from the clutched saman. It oppressed her with its silence, its lack of argument. Perhaps she responded in some obscure portion of her feminine heart. An ant ran silently and fast over her hand. She shook it

off and stared into the green that had swallowed Henry. His precious-
ness to her appeared not enhanced but pointed up by her sense of the
silent violence of growth around her, as if, among the creepers,
windfalls, sagging trees, his face, clear to her love, defined itself as
the absolute essential. Of the rest, blind accidents of power, and
death, and greenness, she could make nothing. Nothing they might
do would surprise her.

There was a wild cocoa bush not ten feet away, dropped into this
paroxysm of growth, thin, tall, struggling for light. She could see the
pendulous gourds in their mysterious stages of ripeness: cucumber
green, yellow, deep rose-bronze, and plum-brown. That plum-brown
was on the voluptuous poles of the bamboos, the great, breeze-
blown, filmy, green-gold stools of bamboo.

She listened for Henry. There was provisional silence, but no real
stillness; hidden streams ran with a deep, secret sound in the throat
of distant ravines, and the air was pierced and tremulous with bird-
calls, flutings, cries, cheeps, whistles, breaks of song; response and
request; somewhere away, lower than all the sounds but that of water,
the single, asking, contemplative note of the mourning dove.

All at once, there was Henry. When she saw him, she realized
that some portion of her had been afraid, as though, like the police
on their little horses, he would melt into the greenness for good.

"Did you realize I'd forgotten my binoculars?" he asked, infuriated
with his stupidity. "Of all idiotic times!"

Suddenly, she flung herself at him, winding her arms about his
neck, linking their legs, covering his face with quick, light kisses.
He held her off to look at her, and then folded her tightly in his
arms, as though she too had come back from somewhere. "We
haven't a flashlight, *either*," he said, "and, if we don't look out, we'll
be plunging about in the dark, breaking everything."

On the way home, they went more rapidly. The birds were almost
completely silent. Now and then one would flash in the tree-crests
far above them, settling to some invisible perch. We've left this
island, Mary thought. There came a turning-point—on a wharf, on a
station platform, in the eyes of a friend—when the movement of
jointure imperceptibly reversed. Now they were faced outward—to
their suitcases, to their plane, to the Port of Spain airport, to Con-
necticut and typewriters. Mary began to worry about the dead snake,
in the thick dusk; she didn't want to brush against its chill with her
bare, sandaled feet. But, when they came to the spot, she saw it at

once. It seemed somehow flatter and older, as though the earth were drawing it in.

As they rounded the bend to the final decline, a sound came to them, stopping them both, Mary with her hand digging into Henry's arm. They thought at first it was an animal in a trap, mistreated or dying. It was a sound of unhuman, concentrated, self-communing pain, a dull, deep crying, with a curious rhythm, as though blood and breath themselves caused pain. "What *is* it?" cried Mary, terrified.

"It's a human being," said Henry.

He was right. Drawn close together, they turned the bend in the road, and saw the group from which the sound came: just up the steep slope to their left, in front of the cabin. Raw light from a kerosene lamp on the porch fell on the heads of the men and women, in an open semicircle. Around this space crawled on her hands and knees a woman. Her head was tied in a red kerchief and the light caught her gold earrings. She pounded the earth with her fist, and round and round she crept in short circles.

Dark faces turned in their direction, but the woman did not stop; on and on went the sound. Alien, shocked, embarrassed by their own presence, the Americans hesitated. Then Henry caught his wife's elbow and steered her, stumbling, down the path.

"Oh, Henry, *Henry* . . ." she whispered frantically to his shadowy face. "Oughtn't we to stop? Couldn't we? . . ."

"They don't *want* us!" he hissed back. "Whatever it is, they don't want *us*."

She knew he was right, but an awful desolation made her stumble sharply again. The sound was fainter now; and then, in a minute or two, gone. Below them, they could see the lightbulb lashed to the trunk of the saman tree, like a dubious star.

Later, Mary was not sure why they said nothing to Mr. Soo. Neither, strangely, did they discuss it between themselves in their bedroom, showering, dressing for dinner. It was as though its significance would have to come later. It was too new, still, too strange; their suspended atmosphere of already-begun departure could not sustain it.

This sense of strangeness, and also, perhaps, the sense of its being their last evening, seemed to constrain them to be more civil to Mr. Soo. Arthur, bringing their Daiquiris, told them there would be a cold supper; the cook was away. His air was apologetic; this was evidently an unexpected arrangement. On the terrace, he set their drinks down on the thick section of a tree bole that served as a stand, and looked through the open casement window into their room, now transforming itself again into Mr. Soo's room: at the open, filled suitcases, the range of empty hangers, the toilet bottles on the dresser.

"You sorry to go?" asked Arthur. "You like it here, and so?"

"Very, very much," said Henry. "We hope we can come back."

"You know, one thing," said Arthur. A gong was struck imperiously. Arthur took his empty tray back through the room. The door closed behind him.

Perhaps it was too late for a more cordial response; perhaps Mr. Soo, too, felt that they were no longer there. Above his arum lilies in their yellow bowl, he was unresponsive. After one or two attempts at conversation, the Driscolls ate their cold supper, talking to each other in tones made artificial by several kinds of constraint. Over coffee, Henry said, "I'd better see him about the bill now—it's all going to be so early in the morning."

Mary waited for him by the huge open window-frames, where they had sat on their first evening, discussing with Mr. Soo their bird-minded friends. The moon, which tonight was going to be purely full, had lost its blemishes of misproportion; it was rising, enormous and perfect, in a bare sky. She could hear very faintly the sound of the tide as she stared out over the invisible bay to the invisible sea.

Behind her, Mr. Soo and Henry approached, their footsteps hushed by the straw, their voices by the silence. Turning, she was confronted by Mr. Soo's face, quite close, and it struck her that the moonlight had drawn and sharpened it, as though it were in pain.

"I hope you and your husband have been happy here," said Mr. Soo.

"Very," said Mary. (Now we're in for a drink, she thought.) "The birds have been wonderful . . ." she began, but Mr. Soo was not listening.

"The driver from the airport will be here at 6.00," he said. He turned and left them, walking slowly over the gleaming rug.

The moon hadn't reached their terrace. Arthur, arriving with the crème de cacao, had to peer at the tree-bole before setting down the little cups. He did not go away, but stood and looked at them. Finally, he said: "Do you remember Vic-tor?"

"Of course," said Henry, and Mary added, "The little boy."

"He's gon," said Arthur.

Henry said with interest, "Gone?"

"Dead, gon." Arthur stood there, holding his tray, and waited for them to speak. When they still did not, he said, "He did go off those high rocks. Back down from he house, those high rocks. He did go to swim in that sea-pussy. Like he grandmother told he not to. He is gon, out to sea; no body. No body a-tall. He was screaming and fighting. Two men fishing, they tried very hard to grab he up, but couldn't never get to he. He go so fast, too fast. They will never have no body—too much current, too many fish. He grandmother told he, but that boy, he gon to swim. He won't even mind he brother, brother Daniel, brought he up," said Arthur, turning away and continuing to talk as he left, "*or* he grandmother, took he in. The cook is gone," said Arthur, faintly, from the distance. "Now Mr. Soo, Mr. Soo is all alone." The door closed.

Mary got up, uncertainly; then she went into the bedroom and began to cry very hard. She cried harder and harder, flinging herself on the bed and burrowing her head in the pillow. She felt Henry's hands on her shoulder blades and told him, "I can't think *why* I'm crying—I didn't even know the child! Yes, he showed me the crabs, but I didn't *know* him! It's not that . . ." She was obsessed by the mystery of her grief. Suddenly, she sat up, the tears still sliding down over her lips. "That was his grandmother," she said.

"It's a pattern," said Henry miserably. "We saw it happen all the way from the beginning, and now it's ended. It had to end this way."

She touched his face. His living body was here beside her. She slid her hand inside his shirt, feeling his flesh, the bones beneath it. The room was filled like a pool with darkness. She ran her finger over his chin, across his lips. He kissed her softly, then more deeply. His strong, warm hand drew her dress apart and closed over her breast.

"I love you," he said.

She did not know when Henry left her bed. She did not, in fact, wake until a sound woke her. Her bed was still in darkness, but the window was a pale blaze from the moon, now high and small. It struck light from the palms' fronds, and against it she saw the figure on the ledge, in the open window. Young and dark and clear, and beautiful as shining carved wood, it looked against all that light, which caught and sparked on the machete's blade. It was gone; she heard a faint thud on the earth below the window. She raised herself on her elbow. In Mr. Soo's moonlit room she stared at Mr. Soo's bed and at what she now made out on the darkening sheet. It was Henry's dark head, fallen forward, and quite separate. His eyes were still closed, as if in an innocent and stubborn sleep.

JAMES BUECHLER was born in Albany and grew up in Schenectady, New York. After graduating from Harvard in 1955 he spent the next year in Europe on a fellowship. He is married, and has worked as a newspaper reporter, a librarian and a teacher. At present, he is a writer-teacher in the Freshman English program at Stanford University, where he is working on his first novel. His stories have appeared in *Mademoiselle*, *The Saturday Evening Post* and *Redbook*. Mr. Buechler's first published story received an O. Henry Award in 1956.

The Second Best Girl

ALL during her high-school years, Shirley was in love with Tom Vinciguerra, the football hero.

Tom didn't even know she was alive. She wasn't a cheerleader, or anything like that. Her marks were good, but even in her marks she wasn't "somebody." She was always just below the leaders, the bright ones who edited the yearbook or were in the plays or who went off to college afterward on scholarships. It seemed unfair to her that she should fall just short in everything, and it made her work very hard. Gradually she raised herself to twelfth in her class. At commencement the first twelve were called forward together, before all the others. The superintendent of schools presented their diplomas while the principal stood by, smiling. He spoke to them all by name. When only Shirley was left, he appeared slightly surprised, as if he couldn't think who she was, but he nodded to her and said, "Congratulations."

She was in love with Tom Vinciguerra—there is no use asking why. These unobtrusive, hard-working, well-behaved girls are attracted just as much as the opposite kind to the particular type of boy, usually wild and reckless, who already possesses the strength and appearance of manhood. Such boys cause the most accidents with automobiles and the most trouble with the police, and get the most girls pregnant. But such things weren't likely to frighten away Shirley, quiet as she looked. She saw plenty of them at the city hospital, where she worked after school. Her trouble was that Tom just didn't know her, and so she loved him from a distance. She realized she had no chance.

She did have another boy, who was not so far away from her. He had grown up in a house four blocks from her own, whereas she never saw Tom except in the highly charged cosmopolitan atmosphere of the big high school. One night in late November, when she was fourteen, Will Schuler had asked if he could walk her home after choir rehearsal, which let out at about nine o'clock. The choir already had begun practicing for Christmas midnight Mass. Will had grown quite tall all of a sudden; he sang bass. Shirley was wearing a red parka; she had on red boots, and a white kerchief tied under her chin. On a small, mid-block street bordered by long back yards, Will pulled her along, his large, bare hand tightly clasping her mittened one, to behind a dark garage where the owner threw his old lumber. There Will sat on a box and Shirley sat on his long knee, which swayed at first with her weight, and she let him kiss her many times. Within its white binding, her cold, smooth face, touched by Will's face, was alive with amusement and happiness. The wind blew around the garage, but they were sheltered behind it. Afterward, when she was home, upstairs in the warm house (she lived on the second floor of a two-family house), her cheek felt a little sore in the place where the collar of Will's big lumber jacket had rubbed against it. Even her lips felt slightly chapped, which made her smile.

After that she "liked" Will Schuler. They both were fourteen years old. Several more times they stopped in the same place after choir rehearsals. On a cold night near Christmas they made their way out to the garage over deep, glowing snow covered with a hard crust. It broke with a punch at every step. Will sat right down, crumbling the snow that capped his box. Shirley shivered and laughed—he might at least have cleaned it off. She liked Will, and she knew Will liked her because at Christmas he gave her a little present. He had even wrapped it in white paper and seals, though there was no card. He gave it to her saying, "Here—this is for you," while they were climbing the steps to the choir loft just before midnight Mass.

After the Mass, however, although it was another cold, bright night, with the same hard and glowing snow spread over the ground like water around the dark shapes of the houses, Will had to go home with his family in their car. The Schulers always opened their presents together after midnight Mass and then slept late on Christmas morning. So Shirley had to walk along the little street to her own house by herself. In a way, she didn't mind being alone. It was a night in her life when she was happy, what with Christmas and the little package Will had given her. As she walked over the hard-packed snow of the road, with patent-leather shoes and new, chilling nylon stockings inside her boots, she could think that at the same time, not very far away, across a distance of only three or four streets, downstairs in a house she knew from the outside very well, there was Will, who liked her. She supposed vaguely that someday she might be married to Will, but it wasn't anything she could picture to herself—for example, living with him upstairs or downstairs in a two-family house. She went home and had something to eat and then slept late herself on Christmas morning.

Before going to bed, though, she unwrapped Will's present. He had given her a fat little diary, the kind you can buy at the ten-cent store, that can be locked shut with a little key. The first things she wrote in it were about herself and Will.

After Christmas she never again saw so much of Will. Now that there was nothing in particular to practice for, he came to choir only rarely. He walked her home those nights that he came. For herself, she still "liked" Will, but she saw that Christmastime, when she had been so happy thinking of what had only begun, had really been the high point of her happiness with him, which she wasn't likely ever to reach again. In June it was she who had to ask Will if he would take her to the graduation dance at the junior high school. She couldn't afford to be bashful. Will accepted. It was the first formal dance she had gone to.

That summer she worked long days in the hospital (she had always wanted to be a nurse) and saved her money. She usually worked weekends, and she didn't know what Will was doing. Probably he worked too—or he might have gone away somewhere. But in the fall he turned up the very first morning in the school bus that carried them both to begin tenth grade at the imposing new high school in another part of town.

In high school her life changed at once. The place was so large.
There were so many people coming from all over. Some of them
were important, were doing things. She felt quite alone and abandoned to herself. Everyone she knew from her own part of the
city seemed to dissolve away among all these other, strange people.
Later on some of them rose into view again as they became important; the others seemed lost forever. The great school upset her, yet
it attracted and excited her. She badly wanted to have a part in it,
but she couldn't seem to find a place, somehow. All during her three
years she seemed only to stand aside and watch what was going on.
She couldn't mingle with the leading people, though she admired
them and wished she were like them. She did what she was told,
she made good marks, but she had no flair. In her last year, when
her first cousin, who lived across town, entered school, Shirley
watched her become somebody almost immediately. Soon more people knew Trish than knew her.

"Trish—what's wrong with me?" she asked one night.

Trish, tiny and lively, a cheerleader already, paused and thought.
"I don't know . . . there isn't anything wrong with you. You do
everything you should." She laughed mischievously. "Maybe you're
too good."

The words struck Shirley, so that she lost heart. "I don't want to be
good. I want to be the same as everybody else. How should I start
being different?" she pleaded. "You know. Tell me."

"Oh . . . I don't know!" The younger girl broke off, exasperated.
She understood very well what Shirley was asking. She knew that she
herself was different from her cousin. But she had her own life.
Her own success exhilarated and preoccupied her. She had to work
very hard at it. She was doing a million things—she had no time.
In a few years she went off to college on a scholarship, left the town
altogether. She never came back afterward except to visit.

At the high school Tom Vinciguerra burst on Shirley's awareness
all at once. For her, he was the excitement and danger and chance
of the whole place—a medium-sized, somewhat brooding, heavy-
set boy, very thick within his clothes. He would sit in the back of the
classroom, watching the teacher with a steady, unafraid look. He was
the best football player the high school had had in many years.
Week after week during Shirley's first autumn the newspapers carried his name and ran pictures of him. The school had never been

good at football before. Now they won almost every game, and Tom Vinciguerra was doing it virtually by himself. He was talked about all over the city. That winter the chamber of commerce chose him as the Athlete of the Year—which meant something, because the city also had someone on the Olympic speed-skating team and a successful racing-car driver. But Tom was more important. He received a trophy, and his picture appeared in the papers once more.

Shirley was working every Saturday, but on Thanksgiving Day she finally could go to a game. She had never seen one. In the strange football clothes with the high, hunching shoulders and the big black shoes, Tom looked much bigger than he did in life. His round white helmet looked like the top of a bottle to her; his suit was red underneath it; he looked like a catsup bottle. She saw the dark ball come flying back to him, he waddled forward clumsily, just shoving people ahead of him as though he wanted to get through a door a little faster than anybody else. So many players crowded around him that eventually he fell down. It didn't make much sense to her, it was all so clumsy and confused, but she saw that it was serious. What convinced her of that was the faces of the players in the other colors when they were close enough to see. Some of them looked quite old. They were dirty and tired. She watched them as they bent down at the beginning of each play and put their heads up and waited for Tom Vinciguerra. They wanted badly to stop Tom, but they couldn't. He did what he wanted with them.

Tom continued to be famous all his and Shirley's three years. Every year he was in at least one class with her, but she could never say she knew him.

She grew more reserved. She didn't smile easily. She went around with an unpleasant, long-faced, horsy expression. Early in her senior year, when someone turned to her with new interest and asked, "Oh! You mean Trish is your cousin?" she softened immediately, and her looks themselves abruptly improved, for she was really fond of Trish. "Yes." She smiled. "Didn't you know that?" But she was asked the same question once too often. In the end it only made her more balky and horsy than ever.

Then something unexpected happened. Will Schuler invited her to the senior ball, which was held the weekend before graduation. Though Will rode on the same school bus, Shirley had not thought much about him for years. She accepted because she wanted to go.

They could have made a good couple. Will was tall and fair, though his skin was blemished. Some girls might have thought him good-looking, and attractive otherwise too. In the morning he was always filled with life, the wit among the boys who sat at the back of the bus; but once in school he put on a pair of small, ridiculous glasses, blinked, looked stupidly serious, and guffawed in a vacuous way with his friends in the halls after lunch. Now, however, in a powder-blue dinner jacket, he was really handsome. They got out of the taxi and walked up to the columned entrance of the school; the walk was lined with onlookers—curious people who lived in the nearby houses, younger students, and some seniors not coming to the dance. Will bent his head; he was self-conscious and so was she. She was thinking she might well take to him again. They entered the vast gymnasium, decorated beyond recognition, its backboards and climbing ropes all hoisted into the dark upper regions of the ceiling. And then, for most of the night, they simply sat at a little-disguised card table with a lighted candle on it and watched the sweep of the long dresses and the matching scissors of black trousers of the dancers at the center.

For high school had infected Will too. With a clumsy inarticulateness he brought out his confusion and admiration. "There's George Becker" (class president, a basketball player). "There's Geordie" (a well-known girl). "Who's that with her? Some college guy?" "There's your cousin Trish, how do you like that, she's only in the tenth grade." "There's Vinciguerra, I'd hate to get in that guy's way. You know they're going to pay him to go to college?"

He talked freely, though he was usually tongue-tied at school. In his own way he was pleased to be there. Finally, while they were dancing, he said to her, "You know, I'm really glad I came with you, though, instead."

Shirley threw back her head and shoulders to look at him as she danced. "Why are you glad about that, Will?" she asked.

He drew closer. "Ah, you know!" he said with an unendurable confidence. "I never have to worry about you, what you're going to think."

He meant it. He was grateful to her. He was overcome by his own feelings.

"Not like some of these characters here," he added moodily, gazing toward the center of the floor.

Shirley didn't answer. She didn't even ask him what he had meant when he said "instead."

The next week, after graduation, she heard that Will had enlisted in the Navy. But she was too busy moving into the student nurses' quarters next to the hospital to care very much.

Not many people are more cut off from the rest of the world than girls in an old-style nursing school. They live under a rigid discipline administered by stern, highly-starched older women. They work hard on the floors, study fat, difficult texts and get two weeks off each year.

In this place Shirley flourished. They knew all about her before-hand. She was the sort of girl for them—she was not playing. On the floors she was capable and managing, even as a student. Mainly she never flinched. She endured all the whining uncertainty of sick people without pity, for she knew she was right. She was held up as a model to the frivolous, and they didn't like her for it. But she was always professionally cheerful.

After graduation she went home to live with her parents. She took a bus to the hospital every day. Some of her old friends thought she had grown unpleasantly hard. "That's the way it is with nurses. They get so used to bossing people. Oh, well. They have to be that way."

About two o'clock in the morning the state police brought in three men from a lonely crossroads to the north known as Four Corners. There was a huge, sagging wooden tavern out there, left over from better days in the 1920s. According to the owner, five men, who were together, had been huddling and talking in loud confusion just before they left, evidently making some sort of plans. Suddenly they all had pushed out of the place into two cars. The cars had backed and cut and run around the ramshackle tavern once in opposite directions, crossed, come out each on a different road, and then rushed into the intersection, where they demolished each other. Two men were crushed or dismembered instantly; one died on the way in; but the last two were still alive by morning.

Because both had been wearing miraculous medals, a priest coming in early to make his visits went to them first. He gave extreme unction to one and then carefully moved his black case and his oils to the bedside of the other.

This man had laid through the night with his eyes open, never quite surrendering consciousness. He had watched the wide-hatted state troopers, the young interns and nurse who had worked over him downstairs. He remembered their bringing him up and settling him in this room and leaving him. It is never fully dark in a hospital. The sounds came down to him of the night nurses talking, desultorily and indifferently, at their desk at the center of the hall. Now he watched the perfunctory ministrations of the priest over the shape of white bedclothes across the room. But when the stout, black-clothed man, eyes tired and circled, still preoccupied with the articles necessary to his task, moved across to him, he went wild. He twisted his upper body powerfully—he had an enormous chest and shoulders, accentuated by the bulk of the dressings—and cried out and swore against the indifference and perfunctoriness that would carry on with things when he himself was in such straits; though he would never plead for pity from that indifference, either. The man was Tom Vinciguerra, grown five years older.

Alarmed, the priest drew back. A male attendant hurried in to hold Tom; a doctor came in and gave him something. He had spent himself anyway.

When he awoke, it was morning again. The daylight fell across the other bed, which was flat and freshly made.

"That one went out last night," said a nurse quietly to another as both stood outside the doorway, looking into the room.

"How about this one?"

"Oh, we could lose him too."

Tom's eyes looked at the doorway with a furious, uncompromising hatred, but the two young women had already gone on down the hall. He could hear a rattle and movement of things on wheels out there. A weak, steamy, coffee tinge reached him; they were serving breakfast.

During the day he lay and watched. Sleep had done him some good. But though he was awake, he would not speak or take notice of anyone who came into the room. The little aide who came around so cheerfully with a fresh water carafe shrugged and went out. He resisted anyone who tried to do anything for him—except the doctors. They had seen resentful patients before, and paid no attention to him. They put his limbs where they wanted them, and if he resisted, they were firmer and it hurt excruciatingly. They paid

no attention to that either. But everyone else Tom fought off. Late
in the afternoon a nurse who was to give him a needle went back to
the desk and complained.

"Oh, he is!" declared, far out there, the nurse in charge.

And she came in swiftly with a smooth but tight-lipped, long-faced
expression, trailed by the other. With a quick little movement she
seized Tom's wrist, which lay along the sheet. She was young, she
wasn't large, she held him only with thumb and forefinger, but
the circlet they made was like an awkward bracelet. The grip pressed
the sharp edges of the bone inside the flesh and actually hurt. All he
could do, in his surprise, was to watch her other hand as, holding the
needle lightly, like a dart, she drew it into the slack flesh of his upper
arm. The fluid was pumped home, his wrist released at once. The first
nurse nodded and was satisfied. The two women went out and Tom
was left alone, wondering and afraid at his weakness.

They treated him like a child. But he was a child; he had no
strength. He was afraid. Let them do what they wanted with him. He
grew apathetic. He slept a great deal. And he began to recover. Before long he was hungry for meals. It all took several days, but he
grew settled, and even contented, in the hospital routine. Though
he said little, he cooperated. He understood that he was better. He
was happy in the solitary, most simple way, just to be alive.

As for Shirley, it might be thought that now that she had Tom
Vinciguerra delivered to her in this way, she would be thrilled. It
wasn't so, however; she knew better than that. It had been eight
years since the first, greatest excitement of her attraction to him, and
she had come to earth long since. There was nothing very wonderful
about his coming—people she knew were continually passing
through the hospital. Tom's fame was so old that it meant nothing
now. Somebody mentioned that he had never finished college, had
never even played on the college team, having been injured soon
after his arrival. He looked much heavier.

She treated him as he needed to be treated, as though he were no
different from anybody else. But from his bed, with the studious
eyes of the football player at the back of the classroom, Tom followed her comings and goings. He saw that she was hard and managed the place. It was something he could appreciate, because for all
his size and strength, he had never been simply a "natural athlete";
he knew that nothing much was ever accomplished against the pain-

ful physical obstacles of life without the grimmest purpose. It was the secret of his success—many boys had been as big as he. Though he dealt in violence, he had never been reckless until, failing, he had returned to his home city.

One morning early she had washed his back and was giving it a rub. "Do you remember me?" he asked her. His voice was uncertain and sounded as though he had a cold.

"Yes. You went to school with me—me and my cousin Trish."

He was silent, thinking. "Was Trish your cousin?" he asked her meekly, but surprised.

Shirley laughed and expanded, as she had the first time the question was asked of her. "Yes—didn't you know that?" For she still thought of Trish with the same admiration. She was proud of her cousin. "Trish is way out in California," she told him. "She's got another year of college, but she's married already. Her husband's going to be a lawyer."

Tom shifted his hips and settled down so that he could see her. "They have good football teams out there . . . I think. They're on television." She was gathering up soap, cloth and ointment. It was quite early, before breakfast, a gray and quiet time in the room. Shirley emptied and rinsed his basin. As she did so her face, momentarily thoughtful of her cousin, appeared in softer, more affectionate, more diffident lines. It was the only time Tom Vinciguerra saw her like that in all the weeks he was at the hospital. But his own mood of convalescent happiness seemed to make him think the best of everyone, and it was the only face he remembered of her once he was out.

After a while he called her up and came to see her. Shirley treated him coldly. He had no job now. In her own work she was quite successful. It really seemed she could hope for something better. But though she was balky and hard and horsy with him, Tom always treated her as if she were some tender beauty. When girls had sought him out in his good days, he never bothered long with any of them; he would not compromise his fame. Now he thought very little of himself and was quite afraid of her.

Shirley did want to learn to drive, though, so she allowed him to teach her. Driving was absolutely new to her; her father had no car. She was much too hesitant, and failed the road test.

That same night, Tom drove her out after supper to a small field that he knew, enclosed by young birch and pine woods, reached by sandy wheel tracks. "Now drive," he told her grimly.

Fearfully she changed gears, but sitting close to her, he crushed her right foot with his own heavy left one. The car (one he had borrowed) jumped forward and bounded over the dry, hard tussocks of orchard grass, smashed down the heads of high goldenrod, ran underneath its charging hood the stalk of a little midfield birch. Inside, they bounced up and down, and when Shirley pulled her foot from under Tom's he pressed harder on the unprotected pedal. His brooding eyes looked outward, straight at the jumping, oncoming trees. Shirley jumped on the brake with all her might, and the vehicle slowed—but kept going. Tom pressed relentlessly; the car would break out again. She jumped on the clutch and they stopped, but the engine wound up and shook as though it would burst. They moved again. She pulled on the wheel. The car jumped and ran, the trees scraping its side. There was no way out. She did nothing but try to stop for she didn't know how long. Tom pressed and Shirley tried to stop. His big hand covered the ignition. Shirley perspired and shouted aloud. She finally got the trick of keeping the car in low gear and turning within the confines of the field. It occurred to her to steer between the trees along the road they had come in by. Tom kept the accelerator down even when they were out on the paved highway—but she held the car in control. Her excitement was up. Though trembling, she laughed in her access to power. Then at last Tom relented; she let the car slow down and turned off the road. "There—now you can drive," he said. She turned and hugged him wholeheartedly.

And so they were married. They lived in a flat just down the street from the hospital, and Tom went back and forth every day to the state teacher's college. Shirley was quite happy. Everybody remarked how she had come out. In two years Tom finished, and was hired as football coach at their old high school. He was very successful. He and Shirley went to all of the school dances as chaperones. Everybody knew who she was—the wife of Mr. Vinciguerra, the football coach.

One morning when she was spending the day at her mother's (she was pregnant and had given up nursing), Will Schuler telephoned.

He talked in a way she had never heard from him before. He had acquired a line, a loud mixture of nervousness and stupid self-esteem that she felt painfully he must really be ashamed to utter. He spoke of all his doings in the Navy, of being stationed here and stationed there, and so on. When he got around to asking her about herself, she said only, "Well, I'm married now, Will."

There was a pause, and he said in the same assertive style, "Yeah? Who's the lucky guy?"

For some reason Shirley found it difficult to answer. "You remember Tom Vinciguerra?" she asked him. She felt very embarrassed. "He's the football coach at school now," she added, as though to mitigate something.

All the rest of the day she felt bad. She sat through the afternoon in her mother's house and waited for Tom to pick her up. It was football season; he would be very late. The baby was expected around Christmas.

Not that she wasn't happy; on the contrary, she had got what she wanted. But only when Will called her up did she think about it that way. Anyway, it wasn't really the same as just getting what you wanted. She felt somewhat better to think that all the joys of her life had come without her asking for them; she hadn't even recognized them when they came. Maybe she wouldn't have been able to stand them otherwise.

JOHN UPDIKE, born in Pennsylvania, lives in Ipswich, Massachusetts, with his wife and four children. He is the author of ten books —three collections of short stories, two volumes of verse, four novels, and a book of parodies and essays. Three of his stories have appeared in earlier O. Henry Prize Story collections—"Wife-Wooing" in 1961, "The Doctor's Wife" in 1962, and "The Bulgarian Poetess," the First Prize winner, in 1966.

Marching Through Boston

THE civil-rights movement had a salubrious effect on Joan Maple. A suburban mother of four, she would return late at night from a non-violence class in Roxbury with rosy cheeks and shining eyes. Her voice, as she phoned evasive local realtors in the campaign for fair housing, grew curiously firm and rather obstinately melodious —a note her husband had never heard her produce before. It seemed to Richard that her posture was improving, her figure filling out, her skin growing lustrous, her very hair gaining body and sheen. Though he had resigned himself, through twelve years of marriage, to a rhythm of apathy and renewal, this raw burst of beauty took him unawares.

He would never forget the night she returned from Alabama. It was three o'clock in the morning. He woke and heard the front door close behind her. He had been dreaming of a parallelogram in the sky that was also somehow a meteor, and the darkened house seemed quadrisected by the four sleeping children he had, with more than paternal tenderness, put to bed. He had caught himself speaking to them of Mommy as of a distant departed spirit, gone to live, invisible, in the newspapers and the television set. The little girl, Bean, had burst into tears. Now the ghost closed the door and walked up the stairs, and came into his bedroom, and fell on the bed.

He switched on the light and saw her sunburned face, her blistered feet. Her ballet slippers were caked with orange mud. She

"Marching Through Boston" – John Updike, *The New Yorker*, © 1966 by The New Yorker Magazine, Inc.

had lived for three days on Coke and dried apricots; she had not gone to the bathroom for sixteen hours. The Montgomery airport had been a madhouse—nuns, social workers, divinity students fighting for space on the northbound planes. They had been in the air when they heard about Mrs. Liuzzo.

He accused her: "It could have been you."

She said, "I was always in a group." But she added guiltily, "How were the children?"

"Fine. Bean cried because she thought you were inside the television set."

"Did you see me?"

"Your parents called long distance to say they thought they did. I didn't. All I saw was Abernathy and King and their henchmen saying, 'Thass right. Say it, man. Thass sayin' it.'"

"Aren't you mean? It was very moving, except that we were all so tired. These teen-age Negro girls kept fainting; a psychiatrist explained to me that they were having psychotic breaks."

"What psychiatrist?"

"Actually, there were three of them, and they were studying to be psychiatrists in Philadelphia. They kind of took me in tow."

"I bet they did. Please come to bed. I'm very tired from being a mother."

She visited the four corners of the upstairs to inspect each sleeping child and, returning, undressed in the dark. She removed underwear she had worn for seventy hours and stood there shining. To the sleepy man in the bed it seemed a visitation, quite wonderful and quite beyond his control.

She spoke on the radio; she addressed local groups. In garages and supermarkets he heard himself being pointed out as her husband. She helped organize meetings at which dapper young Negroes ridiculed and abused the applauding suburban audience. Richard marvelled at Joan's public composure. Her shyness stayed with her, but it had become a kind of weapon, as if the doctrine of nonviolence had given it point. He grew jealous and irritable. He found himself insisting, at parties, on the Constitutional case for states' rights, on the misfortunes of African independence, on the tangled history of the Reconstruction. Yet she had little trouble persuading him to march with her in Boston.

He promised, though he could not quite grasp the object of the march. Indeed, his brain, as if surgically deprived, quite lacked the

faculty of believing in people considered generically. All movements, of masses or of ideas supposedly embodied in masses, he
secretly felt to be phantasmal. Whereas his wife, a minister's daughter, lived by abstractions; her blood returned to her heart enriched
and vivified by the passage through some capillarious figment. He
was struck, and subtly wounded, by the ardor with which she re-
warded his promise; under his hands her body felt baroque and her
skin smooth as night.

The march was in April. Richard awoke that morning with a
fever. He had taken something foreign into himself and his body
was making resistance. Joan offered to go alone; as if something fun-
damental to his dignity, to their marriage, were at stake, he refused
the offer. The day, dawning cloudy, had been forecast as sunny,
and he wore a summer suit that enclosed his hot skin in a slipping,
weightless unreality. At a highway drugstore they bought some pills
designed to detonate inside him through a twelve-hour period. They
parked near her aunt's house in Louisburg Square and took a taxi
toward the headwaters of the march, a playground in Roxbury. The
cab was turned aside by a sullen policeman; the Maples got out and
walked down a broad boulevard lined with barbershops, shoe-repair
nooks, pizzerias, and friendliness associations. On stoops and stair-
ways male Negroes loitered, blinking and muttering toward one another as if a vast, decrepit conspiracy had assigned them their positions and then collapsed.

"Lovely architecture," Joan said, pointing toward a curving side
street, a neo-Georgian arc suspended in the large urban sadness.

Though she pretended to know where she was, Richard doubted
that they were going the right way. But then he saw ahead of them,
scattered like the anomalous objects with which Dali punctuates his
perspectives, receding black groups of white clergymen. In the distance, red lights of police cars wheeled within a twinkling mob. As
they drew nearer, colored girls adorned with bouffant hairdos and
bangle earrings multiplied beside them. The most queenly wore
cerise stretch pants and the golden sandals of a heavenly cup-
bearer, and held pressed against her ear a transistor radio tuned to
WMEX. On this thin stream of music they all together poured into
a playground surrounded by a link fence.

A loose crowd of thousands swarmed on the crushed grass. Bob-
bing placards advertised churches, brotherhoods, schools, towns. Pop-

sicle venders lent an unexpected touch of carnival. Suddenly at
home, Richard bought a bag of peanuts and looked around—as if
this were the playground of his childhood—for friends.

But it was Joan who found some. "My God," she said. "There's
my old analyst." At the fringe of some Unitarians stood a plump,
doughy man with the troubled squint of a baker who has looked into
too many ovens. Joan turned to go the other way.

"Don't suppress," Richard told her. "Let's go and be friendly and
normal."

"It's too embarrassing."

"But it's been years since you went. You're cured."

"You don't understand. You're never cured. You just stop going."

"O.K., come this way. I think I see my Harvard section man in
Plato to Dante."

But, even while arguing against it, she had been drifting them
toward her psychiatrist, and now they were caught in the pull of his
gaze. He scowled and came toward them, flat-footedly. Richard had
never met him and, shaking hands, felt himself as a putrid heap of
anecdotes, of detailed lusts and abuses. "I think I need a doctor," he
madly blurted.

The other man produced, like a stiletto from his sleeve, a nimble
smile. "How so?" Each word seemed precious.

"I have a fever."

"Ah." The psychiatrist turned sympathetically to Joan, and his
face issued a clear commiseration: *So he is still punishing you.*

Joan said loyally, "He really does. I saw the thermometer."

"Would you like a peanut?" Richard asked. The offer felt so sym-
bolic, so transparent, that he was shocked when the other man took
one, cracked it harshly, and substantially chewed.

Joan asked, "Are you with anybody? I feel a need for group
security."

"Come meet my sister." The command sounded strange to Richard; "sister" seemed a piece of psychological slang, a euphemism for
"mistress."

But again things were simpler than they seemed. His sister was
plainly from the same batter. Ruddy and yeasty, she seemed to have
been enlarged by the exercise of good will and wore a saucer-sized
S.C.L.C. button in the lapel of a coarse green suit. Richard coveted
the suit; it looked warm. The day was continuing overcast and chilly.

Something odd, perhaps the successive explosions of the antihista-mine pill, was happening inside him, making him feel elegantly elongated; the illusion crossed his mind that he was destined to se-duce this woman. She beamed and said, "My daughter Trudy and her *best* friend, Carol."

They were girls of sixteen or so, one size smaller in their bones than women. Trudy had the family pastry texture and a darting frown. Carol was homely, fragile, and touching; her upper teeth were a gray blur of braces and her arms were protectively folded across her skimpy bosom. Over a white blouse she wore only a thin blue sweater, unbuttoned. Richard told her, "You're freezing."

"I'm freezing," she said, and a small love was established between them on the basis of this demure repetition. She added, "I came along because I'm writing a term paper."

Trudy said, "She's doing a history of the labor unions," and laughed.

The girl shivered. "I thought they might be the same. Didn't the unions use to march?" Her voice, moistened by the obtrusion of her braces, had a sprayey faintness in the raw gray air.

The psychiatrist's sister said, "The *way* they *make* these poor children *study* nowadays! The *books* they have them *read*! Their *English* teacher *assigned* them 'Tropic of *Cancer*'! I picked it *up* and read *one page*, Trudy reassured me, 'It's all *right*, Mother, the teacher says he's a Transcen*dent*alist!'"

It felt to Richard less likely that he would seduce her. His sense of reality was expanding in the nest of warmth these people pro-vided. He offered to buy them all popsicles. His consciousness ven-tured outward and experienced the joy of so many Negro presences, the luxury of immersion in a race so buoyantly courteous and free of rancor. He drifted happily through the crosshatch of their oblique sardonic hooting and blurred voices, searching for the popsicle vender. The girls and Trudy's mother had said they would take one; the psychiatrist and Joan had refused. The crowd was formed of jiggling fragments. Richard waved at the rector of a church whose nursery school his children had attended; winked at a folk singer he had seen on television and who looked lost and wan in depth; assumed a stony face in passing a long-haired youth guarded by police and draped in a signboard proclaiming "MARTIN LUTHER KING A TOOL OF THE COMMUNISTS"; and tapped a tall sandy-haired man on the shoulder. "Remember me? Dick Maple, Plato to Dante, B-plus."

The section man turned, bespectacled and pale. It was shocking; he had aged.

The march was slow to start. Trucks and police cars appeared and disappeared at the playground gate. Officious young seminarians tried to organize the crowd into lines. Unintelligible announcements crackled within the loudspeakers. Martin Luther King was a dim religious rumor on the playground plain—now here, now there, now dead, now alive. The sun showed as a kind of sore spot burning through the clouds. Carol nibbled her popsicle and shivered. He and Joan argued whether to march under the Lexington banner with the psychiatrist or with the Unitarians because her father was one. In the end it did not matter; King invisibly established himself at their head, a distant truck loaded with singing women lurched forward, a far corner of the crowd began to croon, "Which side are you on, boy?," and they were marching.

On Columbus Avenue they were shuffled into lines ten abreast. The Maples were separated. Joan turned up between her psychiatrist and a massive, doleful African wearing tribal scars, sneakers, and a Harvard Athletic Association sweatshirt. Richard found himself at the end of the line ahead, with Carol beside him. The man behind him, a forward-looking liberal, stepped on his heel, giving the knit of his loafer such a wrench that he had to walk the three miles through Boston with a floppy shoe and a dragging limp. He had been born in West Virginia, near the Pennsylvania line, and did not understand Boston. In ten years he had grown familiar with some of its districts, but was still surprised by the quick curving manner in which these districts interlocked. For a few blocks they marched between cheering tenements from whose topmost windows hung banners that proclaimed "END DE FACTO SEGREGATION" and "RETIRE MRS. HICKS." Then the march turned left, and Richard was passing Symphony Hall, within whose rectangular vault he had often dreamed his way along the deep-grassed meadows of Brahms and up the agate cliffs of Strauss. At this corner, from the Stygian subway kiosk, he had emerged with Joan, Orpheus and Eurydice, when both were students; in this restaurant, a decade later, he and she, on four drinks apiece, had decided not to get a divorce. The new Prudential Tower, taller and somehow dimmer than any other build-

ing, haunted each twist of their march, before their faces like a
mirage, at their backs like a memory. A leggy nervous colored girl
wearing the orange fireman's jacket of the Security Unit shepherded
their section of the line, clapping her hands, shouting freedom-song
lyrics for a few bars. These songs struggled through the miles of the
march, overlapping and eclipsing one another in a kind of embarrassment. "Which side are you on, boy, which side are you on . . .
like a tree-ee planted by the wah-ha-ter, we shall not be moved . . .
this little light of mine, gonna shine on Boston, Mass., this little
light of mine . . ." The day continued cool and without shadows.
Newspapers that he had folded inside his coat for warmth slipped
and slid. Carol beside him plucked at her little sweater, gathering it
at her breast but unable, as if under a spell, to button it. Behind him,
Joan, serenely framed between her id and superego, stepped along
masterfully, swinging her arms, throwing her ballet slippers alter-
nately outward in a confident splaying stride. ". . . let 'er shine, let
'er shine . . ."

Incredibly, they were traversing a cloverleaf, an elevated concrete
arabesque devoid of cars. Their massed footsteps whispered; the city
yawned beneath them. The march had no beginning and no end
that he could see. Within him, the fever had become a small glassy
scratching on the walls of the pit hollowed by the detonating pills.
A piece of newspaper spilled down his leg and blew into the air.
Impalpably medicated, ideally motivated, he felt, strolling along
the curve of the cloverleaf, gathered within an infinitely populated
ascent. He asked Carol, "Where are we going?"

"The newspapers said the Common."

"Do you feel faint?"

Her gray braces shyly modified her smile. "Hungry."

"Have a peanut." A few still remained in his pocket.

"Thank you." She took one. "You don't have to be paternal."

"I want to be." He felt strangely exalted and excited, as if destined to give birth. He wanted to share this sensation with Carol,
but instead he asked her, "In your study of the labor movement,
have you learned much about the Molly Maguires?"

"No. Were they goons or finks?"

"I think they were either coal miners or gangsters."

"Oh. I haven't studied about anything earlier than Gompers."

"I think you're wise." Suppressing the urge to tell her he

loved her, he turned to look at Joan. She was beautiful, like a poster, with far-seeing blue eyes and red lips parted in song.

Now they walked beneath office buildings where like mounted butterflies secretaries and dental technicians were pressed against the glass. In Copley Square, stony shoppers waited forever to cross the street. Along Boylston, there was Irish muttering; he shielded Carol with his body. The desultory singing grew defiant. The Public Garden was beginning to bloom. Worthy statues—Channing, Kosciusko, Cass, Phillips—were trundled by beneath the blurring trees; Richard's dry heart cracked like a book being opened. The march turned left down Charles and began to press against itself, to link arms, to fumble for love. He lost sight of Joan in the crush. Then they were walking on grass, on the Common, and the first drops of rain, sharp as needles, touched their faces.

"Did we have to stay to hear every damn speech?" Richard asked. They were at last heading home; he felt too sick to drive and huddled, in his soaked slippery suit, toward the heater. The windshield wiper seemed to be squeaking *free-dom, free-dom.*

"I wanted to hear King."

"You heard him in Alabama."

"I was too tired to listen."

"Did you listen this time? Didn't it seem corny and forced?"

"Somewhat. But does it matter?" Her white profile was serene; she passed a trailer truck on the right, and her window was spattered as if with applause.

"And that Abernathy. God, if he's John the Baptist, I'm Herod the Great. 'Onteel de Frenchman go back t'France, onteel de Ahrishman go back t'Ahrland, onteel de Mexican he go back tuh—'"

"Stop it."

"Don't get me wrong. I didn't mind them sounding like demagogues; what I minded was that god-awful boring phony imitation of a revival meeting. 'Thass right, yossuh. Yoh-*suh!*'"

"Your throat sounds sore. Shouldn't you stop using it?"

"*How* could you crucify me that way? *How* could you make this miserable sick husband stand in the icy rain for hours listening to boring stupid speeches that you'd heard before anyway?"

"I didn't think the speeches were that great. But I think it was important that they were given and that people listened. You were there as a witness, Richard."

"Ah witnessed. Ah believes. Yossuh."

"You're a very sick man."

"I know, I *know* I am. That's why I wanted to *leave*. Even your pastry psychiatrist left. He looked like a dunked doughnut."

"He left because of the girls."

"I loved Carol. She respected me, despite the color of my skin."

"You didn't have to go."

"Yes I did. You somehow turned it into a point of honor. It was a sexual vindication."

"How you go on."

" 'Onteel de East German goes on back t'East Germany, onteel de Luxembourgian hies hisself back to Luxembourg—' "

"Please stop it."

But he found he could not stop, and even after they reached home and she put him to bed, the children watching in alarm, his voice continued its slurred plaint. "Ah'ze all riaight, Missy, jes' a tech o' double pneu*mon*ia, don't you fret none, we'll get the cotton in."

"You're embarrassing the children."

"Shecks, doan min' me, chilluns. Ef Ah could jes' res' hyah foh a spell in de shade o' dis watuhmelon patch, res' dese ol' bones . . . Lawzy, dat do feel good!"

"Daddy has a tiny cold," Joan explained.

"Will he die?" Bean asked, and burst into tears.

"Now, effen," he said, "bah some un*foh*-choonut chayance, mah spirrut should pass owen, bureh me bah de levee, so mebbe Ah kin heeah de singin' an' de banjos an' de cotton bolls a-bustin' . . . an' mebbe even de white folks up in de Big House kin shed a homely tear . . ." He was almost crying; a weird tenderness had come over him in bed, as if he had indeed given birth, birth to this voice, a voice crying from the depths of oppression for attention. High in the window, the late afternoon sky blanched as the storm lifted. In the warmth of the bed, he crooned to himself, and once started up, crying out, "Missy! Missy! Doan you worreh none, ol' Tom'll see anotheh sun-up!"

But Joan was downstairs, talking firmly on the telephone.

ERNEST J. FINNEY lives in San Francisco, California. "The Investigator" is his first published short story.

The Investigator

He sat on the floor of the closet, behind an overcoat that smelled of tobacco. His knees were drawn up nearly to his chin, and his back rested against the lath and plaster wall. He was not uncomfortable, or at least he never thought of the different things he did on the job as good or bad, just or unjust, comfortable or uncomfortable. He knew what had to be done on each case and did it, no matter what the situation or how much his back hurt. He was efficient and had more work than he could handle, but he'd never even considered hiring an assistant.

His present case demanded unequivocal evidence of infidelity. It would be written in the court records as McLain versus McLain; Mr. McLain was committing adultery with a Mrs. Richard Canta. They should be done eating now and on their way to the room which Mr. McLain, a contractor, rented. He would listen, and later write up the special evidence in a report, to be mailed to the lawyer. They would spend an hour in the room; at least that was how long they had stayed the two previous times he had watched from across the street. Listening from the closet was not really necessary; if there had been a room vacant on either side he could have listened from it, but he had not even bothered to ask the landlady. It was against the law; he could be charged with breaking and entering; the evidence he would get in the closet could not be used in court; but it was always the one thing that really clinched the case. His employer, the lawyer representing Mrs. McLain, would have a talk with Mr. McLain. The lawyer would tell him of the anguish and despair that Mrs. McLain had suffered at his hands, and that there must be restitution made to compensate, and support for the children. Ordinarily a Mr. McLain, not suspecting that his infidelity had been observed and recorded, would sit quietly and listen politely and, when the lawyer was finished, announce that he too had a lawyer and they would be hearing from him soon, and get up to leave. Then the lawyer would quickly read off the report sheet. Mr. McLain was seeing a Mrs. Canta. He had bought her a $70.00 watch. He had taken her to dinner twenty-seven times. He had given her son Gerald, age nine, an electric train valued at $40.00. He had rented a room from Mrs. Sheridan for $23.00 a week on November fourth, and had taken Mrs. Canta there numerous times. If Mr. McLain still protested, and said he was going to fight all the way to the supreme court, he'd burn all the money he had ever saved before he'd give it to his wife, and furthermore he'd never pay alimony because he was leaving the country, the lawyer would continue reading, loud enough to be heard out in the waiting room. It would be Mr. McLain who asked the lawyer to lower his voice, listening intently, now looking only at his hands, as the lawyer read what Albert Morris, Investigator, had heard.

"My wife won't take off her clothes in front of me, and sleeps in a nightgown and girdle. She slept with her mother until she was eighteen, and when her mother remarried, her stepfather had to lock the bedroom door so she wouldn't slip in. He told me so himself. Three months after we were married she made me a silk nightgown and if I didn't wear it she refused to sleep in the same bed with me. It was green, and had pull strings at the neck and wrists. When I was finally able to rip it up bad enough that she couldn't fix it, she made two others; another green and one a black one. I only married her because I knocked her up and her mother was going to call the police if I didn't."

It had never failed yet: Mr. McLain would turn red, pleading enough, enough, and then quickly come to terms. Albert was always pleased when the lawyer told him the evidence was sufficient and the case was closed. The special evidence always had the same effect; it brought the prospective antagonist to his knees in a hurry.

Albert had once thought of using a tape recorder, a device that would have made the job of getting special evidence much easier. The microphone was concealed in their room, hooked inside a lampshade, and he waited, sitting next to the shiny plastic spools, ready to press the on button with his thumb. From the window he could see the principals in the case coming down the sidewalk, arm in arm. It was Vester versus Vester: Mrs. Vester, a mother of three, at forty-four was committing adultery with Roland Flish. Albert knew the recorder would be accurate, possibly even more accurate than himself. He fidgeted on the chair, clasping his hands and then putting them in his pockets. He could hear them on the stairs and he pressed his hovering thumb down on the on button and the plastic spools began to rotate. They had not entered the room yet and he listened, his head cocked to one side, his eyes peering into space. When the door slammed shut he jumped up and walked quickly around the room, his eyes on the rotating plastic spools. He could not hear; the recorder was doing the work; all he could do was watch the two rotating spools. He knew the glass would be in the metal cabinet if it wasn't on the sink: he picked it up and wiped it carefully with his handkerchief. He pulled the chair up near the wall, sat down, placed the glass to the wall, his ear to the bottom of the glass, and turned off the recorder. He could hear perfectly; he had always been able to; he relaxed and listened. He stared intently at the other wall, never changing expression, never moving, for over an hour. When the door slammed shut he took the glass from the wall. His ear was red and warm from pressing it so hard against the bottom of the glass. He rubbed it, smiling to himself: the evidence was satisfactory; the case, as far as he was concerned, was closed. Mr. Vesper would have the evidence needed to gain custody of the children. As he left the apartment building he passed Mrs. Vesper and Mr. Flish, who were looking in a store window: he did not look in their direction nor did he think of what he had heard five minutes before. The case was closed.

They should have been here by now, he thought. He looked at his watch and stretched out his legs. They must have stopped for a drink or at a store; he knew Mr. McLain went back to his wife every night after taking Mrs. Canta home from the room. Mrs. McLain had been very explicit in her information regarding her husband's activities, even to the point of explaining that they slept in different rooms now and made a point of not talking to each other. She refused to cook for him and would not send his laundry out to be cleaned. Or so the lawyer related; for the last seven years Albert had not met or spoken directly to a client; it was all handled through a lawyer who phoned the necessary information to his apartment. If he needed photographs or other data that could not be communicated over the phone, the lawyer sent it by mail. When he had finished the case he sent the information to the lawyer, and received his pay the same way.

In the beginning he had had an office and the clients had come to him, distraught and anxious over a domestic disaster. He had always tried to do an efficient job for his clients. He had succeeded in satisfying their desires to know exactly what the errant husband or wife was doing; to confirm each outrage. He had worked with their lawyers and had gone to court to testify in their behalf and accepted their gratitude after the court's proceedings. It was Morris White, attorney at law, who suggested that they work more closely together. It was Morris White who felt it was a lawyer's place to make the initial contact with the prospective client. Albert agreed, and was satisfied to be called in for the investigation, thus avoiding the clients and any false alarms from jealous husbands and wives. He liked it much better this way; he had always felt uncomfortable in trying to investigate a case while at the same time confronting the client to report his progress on the client's deteriorating marriage. He had had, when he still had the office, a client who in the course of five years had married three times, coming each time to him to have her husband investigated for infidelity. Each time she would come into the office and sit in the chair facing his desk, sobbing, telling him of her suspicions, which had always been correct. The last time she had kept demanding to know what was wrong with her; why did her husbands always need someone else; what was wrong. He did not know what to say: he pushed the kleenex box closer to her, and got her cup after cup of water from the cooler.

Her last husband, ten years younger than she, had always gone to motels, which made it difficult to obtain the special evidence. The first time, after he followed them through night clubs, restaurants, and dark streets, he lost them at a motel. He was unable to rent either of the units siding theirs. The second time the walls were too thick, or insulated too well to hear through. He waited patiently, knowing sooner or later he would be able to listen. Then Mr. Carson rented a cabin in the woods from a real estate agent for the weekend. Albert had followed them up the switchback road, driving past as they parked in the garage. He waited nearly half an hour, listening to rain strike the metal roof of his car. He was excited as he walked through the trees toward the cabin. The case had taken too long and now the opportunity had come to end it, tonight. If only they would talk of Mrs. Carson; that was important. Sometimes they didn't; sometimes it would be arguments, or politics, or discussions of each other's families or their love for each other. But sooner or later they talked of their wives or husbands, and Albert would be there to hear it all. He circled the house, creeping near the walls, and stopped near a lighted window. He could not see in but he could hear them as if he too were in the room. A medium sized acacia tree, with branches that shaded the window from the sun in the summer, was easy to climb; he spread himself around a thick branch. He could feel the rain soaking through his clothes, wetting his skin. But he could see perfectly, and forgot the rain and his precarious perch. They were eating by candle light, toasting each other with red wine, holding their glasses by the stem. The glasses caught the candle light and flashed triangles of light out the window into the night, toward him. It was getting colder; his nose ran and the wind made the limbs of the tree sway. He watched, fascinated, as they ate, and he could hear their voices and her laughter, and see the smiles exchanged like caresses. The longer he watched the more he felt he was in the room, holding a glass, feeling the warmth of the fire. He smiled when they smiled, and started to laugh once, but stopped when Mr. Carson looked out the window into the darkness. Then the husband, smiling, said something, and the woman, her eyes nearly closed and her white breasts two thirds exposed by a low cut dress, smiled back. Albert smiled too. The husband wet his thumb and forefinger with his tongue and snuffed out the candles. Albert almost cried out "No, no; continue, continue." He could see their shadows as they moved in front of the fire and then they were gone. He climbed down quickly, slipping, hitting the ground with his shoulders and the back of his head. He got up and ran to the bedroom window, put his ear to the glass and listened. They weren't ready yet. He could hear the shower, and see the light from the bathroom and the steam pouring out the open door. They giggled and made the metal shower stall rattle and shake. The husband dried her. She stood brushing her hair, laughing, as he kneeled to dry her feet. The fire in the other room cast strange dancing reliefs on the ceiling.

Later they talked. He was going to marry her as soon as he was able to convince his wife to sell some more of her property, and with the money he had already received they would go to Mexico, Europe, everywhere, Mr. Carson shouted, clapping his hands together with a loud smack. They laughed, and Albert caught himself in time and only smiled. Mr. Carson had even taken one of his wife's rings: fumbling with his trousers lying on the floor, he slipped the ring on her finger. Albert left then, walking down the dark road to his car, coughing fog into the cold air. Later the lawyer, after receiving the evidence, phoned, congratulating Albert. He, the lawyer, had convinced the husband that by stealing the ring he faced fourteen years in prison, and the husband had agreed to all terms.

Albert kept remembering the two candles and the goblets catching their light. He was able to find the same kind of candles, but had to settle for two goblets with stems that seemed shorter than those he remembered. The first time he used the goblets and candles he felt someone might see him and kept his eyes on his plate, away from the empty goblet across the table. When he sat down to eat the second time, he was more relaxed, and drank the red wine and smiled across the table to the empty chair.

How long had he been in the business; fifteen, nineteen years, that long. He thought of all the things he had seen and heard in those nineteen years. It was annoying that time had passed so quickly with nothing more memorable to recall than the cases he had worked on. He was forty-two; that was all; forty-two years of moving his body from one place to another. He had never married and never regretted it. He was not soured by the men and women filing past his ears and eyes who had not succeeded in marriage; it was simply something that had never occurred to him. He thought about it rarely, deciding, after his sister had invited him over on his birthday, that it might still happen: who really knew about these things.

His brother-in-law and three nieces sat around the table. When his sister brought in the cake one of the children turned off the lights and all forty candles burned persistently over the children's squeals and waving hands. He sat there in the dark, pleased that they had invited him, pleased with the cake. The children shrieked and jumped in their chairs as the candles burned, dripping wax over the white sugar frosting. On the cake was printed Happy Birthday Al in large pink letters. Albert thought of the candles wrapped neatly in newspaper in a shoe box with the two goblets. He smiled across the table at his sister, who smiled back. His brother-in-law urged him to blow out the candles before they all melted. The children yelled

"Make a wish!" as he exhaled all the air his bulging cheeks would hold. The candles went out under the blast and it was dark in the room; he had forgotten to make a wish.

Where were they, they should have been here nearly fifteen minutes ago, he thought. Maybe they decided not to come, maybe he had told her he was going to stay with his wife, or they argued. It could happen, anything could happen, he thought. He would wait, though; they still might come. He was irritated; he had taken the risk of actually being in the room with them, something he normally would never do, and now they hadn't shown up. He hadn't even bothered to ask the landlady if the room on either side was vacant. He shouldn't take such risks; they weren't worth it; if he were caught, then what: a scene, possibly the police; they might even take his license away. He tried to push the thought of discovery from his mind; he would stay and see if they would come.

He had before, too, under a large wrought iron bed. He smiled in the dark when he thought of that time. He had gone into the room to see how far the bed was from the wall which his rented room sided. When he heard the footsteps coming up the stairs he had waited, listening to them come closer and closer. It was not time for him, the husband he was investigating, to arrive. He knew it must be the landlady, or a roomer. When the key was inserted in the lock he panicked, taking two steps away from the bed, pivoting around again, as if possessed to perform some strange dance. He closed his eyes and slid under the bed. There had been no closet. He lay there, his head against the wall, his buttocks pressed against the springs, his eyes still closed. They got into bed quickly, and the springs gently pressed against his buttocks and shoulder blades. Even then he had been over weight, but the springs did not injure him and after a while he had enjoyed the rhythmical bouncing. When they had finished they lay on the bed and ate sandwiches—she had to be back earlier that day, and they had no time for dinner at their regular restaurant. She had not liked pickles and had thrown three of them on the floor next to the bed. Albert, whose eyes were level with the three small disks, watched them carefully, as if they might possibly move of their own accord. They did not; however, the two occupants of the bed did some twenty minutes later, leaving Albert alone again to crawl out from under the bed, to stand in the middle of the room, listening to their footsteps disappearing, brushing the

dust off the front of his protruding suit coat. He had been careful
since then never to take any unnecessary chances of being discovered.

He could not help smiling as he remembered the time under the
bed. In the dark of the closet he looked at his watch again. They
were an hour late now: they weren't coming, he thought. He should
leave, get up and leave, and go home and eat dinner. He was
hungry, and his stomach, straining against his shirt buttons, gurgled
for food. Until six months ago he had always eaten alone in his
apartment, cooking huge quantities of food. No matter how much
he ate, which was always a great deal, there was food left over to eat
later that night or the next day for breakfast—steaks that hung over
the curved edges of the large frying pan, a half dozen baked potatoes,
a loaf of french bread slit down the middle and put in the oven with
cheese spread over the top. He thought of the meal he would have
when he got up and left the closet and could almost feel the heat
from the oven where he'd be cooking the squash. When he had
invited the woman across the hall he had cooked squash then too,
with butter and brown sugar melted over the top. It had taken a
full two weeks to get enough courage just to invite her. She had
accepted, pleased that he asked. He heard her come home that
night, walking down the hall, opening the door to her apartment;
then he heard music, the music went off, and her door opened and
shut. She came in smiling, telling him what nice furniture he had,
how well the table looked, and candle light too, she exclaimed. He
stood, his tie tucked into his shirt to keep it out of the food, offering
her a plate of assorted nuts and a plate heaped with thick slices of
salami and round crackers. She sat down and talked to him while
he cooked. He knew nothing about her other than her name, which
he had read on her mail box. When he put the food on the table she
helped him slide the plate of potatoes over, making room for the
squash, the steaming bowl of green beans, the bread and platter of
steaks. She had eaten as much as he, and the yellow candles flickered,
catching the two goblets of red wine in their light. He had smiled
continuously at her as she ate; when she looked up, she smiled back.
When they finished she poured more wine, spilling some on her
white blouse, talking, telling him what an excellent cook he was.
She had been telling him about her job when he interrupted and
asked if she would like to take a shower. She had looked more
puzzled than surprised, asking "What?" twice after he had spoken.
He said it again in the same even tone, looking straight into her

face, smiling. She pulled herself up from the back of the couch and sat on the edge, holding her glass in her left hand, the right pulling the lobe of her ear. "Why not," she said, "why not," and stood up and took off the belt from around her waist. She continued to drink while she undressed. He watched her from the couch, annoyed that she actually was taking off her clothes. He unlaced his shoes and kicked them off, watching her still as she slipped off her blouse. She could hardly see him, he thought. He had snuffed the candles, and the only light came from the stove light in the kitchen. She stopped and refilled her glass. When she straightened he could see her silhouette. Without her blossoming skirt she was too fat; not as fat as he, but still her stomach looked like the second ball of the snowmen he and his sister used to make during the winter. Like some enormous extended pregnant woman's stomach. But she was not pregnant, nor young for that matter: possibly she was as old as he was, in her forties at least.

He had asked her to dinner in the same way he had asked her to take a shower, without really thinking of the dinner or the shower or that either would actually take place: it was as if there was nothing else for him to say and so he had said what he did as if he were asking if she'd like more potatoes. Now she, not he, was undressed: completely naked except for the scarf around her neck, she sat sipping her wine, looking over the edge of the glass at him. He was not inexperienced in these matters; he had had his share of the fruits of love; she was not the first woman to come to his apartment to be taken, sooner or later, into the bedroom. In fact, he had bragged of it to his sister when she had asked him why he didn't marry. He had not even been thirty then; he was young and just starting out in the business. "Why should I buy a cow when I can get all the free milk I want," he had answered. It was true then. The women who came into his office, bereaved, disgusted with themselves, their husbands, would most willingly with practically no encouragement lie on the floor or the top of the desk, and when he bought a small cot within four months it filled the office with the odor of semen, sweat and perfume. He had to get rid of it and buy another, washable this time. It was actually a relief to be rid of the office and handle the business by phone. He had always felt that he was taking advantage of the clients, but it hadn't stopped him from buying the washable couch and putting another lock on the door. With the apartment it had changed; no women came charging in, tearing their clothes off ten minutes after he closed the door. Except this one, who kept smiling at him over her glass. She seemed as satisfied sitting there naked as she did clothed.

She's waiting for me, he thought. To take a shower with her, to take off my clothes and then take a shower. He could not seem to loosen his tie, much less take off his clothes. He finished the wine in his goblet and then refilled his glass. She held out her glass and he filled that too, spilling some on her leg. He watched the small red stream run down each side of her leg, as if some invisible knife had cut through the soft white flesh. She did not seem to notice; she sipped her wine and continued to smile. He had an insane desire to ask her if she would like another piece of lemon chiffon pie. She would probably take it, too, and then he would have a piece and they could sit there eating, forgetting about the shower. Her naked body reminded him of the picture he had seen once in the office of a lawyer. There were two clothed men and one naked woman sitting on the ground; another, with only a towel around her waist, was washing her feet in a pond, and they were having a picnic. At the time he thought it was a very strange thing to paint. Would a woman actually take off her clothes and sit there so calmly with the men still dressed? It did not seem possible at the time. He even had asked the lawyer why the woman was naked and not at least one of the men, and why she was sitting so contentedly. The lawyer had said he didn't know; his wife had given him the reproduction for a birthday present and it didn't make much sense to him either, but it looked like statutory rape. "Maybe she was a whore and was just showing her wares," the lawyer added. She hadn't looked like a whore, though; it was very strange.

He decided he should stop playing around and get down to business: she would not remain that way forever. He pulled at his tie and unbuttoned his cuffs. He did not look at her as he undressed. He took off all of his clothes but his undershirt; he couldn't bring himself to pull it up over his head. He left her sitting there, not daring to look back, sucking his stomach in as he walked to the bathroom. He let the water run, filling the bathroom with steam. It enveloped the red tile floor, the mirror over the sink, and finally himself. He adjusted the water, turned off the light, and yelled from the door, "Come on, ready or not."

He was already under the warm spray when she came in. He moved over, his back against the cold tile wall. The water did not touch him there and he held his breath, trying not to touch her. She had taken off her scarf, and stood directly under the spray, letting the water beat down on her head. It was extremely crowded; when she tried to bend down to wash her legs he was pressed against the wall. He stood straight, his back still against the wall, his stomach sucked in even more than before. He breathed through his nose in short gasps, wondering why he had ever suggested a shower in the first place. He had never taken a shower with a woman before and he promised himself that this would be the last time. She offered to wash his back and he turned around, his forehead resting against the tile, his body stiff, as if he expected to be flogged. When she was finished she adjusted the water nozzle and the spray washed off the soap. She readjusted the nozzle so that the water struck her back, and faced him. Even in the dark he could see her nose and the outline of her chin. They both remained that way, the drain gurgling up the water at their feet. He thought he might stay that way forever, but the water that bounced off the tile began to be lukewarm, and then colder. He started to shiver, but she remained under the stream of water. It was almost ice cold now, and his whole body trembled. "Don't you love a nice cold shower?" she said, raising her arms over her head, pirouetting under the spray. He did not answer: his teeth were clattering and he didn't trust himself to open his mouth. He thought his partial plate, which had always been loose, might slip and fall out of his mouth.

When she turned off the water he was the first one out of the stall. Racing to the floor furnace, he turned the thermostat as high as it would go. He straddled the grate and stood trembling in the first blast of cold air. She brought him a towel and he dried himself, rubbing as hard as he could against his shaking body. It seemed as if he would never stop shaking; the warm blasts of air did not penetrate his cold. He could see her sitting on the edge of the bed with a glass of wine, her head turned in his direction, watching. In self defense he said, "I don't feel good," and put the towel around his waist. She didn't answer, and poured another drink from the bottle at her feet. Slowly the shaking stopped; warm blast after warm blast enveloped his body; the insides of his legs felt red hot, and he enjoyed the pain before he stepped away from the furnace. He was hesitant, not knowing exactly how he should continue or if he should cease all thoughts of continuing. He decided on the latter, articulating slowly, "I don't feel good." She asked him if he wanted her to go. He said if she didn't mind. She got up and walked to the couch, with the goblet still in her hand, picked up her clothes, and walked out the door. When the door closed he ran across the room and fastened the latch. The next morning, when he was ready to leave, the goblet, washed, was standing next to the door jamb. He made a point of not meeting her again for a year; then she moved away.

His buttocks were numb, his back ached, and his right foot had gone to sleep. They weren't coming; over an hour late: he'd better get up and go; he wasn't doing any good here. He pushed up and forward onto his knees, moving his right foot back and forth to get the circulation to return. He crawled over to the door, listened a minute before opening it, and then stood up. He limped across the room, leaning heavily on the bannister as he went down the stairs. The night air woke him up as he walked toward his apartment. For the last six months he had not cooked dinner for himself: only in the morning did he bother to fix himself something, usually corn flakes and milk and sugar. At lunch he would stop somewhere for a sandwich, not even considering going home for a big lunch as he once had, and then sleep for an hour before going back to work. Every night since he had stopped cooking he left work intending to go home and defrost something in the freezer for his meal. Sitting instead, in a nearby cafe, waiting for his food, he would tell himself, tomorrow night I'll start cooking again.

There were few people in the cafe: he sat in one of the booths, ordered, and waited for the soup. He wondered what had happened to Mr. McLain; it was unusual that he should not come, and it was going to delay closing the case. He had always worked one case at a time, never letting anything interfere with its conclusions. It had been slower that way, but there was a certain procedure to his investigations. McLain versus McLain was taking too much time; he should have ended the case four days ago. Now he would have to get in position again tomorrow, losing another day. There were three other cases to work on too; he'd have to hope they'd be easy, and not involve too much time. He finished his soup and the waitress brought the salad with roquefort dressing. She had blond hair and heavily rouged cheeks, and her eyebrows, painted on, gave her face a look of perpetual surprise. He thought of the woman he had invited to take a shower. What a mistake, he thought, to rush right into something like that without first knowing the person better. I haven't had a woman up since. He thought again of her raised arm, the cold water striking her in the face, and the words don't you just love cold showers. It was not cold in the cafe but he moved his feet uneasily and shivered. It was a mistake, he thought. She was the wrong person to invite. He pictured the waitress, who was wiping off the counter, sitting across the table, eating, drinking wine from a goblet. He watched steadily as she pressed the tabs of the cash register, making change for a customer who wanted to buy cigarettes. No, she wouldn't be the right one either; it would have to be someone special. He would know when the time came. When he finished his dinner he sat over the empty coffee cup planning the following day. He would phone the lawyer to see if there had been a reconciliation between the McLains. Reassure the lawyer that the other cases would be taken care of soon. Then see if Mr. McLain went to Mrs. Canta's for lunch. See if one of the other rooms could be rented. The closet was out; it was too risky; why take such unnecessary chances when the job could be done just as easily from the next room, if there was one vacant. If they didn't come he would start on the next case, Best versus Best. He couldn't spend any more time on the McLains; the lawyers would start to get sarcastic when he phoned, asking if they should hire another investigator to assist him. He left a dollar tip near the cup, paid the waitress at the cash register. He smiled at her and she steadily counted his change into the palm of his right hand, looking glum.

The next morning the lawyer, in a pleasant, confidential voice, told him Mr. McLain was still estranged from his wife so far as he knew, and he would probably have two new cases for him the following week. Albert replied that he was nearly finished with the case and would have the other three completed soon. The lawyer sounded pleased and wished him good luck. Albert never knew which lawyer he had talked to over the phone: there were three of them in the same office, specializing in marital cases, and any one of them would pick up the phone and talk to him once he had told the secretary his name. The lawyer did not seem displeased at the length of time the case was taking. Probably they were busy too, handling cases that didn't require his services. It was near the end of the year; there were always more divorces at this time than any other—people seemed to want to start the year fresh.

He watched Mr. McLain stop for Mrs. Canta and take her to lunch. Then he went back to his apartment, read the newspaper, and made himself a sandwich. He took a steak out of the freezing compartment and put it in the sink. He would cook tonight. He was pleased with himself, and vacuumed the rug. Later he went to the rooming house and rented the vacant room next to Mr. McLain's. He had brought along in his briefcase both goblets, and the two candles and their holders. He had told himself he might use the goblets for listening through the wall; they might be better even than ordinary glasses. The new candles he had put in the briefcase automatically; they were always used with the goblets and there was no reason not to take them. The room he rented for a week, putting down his occupation as cook.

Since he had plenty of time he decided to see the other room. It was the same as he had left it. The bed was still slightly mussed where Mrs. Canta had hastily thrown the cover back, and the left side of the chenille was hanging to the floor. He sat down on the edge of the bed, his elbows resting on his knees, his eyes focussed on the wall. He had plenty of time, he thought, and lay back on the bed. He would be glad when this case was over. The next would be Best versus Best, another husband who, according to the information, was keeping two different women. It should be an easy case, especially since he took them to an apartment, which his wife had already found. The address was in the file, too. He looked at his watch. It was almost time, and he got up and went to the window. The street was empty and he stood there waiting. He wasn't sure it was them when they turned the corner: they were walking arm in arm; her head was turned; she was saying something to him. He was laughing—now Albert could see his teeth—and he put his arm around her waist. He left the room and went to his, closing both doors quietly. He listened to them coming up the stairs, their words echoing through the stairway. He quietly lifted the chair and put it next to the wall, opened his briefcase and got out one of the goblets, wiped it clean with his handkerchief and held it to the wall as they closed the door. It didn't work; he couldn't hear anything. He tried his other ear, twisting around in the chair. Nothing again; he could hear better without the goblet. He got the glass from the sink and put that to the wall. It worked, he could hear them now. He listened as if to a record he had heard many times before, listening as if each time he played the record he would discover something new, something he could use for his own. He did not, though: he never did; it was the same thing. Mr. McLain was going to divorce his wife, charging mental cruelty. Mrs. Canta would also get a divorce from her husband, who had deserted her two years ago. He would adopt Jerry; he liked him more than his own two daughters, who were exactly like their mother. No one knew about these meetings; he would be able to get a small alimony settlement, with the things he could charge his wife with, if he acted first.

Albert listened the whole time they were in the room, and continued to hold the glass up to the wall even after they were gone. He put the glass down on the floor and sat quietly; the case was over; he could start on the next tomorrow. He picked up the briefcase and left the room. At the first booth he came to he phoned the lawyer's office. The lawyer was pleased. Albert thanked him and hung up. He walked on, thinking of what he would have to do tomorrow. Best versus Best: he would have to find out if there was a vacant apartment on either side, and what time Mr. Best used his. It was cold and the hand that held the briefcase felt numb; he put the briefcase under his arm and his hand in his pocket. He remembered the steak he had taken out after he slid into the booth. It will keep, he thought, and ordered his dinner. The same waitress brought him the soup. He broke three crackers over the bowl and with the briefcase on his lap he began to eat.

DIANE OLIVER was born in Charlotte, North Carolina, in 1943; she was killed in an automobile accident in 1966. She was a graduate of the University of North Carolina at Greensboro and was awarded an M.F.A. by Iowa University in 1966. Stories by Miss Oliver have appeared in *Red Clay Reader*, *The Negro Digest*, *The Sewanee Review*, and *New Writing of the Sixties*.

Neighbors

THE bus turning the corner of Patterson and Talford Avenue was dull this time of evening. Of the four passengers standing in the rear, she did not recognize any of her friends. Most of the people tucked neatly in the double seats were women, maids and cooks on their way from work or secretaries who had worked late and were riding from the office building at the mill. The cotton mill was out from town, near the house where she worked. She noticed that a few men were riding too. They were obviously just working men, except for one gentleman dressed very neatly in a dark grey suit and carrying what she imagined was a push-button umbrella.

He looked to her as though he usually drove a car to work. She immediately decided that the car probably wouldn't start this morning so he had to catch the bus to and from work. She was standing in the rear of the bus, peering at the passengers, her arms barely reaching the over-head railing, trying not to wobble with every lurch. But every corner the bus turned pushed her head toward a window. And her hair was coming down too, wisps of black curls swung between her eyes. She looked at the people around her. Some of them were white, but most of them were her color. Looking at the passengers at least kept her from thinking of tomorrow. But really she would be glad when it came, then everything would be over.

She took a firmer grip on the green leather seat and wished she had on her glasses. The man with the umbrella was two people ahead of her on the other side of the bus, so she could see him between other people very clearly. She watched as he unfolded the evening newspaper, craning her neck to see what was on the front page. She stood, impatiently trying to read the headlines, when she realized he was staring up at her rather curiously. Biting her lips she turned her head and stared out the window until the downtown section was in sight.

She would have to wait until she was home to see if they were in the newspaper again. Sometimes she felt that if another person snapped a picture of them she would burst out screaming. Last Monday reporters were already inside the pre-school clinic when she took Tommy for his last polio shot. She didn't understand how anybody could be so heartless to a child. The flashbulb went off right when the needle went in and all the picture showed was Tommy's open mouth.

The bus pulling up to the curb jerked to a stop, startling her and confusing her thoughts. Clutching in her hand the paper bag that contained her uniform, she pushed her way toward the door. By standing in the back of the bus, she was one of the first people to step to the ground. Outside the bus, the evening air felt humid and uncomfortable and her dress kept sticking to her. She looked up and remembered that the weatherman had forecast rain. Just their luck—why, she wondered, would it have to rain on top of everything else?

As she walked along, the main street seemed unnaturally quiet but she decided her imagination was merely playing tricks. Besides, most of the stores had been closed since five o'clock.

She stopped to look at a reversible raincoat in Ivey's window, but although she had a full time job now, she couldn't keep her mind on clothes. She was about to continue walking when she heard a horn blowing. Looking around, half-scared but also curious, she saw a man beckoning to her in a grey car. He was nobody she knew but since a nicely dressed woman was with him in the front seat, she walked to the car.

"You're Jim Mitchell's girl, aren't you?" he questioned. "You Ellie or the other one?"

She nodded yes, wondering who he was and how much he had been drinking.

"Now honey," he said leaning over the woman, "you don't know me but your father does and you tell him that if anything happens to that boy of his tomorrow we're ready to set things straight." He looked her straight in the eye and she promised to take home the message.

Just as the man was about to step on the gas, the woman reached out and touched her arm. "You hurry up home, honey, it's about dark out here."

Before she could find out their names, the Chevrolet had disappeared around a corner. Ellie wished someone would magically appear and tell her everything that had happened since August. Then maybe she could figure out what was real and what she had been imagining for the past couple of days.

She walked past the main shopping district up to Tanner's where Saraline was standing in the window peeling oranges. Everything in the shop was painted orange and green and Ellie couldn't help thinking that poor Saraline looked out of place. She stopped to wave to her friend who pointed the knife to her watch and then to her boyfriend standing in the rear of the shop. Ellie nodded that she understood. She knew Sara wanted her to tell her grandfather that she had to work late again. Neither one of them could figure out why he didn't like Charlie. Saraline had finished high school three years ahead of her and it was time for her to be getting married. Ellie watched as her friend stopped peeling the orange long enough to cross her fingers. She nodded again but she was afraid all the crossed fingers in the world wouldn't stop the trouble tomorrow.

She stopped at the traffic light and spoke to a shrivelled woman hunched against the side of a building. Scuffing the bottom of her sneakers on the curb she waited for the woman to open her mouth and grin as she usually did. The kids used to bait her to talk, and since she didn't have but one tooth in her whole head they called her Doughnut Puncher. But the woman was still, the way everything else had been all week.

From where Ellie stood, across the street from the Sears and Roebuck parking lot, she could see their house, all of the houses on the single street white people called Welfare Row. Those newspaper men always made her angry. All of their articles showed how rough the people were on their street. And the reporters never said her family wasn't on welfare, the papers always said the family lived on that street. She paused to look across the street at a group of kids pouncing on one rubber ball. There were always white kids around their neighborhood mixed up in the games, but playing with them was almost an unwritten rule. When everybody started going to school, nobody played together any more.

She crossed at the corner ignoring the cars at the stop light and the closer she got to her street the more she realized that the newspaper was right. The houses were ugly, there were not even any trees, just patches of scraggly bushes and grasses. As she cut across the sticky asphalt pavement covered with cars she was conscious of the parking lot floodlights casting a strange glow on her street. She stared from habit at the house on the end of the block and except for the way the paint was peeling they all looked alike to her. Now at twilight the flaking grey paint had a luminous glow and as she walked down the dirt sidewalk she noticed Mr. Paul's pipe smoke added to the hazy atmosphere. Mr. Paul would be sitting in that same spot waiting until Saraline came home. Ellie slowed her pace to speak to the elderly man sitting on the porch.

"Evening, Mr. Paul," she said. Her voice sounded clear and out of place on the vacant street.

"Eh, who's that?" Mr. Paul leaned over the rail, "What you say, girl?"

"How are you?" she hollered louder. "Sara said she'd be late tonight, she has to work." She waited for the words to sink in.

His head had dropped and his eyes were facing his lap. She could see that he was disappointed. "Couldn't help it," he said finally. "Reckon they needed her again." Then as if he suddenly remembered he turned toward her.

"You people be ready down there? Still gonna let him go tomorrow?"

She looked at Mr. Paul between the missing rails on his porch, seeing how his rolled up trousers seemed to fit exactly in the vacant bannister space.

"Last I heard this morning we're still letting him go," she said.

Mr. Paul had shifted his weight back to the chair. "Don't reckon they'll hurt him," he mumbled, scratching the side of his face. "Hope he don't mind being spit on though. Spitting ain't like cutting. They can spit on him and nobody'll ever know who did it," he said, ending his words with a quiet chuckle.

Ellie stood on the sidewalk grinding her heel in the dirt waiting for the old man to finish talking. She was glad somebody found something funny to laugh at. Finally he shut up.

"Goodbye, Mr. Paul," she waved. Her voice sounded loud to her own ears. But she knew the way her head ached intensified noises. She walked home faster, hoping they had some aspirin in the house and that those men would leave earlier tonight.

From the front of her house she could tell that the men were still there. The living room light shone behind the yellow shades, coming through brighter in the patched places. She thought about moving the geranium pot from the porch to catch the rain but changed her mind. She kicked a beer can under a car parked in the street and stopped to look at her reflection on the car door. The tiny flowers of her printed dress made her look as if she had a strange tropical disease. She spotted another can and kicked it out of the way of the car, thinking that one of these days some kid was going to fall and hurt himself. What she wanted to do she knew was kick the car out of the way. Both the station wagon and the Ford had been parked in front of her house all week, waiting. Everybody was just sitting around waiting.

Suddenly she laughed aloud. Reverend Davis' car was big and black and shiny just like, but no, the smile disappeared from her face, her mother didn't like for them to say things about other people's color. She looked around to see who else came, and saw Mr. Moore's old beat up blue car. Somebody had torn away half of his NAACP sign. Sometimes she really felt sorry for the man. No matter how hard he glued on his stickers somebody always yanked them off again.

Ellie didn't recognize the third car but it had an Alabama license plate. She turned around and looked up and down the street, hating to go inside. There were no lights on their street, but in the distance she could see the bright lights of the parking lot. Slowly she did an about face and climbed the steps.

She wondered when her mama was going to remember to get a yellow bulb for the porch. Although the lights hadn't been turned on, usually June bugs and mosquitoes swarmed all around the porch. By the time she was inside the house she always felt like they were crawling in her hair. She pulled on the screen and saw that Mama finally had made Hezekiah patch up the holes. The globs of white adhesive tape scattered over the screen door looked just like misshapen butterflies.

She listened to her father's voice and could tell by the tone that the men were discussing something important again. She rattled the door once more but nobody came.

"Will somebody please let me in?" Her voice carried through the screen to the knot of men sitting in the corner.

"The door's open," her father yelled. "Come on in."

"The door is not open," she said evenly. "You know we stopped leaving it open." She was feeling tired again and her voice had fallen an octave lower.

"Yeah, I forgot, I forgot," he mumbled walking to the door.

She watched her father almost stumble across a chair to let her in. He was shorter than the light bulb and the light seemed to beam down on him, emphasizing the wrinkles around his eyes. She could tell from the way he pushed open the screen that he hadn't had much sleep either. She'd overheard him telling Mama that the people down at the shop seemed to be piling on the work harder just because of this thing. And he couldn't do anything or say anything to his boss because they probably wanted to fire him.

"Where's Mama?" she whispered. He nodded toward the back.

"Good evening, everybody," she said looking at the three men who had not looked up since she entered the room. One of the men half stood, but his attention was geared back to something another man was saying. They were sitting on the sofa in their shirt sleeves and there was a pitcher of ice water on the window sill.

"Your mother probably needs some help," her father said. She looked past him trying to figure out who the white man was sitting on the end. His face looked familiar and she tried to remember where she had seen him before. The men were paying no attention to her. She bent to see what they were studying and saw a large sheet of white drawing paper. She could see blocks and lines and the man sitting in the middle was marking a trail with the eraser edge of the pencil.

The quiet stillness of the room was making her head ache more. She pushed her way through the red embroidered curtains that led to the kitchen.

"I'm home, Mama," she said, standing in front of the back door facing the big yellow sun Hezekiah and Tommy had painted on the wall above the iron stove. Immediately she felt a warmth permeating her skin. "Where is everybody?" she asked, sitting at the table where her mother was peeling potatoes.

"Mrs. McAllister is keeping Helen and Teenie," her mother said.

"Your brother is staying over with Harry tonight." With each name she uttered, a slice of potato peeling tumbled to the newspaper on the table. "Tommy's in the bedroom reading that Uncle Wiggily book."

Ellie looked up at her mother but her eyes were straight ahead. She knew that Tommy only read the Uncle Wiggily book by himself when he was unhappy. She got up and walked to the kitchen cabinet.

"The other knives dirty?" she asked.

"No," her mother said, "look in the next drawer."

Ellie pulled open the drawer, flicking scraps of white paint with her fingernail. She reached for the knife and at the same time a pile of envelopes caught her eye.

"Any more come today?" she asked, pulling out the knife and slipping the envelopes under the dish towels.

"Yes, seven more came today," her mother accentuated each word carefully. "Your father has them with him in the other room."

"Same thing?" she asked picking up a potato and wishing she could think of some way to change the subject.

The white people had been threatening them for the past three weeks. Some of the letters were aimed at the family, but most of them were directed to Tommy himself. About once a week in the same handwriting somebody wrote that he'd better not eat lunch at school because they were going to poison him.

They had been getting those letters ever since the school board made Tommy's name public. She sliced the potato and dropped the pieces in the pan of cold water. Out of all those people he had been the only one the board had accepted for transfer to the elementary school. The other children, the members said, didn't live in the district. As she cut the eyes out of another potato she thought about the first letter they had received and how her father just set fire to it in the ashtray. But then Mr. Bell said they'd better save the rest, in case anything happened, they might need the evidence for court.

She peeped up again at her mother, "Who's that white man in there with Daddy?"

"One of Lawyer Belk's friends," she answered. "He's pastor of the church that's always on television Sunday morning. Mr. Belk seems to think that having him around will do some good." Ellie saw that her voice was shaking just like her hand as she reached for the last potato. Both of them could hear Tommy in the next room mumbling to himself. She was afraid to look at her mother.

Suddenly Ellie was aware that her mother's hands were trembling violently. "He's so little," she whispered and suddenly the knife slipped out of her hands and she was crying and breathing at the same time.

Ellie didn't know what to do but after a few seconds she cleared away the peelings and put the knives in the sink. "Why don't you lie down?" she suggested. "I'll clean up and get Tommy in bed." Without saying anything her mother rose and walked to her bedroom.

Ellie wiped off the table and draped the dishcloth over the sink. She stood back and looked at the rusting pipes powdered with a whitish film. One of these days they would have to paint the place. She tiptoed past her mother who looked as if she had fallen asleep from exhaustion.

"Tommy," she called softly, "come on and get ready for bed."

Tommy sitting in the middle of the floor did not answer. He was sitting the way she imagined he would be, crosslegged, pulling his ear lobe as he turned the ragged pages of *Uncle Wiggily at the Zoo*.

"What you doing, Tommy?" she said, squatting on the floor beside him. He smiled and pointed at the picture of the ducks.

"School starts tomorrow," she said, turning a page with him. "Don't you think it's time to go to bed?"

"Oh Ellie, do I have to go now?" She looked down at the serious brown eyes and the closely cropped hair. For a minute she wondered if he questioned having to go to bed now or to school tomorrow.

"Well," she said, "aren't you about through with the book?" He shook his head. "Come on," she pulled him up, "you're a sleepy head." Still he shook his head.

"When Helen and Teenie coming home?"

"Tomorrow after you come home from school they'll be here."

She lifted him from the floor, thinking how small he looked to be facing all those people tomorrow.

"Look," he said, breaking away from her hand and pointing to a blue shirt and pair of cotton twill pants, "Mama got them for me to wear tomorrow."

While she ran water in the tub, she heard him crawl on top of the bed. He was quiet and she knew he was untying his sneakers.

"Put your shoes out," she called through the door, "and maybe Daddy will polish them."

"Is Daddy still in there with those men? Mama made me be quiet so I wouldn't bother them."

He padded into the bathroom with bare feet and crawled into the water. As she scrubbed him they played Ask Me A Question, their own version of Twenty Questions. She had just dried him and was about to have him step into his pajamas when he asked: "Are they gonna get me tomorrow?"

"Who's going to get you?" She looked into his eyes and began rubbing him furiously with the towel.

"I don't know," he answered. "Somebody I guess."

"Nobody's going to get you," she said, "who wants a little boy who gets bubblegum in his hair anyway—but us?" He grinned but as she hugged him she thought how much he looked like his father. They walked to the bed to say his prayers and while they were kneeling she heard the first drops of rain. By the time she covered him up and tucked the spread off the floor the rain had changed to a steady downpour.

When Tommy had gone to bed her mother got up again and began ironing clothes in the kitchen. Something, she said, to keep her thoughts busy. While her mother folded and sorted the clothes Ellie drew up a chair from the kitchen table. They sat in the kitchen for a while listening to the voices of the men in the next room. Her mother's quiet speech broke the stillness in the room.

"I'd rather," she said, making sweeping motions with the iron, "that you stayed home from work tomorrow and went with your father to take Tommy. I don't think I'll be up to those people."

Ellie nodded, "I don't mind," she said, tracing circles on the oilcloth covered table.

"Your father's going," her mother continued. "Belk and Reverend Davis are too. I think that white man in there will probably go."

"They may not need me," Ellie answered.

"Tommy will," her mother said, folding the last dish towel and storing it in the cabinet.

"Mama, I think he's scared," the girl turned toward the woman. "He was so quiet while I was washing him."

"I know," she answered, sitting down heavily. "He's been that way all day." Her brown wavy hair glowed in the dim lighting of the kitchen. "I told him he wasn't going to school with Jakie and Bob any more but I said he was going to meet some other children just as nice."

Ellie saw that her mother was twisting her wedding band around and around on her finger.

"I've already told Mrs. Ingraham that I wouldn't be able to come out tomorrow." Ellie paused, "She didn't say very much. She didn't even say anything about his pictures in the newspaper. Mr. Ingraham said we were getting right crazy but even he didn't say anything else."

She stopped to look at the clock sitting near the sink. "It's almost time for the cruise cars to begin," she said. Her mother followed Ellie's eyes to the sink. The policemen circling their block every twenty minutes was supposed to make them feel safe, but hearing the cars come so regularly and that light flashing through the shade above her bed only made her nervous.

She stopped talking to push a wrinkle out of the shiny red cloth, dragging her finger along the table edges. "How long before those men going to leave?" she asked her mother. Just as she spoke she heard one of the men say something about getting some sleep. "I didn't mean to run them away," she said, smiling. Her mother half-smiled too. They listened for the sound of motors and tires and waited for her father to shut the front door.

In a few seconds her father's head pushed through the curtain. "Want me to turn down your bed now, Ellie?" She felt uncomfortable staring up at him, the whole family looked drained of all energy.

"That's all right," she answered. "I'll sleep in Helen and Teenie's bed tonight."

"How's Tommy?" he asked looking toward the bedroom. He came in and sat down at the table with them.

They were silent before he spoke. "I keep wondering if we should send him." He lit a match and watched the flame disappear into the ashtray, then he looked into his wife's eyes. "There's no telling what these fool white folks will do."

Her mother reached over and patted his hand. "We're doing what we have to do, I guess," she said. "Sometimes though I wish the others weren't so much older than him."

"But it seems so unfair," Ellie broke in, "sending him there all by himself like that. Everybody keeps asking me why the MacAdams didn't apply for their children."

"Eloise." Her father's voice sounded curt. "We aren't answering for the MacAdams, we're trying to do what's right for your brother. He's not old enough to have his own say so. You and the others could decide for yourselves, but we're the ones that have to do for him."

She didn't say anything but watched him pull a handful of envelopes out of his pocket and tuck them in the cabinet drawer. She knew that if anyone had told him in August that Tommy would be the only one going to Jefferson Davis they would not have let him go.

"Those the new ones?" she asked. "What they say?"

"Let's not talk about the letters," her father said. "Let's go to bed."

Outside they heard the rain become heavier. Since early evening she had become accustomed to the sound. Now it blended in with the rest of the noises that had accumulated in the back of her mind since the whole thing began.

As her mother folded the ironing board they heard the quiet wheels of the police car. Ellie noticed that the clock said twelve-ten and she wondered why they were early. Her mother pulled the iron cord from the switch and they stood silently waiting for the police car to turn around and pass the house again, as if the car's passing were a final blessing for the night.

Suddenly she was aware of a noise that sounded as if everything had broken loose in her head at once, a loudness that almost shook the foundation of the house. At the same time the lights went out and instinctively her father knocked them to the floor. They could hear the tinkling of glass near the front of the house and Tommy began screaming.

"Tommy, get down," her father yelled.

She hoped he would remember to roll under the bed the way they had practiced. She was aware of objects falling and breaking as she lay perfectly still. Her breath was coming in jerks and then there was a second noise, a smaller explosion but still drowning out Tommy's cries.

"Stay still," her father commanded. "I'm going to check on Tommy. They may throw another one."

She watched him crawl across the floor, pushing a broken flower vase and an iron skillet out of his way. All of the sounds, Tommy's crying, the breaking glass, everything was echoing in her ears. She felt as if they had been crouching on the floor for hours but when she heard the police car door slam, the luminous hands of the clock said only twelve-fifteen.

She heard other cars drive up and pairs of heavy feet trample on the porch. "You folks all right in there?"

She could visualize the hands pulling open the door, because she knew the voice. Sergeant Kearns had been responsible for patrolling the house during the past three weeks. She heard him click the light switch in the living room but the darkness remained intense.

Her father deposited Tommy in his wife's lap and went to what was left of the door. In the next fifteen minutes policemen were everywhere. While she rummaged around underneath the cabinet for a candle, her mother tried to hush up Tommy. His cheek was cut where he had scratched himself on the springs of the bed. Her mother motioned for her to dampen a cloth and put some petroleum jelly on it to keep him quiet. She tried to put him to bed again but he would not go, even when she promised to stay with him for the rest of the night. And so she sat in the kitchen rocking the little boy back and forth on her lap.

Ellie wandered around the kitchen but the light from the single candle put an eerie glow on the walls making her nervous. She began picking up pans, stepping over pieces of broken crockery and glassware. She did not want to go into the living room yet, but if she listened closely, snatches of the policemen's conversation came through the curtain.

She heard one man say that the bomb landed near the edge of the yard, that was why it had only gotten the front porch. She knew from their talk that the living room window was shattered completely. Suddenly Ellie sat down. The picture of the living room window kept flashing in her mind and a wave of feeling invaded her body making her shake as if she had lost all muscular control. She slept on the couch, right under that window.

She looked at her mother to see if she too had realized, but her mother was looking down at Tommy and trying to get him to close his eyes. Ellie stood up and crept toward the living room trying to prepare herself for what she would see. Even that minute of determination could not make her control the horror that she felt. There were jagged holes all along the front of the house and the sofa was covered with glass and paint. She started to pick up the picture that had toppled from the book shelf, then she just stepped over the broken frame.

Outside her father was talking and, curious to see who else was with him, she walked across the splinters to the yard. She could see pieces of the geranium pot and the red blossoms turned face down. There were no lights in the other houses on the street. Across from their house she could see forms standing in the door and shadows being pushed back and forth. "I guess the MacAdams are glad they just didn't get involved." No one heard her speak, and no one came over to see if they could help; she knew why and did not really blame them. They were afraid their house could be next.

Most of the policemen had gone now and only one car was left to flash the revolving red light in the rain. She heard the tall skinny man tell her father they would be parked outside for the rest of the night. As she watched the reflection of the police cars returning to the station, feeling sick on her stomach, she wondered now why they bothered.

Ellie went back inside the house and closed the curtain behind her. There was nothing anyone could do now, not even to the house. Everything was scattered all over the floor and poor Tommy still would not go to sleep. She wondered what would happen when the news spread through their section of town, and at once remembered the man in the grey Chevrolet. It would serve them right if her father's friends got one of them.

Ellie pulled up an overturned chair and sat down across from her mother who was crooning to Tommy. What Mr. Paul said was right, white people just couldn't be trusted. Her family had expected anything but even though they had practiced ducking, they didn't really expect anybody to try tearing down the house. But the funny thing was the house belonged to one of them. Maybe it was a good thing her family were just renters.

Exhausted, Ellie put her head down on the table. She didn't know what they were going to do about tomorrow, in the day time they didn't need electricity. She was too tired to think any more about Tommy, yet she could not go to sleep. So, she sat at the table trying to sit still, but every few minutes she would involuntarily twitch. She tried to steady her hands, all the time listening to her mother's sing-songy voice and waiting for her father to come back inside the house.

She didn't know how long she lay hunched against the kitchen table, but when she looked up, her wrists bore the imprints of her hair. She unfolded her arms gingerly, feeling the blood rush to her fingertips. Her father sat in the chair opposite her, staring at the vacant space between them. She heard her mother creep away from the table, taking Tommy to his room.

Ellie looked out the window. The darkness was turning to grey and the hurt feeling was disappearing. As she sat there she could begin to look at the kitchen matter-of-factly. Although the hands of the clock were just a little past five-thirty, she knew somebody was going to have to start clearing up and cook breakfast.

She stood and tipped across the kitchen to her parents' bedroom. "Mama," she whispered, standing near the door of Tommy's room. At the sound of her voice, Tommy made a funny throaty noise in his sleep. Her mother motioned for her to go out and be quiet. Ellie knew then that Tommy had just fallen asleep. She crept back to the kitchen and began picking up the dishes that could be salvaged, being careful not to go into the living room.

She walked around her father, leaving the broken glass underneath the kitchen table. "You want some coffee?" she asked.

He nodded silently, in strange contrast she thought to the water faucet that turned with a loud gurgling noise. While she let the water run to get hot she measured out the instant coffee in one of the plastic cups. Next door she could hear people moving around in the Williams' kitchen, but they too seemed much quieter than usual.

"You reckon everybody knows by now?" she asked, stirring the coffee and putting the saucer in front of him.

"Everybody will know by the time the city paper comes out," he said. "Somebody was here last night from the *Observer*. Guess it'll make front page."

She leaned against the cabinet for support watching him trace endless circles in the brown liquid with the spoon. "Sergeant Kearns says they'll have almost the whole force out there tomorrow," he said.

"Today," she whispered.

Her father looked at the clock and then turned his head.

"When's your mother coming back in here?" he asked, finally picking up the cup and drinking the coffee.

"Tommy's just off to sleep," she answered. "I guess she'll be in here when he's asleep for good."

She looked out the window of the back door at the row of tall hedges that had separated their neighborhood from the white people for as long as she remembered. While she stood there she heard her mother walk into the room. To her ears the steps seemed much slower than usual. She heard her mother stop in front of her father's chair.

"Jim," she said, sounding very timid, "what we going to do?" Yet as Ellie turned toward her she noticed her mother's face was strangely calm as she looked down on her husband.

Ellie continued standing by the door, listening to them talk. Nobody asked the question to which they all wanted an answer.

"I keep thinking," her father said finally, "that the policemen will be with him all day. They couldn't hurt him inside the school building without getting some of their own kind."

"But he'll be in there all by himself," her mother said softly. "A hundred policemen can't be a little boy's only friends."

She watched her father wrap his calloused hands, still splotched with machine oil, around the salt shaker on the table.

"I keep trying," he said to her, "to tell myself that somebody's got to be the first one and then I just think how quiet he's been all week."

Ellie listened to the quiet voices that seemed to be a room apart from her. In the back of her mind she could hear phrases of a hymn her grandmother used to sing, something about trouble, her being born for trouble.

"Jim, I cannot let my baby go." Her mother's words, although quiet, were carefully pronounced.

"Maybe," her father answered, "it's not in our hands. Reverend Davis and I were talking day before yesterday how God tested the Israelites, maybe he's just trying us."

"God expects you to take care of your own," his wife interrupted. Ellie sensed a trace of bitterness in her mother's voice.

"Tommy's not going to understand why he can't go to school," her father replied. "He's going to wonder why, and how are we going to tell him we're afraid of them?" Her father's hand clutched the coffee cup. "He's going to be fighting them the rest of his life. He's got to start sometime."

"But he's not on their level. Tommy's too little to go around hating people. One of the others, they're bigger, they understand about things."

Ellie still leaning against the door saw that the sun covered part of the sky behind the hedges, and the light slipping through the kitchen window seemed to reflect the shiny red of the table cloth.

"He's our child," she heard her mother say. "Whatever we do, we're going to be the cause." Her father had pushed the cup away from him and sat with his hands covering part of his face. Outside Ellie could hear a horn blowing.

"God knows we tried but I guess there's just no use." Her father's voice forced her attention back to the two people sitting in front of her. "Maybe when things come back to normal, we'll try again."

He covered his wife's chunky fingers with the palm of his hand and her mother seemed to be enveloped in silence. The three of them remained quiet, each involved in his own thoughts, but related, Ellie knew, to the same thing. She was the first to break the silence.

"Mama," she called after a long pause, "do you want me to start setting the table for breakfast?"

Her mother nodded.

Ellie turned the clock so she could see it from the sink while she washed the dishes that had been scattered over the floor.

"You going to wake up Tommy or you want me to?"

"No," her mother said, still holding her father's hand, "let him sleep. When you wash your face, you go up the street and call Hezekiah. Tell him to keep up with the children after school, I want to do something to this house before they come home."

She stopped talking and looked around the kitchen, finally turning to her husband. "He's probably kicked the spread off by now," she said. Ellie watched her father, who without saying anything walked toward the bedroom.

She watched her mother lift herself from the chair and automatically push in the stuffing underneath the cracked plastic cover. Her face looked set, as it always did when she was trying hard to keep her composure.

"He'll need something hot when he wakes up. Hand me the oatmeal," she commanded, reaching on top of the icebox for matches to light the kitchen stove.

M. R. KURTZ was born in Santa Ana, California, and lives on Fire Island, New York, with her husband and young son. She is a graduate of UCLA and has worked as a magazine editor in New York City. Stories by Mrs. Kurtz have appeared in *McCall's* and *Good Housekeeping*.

Waxing Wroth

WAKING, for George Pastorius, was like a blow on the head. Stunned, he lay on this Saturday morning in the bedroom of his beach house on an island not far from New York City, listening to the wash of the ocean, listening to the damn birds, listening to his wife and children being quiet. Then he remembered that they were all going to play volleyball, no matter what, and it came to him that if he just lay still he might in time be able to get up, might even feel a twinge of eagerness. Then he remembered what had gone on in the analyst's office yesterday.

It had been what Le Petit Booby Docteur called a significant hour. Turned out George was one mass of festering anger. Yes, yes, yes, cried The Good Gray Doctor, beside himself with excitement, yes!—those spells of depression, that pervasive hopelessness, those attacks of colitis, all due to anger, unrecognized and unexpressed anger. (If the doctor had worn his hair in a bun and if he hadn't smoked cigars, he would have looked like a jolly grandmother, what with his pudding face and his thimble nose and his merry glasses.) It struck George that feeling anger and acting on it might be a fairly messy business, especially if one were a novice at it, especially if one might be in the wrong. Out loud he wondered if maybe anger weren't something that people didn't much like to feel, it took so many words to say it. With other passions you could be direct: I hate you, I love you. But you couldn't say I wrath you, I fury you; you had to say I am infuriated at, I am enraged at, I am wrathful at.

"Semantics," said the doctor. "At whom do you feel anger?"

"I feel anger at anti-Semites."

"Do you know any?"

"No."

"Um."

"Well then," said George, "I am angry at southern sheriffs."

"Try closer to home," said the doctor.

Not Ellie! Surely not Ellie. George liked his wife and expected, after another year of analysis, to find out he loved her. There was only that one thing about her—

"I am angry at my parents," said George, which was being ridiculous, since they were dead; and he felt that prickling under the eyelids which he always felt when he thought of them, and he knew he could only be angry at them for their single hostile act which was that they died too soon, too early left him to kick around alone.

All right then, said George silently, you. I'm angry at you, I'm in a fury at you, you who make goldfish-popping noises when you light your cigar, you who stir things up. But you couldn't go around telling people you were angry at them when you were flat on your back and they were sitting up straight behind you; you didn't expect them to reach over and punch you in the stomach, but they might reach over and flick cigar ash on you.

"I'm angry at my boss," said George. He was. His boss published a trade journal and George edited it. His boss was always saying, "Editors are a dime a dozen." His boss was always saying, "Call me Ken, we're just one big family here." His boss was always saying, "Well, Pastorius, I guess we won't be seeing you on Yom Ki-poor," when George never took any of the holidays off. His boss was always sending George out to bring him back his carrot juice and his whole-grain cutlets. His boss was always making George write editorials on honesty and then making George give the most coverage to the firms that took the most ads. Once, when George was practicing courage, he brought this up and his boss, who had little raisin eyes, said, "Knuckle down, Pastorius." Ever after, having knuckled under, George smouldered at his boss, but his boss couldn't fire him because of Mr. Spurgeon. Mr. Spurgeon made an unmentionable product and took full pages in the mass magazines in order not to mention it, pages of clouds or cherry blossoms or sunbeams, with just "Spurgeon" at the bottom. Mr. Spurgeon also made other products which he liked to mention and he was George's boss's biggest advertiser. Mr. Spurgeon couldn't stand George's boss and would deal only with George. He liked George because George took an interest in his hobby, which was making cloisonné. Mr. Spurgeon had an electric kiln in his office.

"I'm angry at Rudd," said George, tightening his tie since the hour was over. "Rudd's the man who moved the volleyball court."

"This has been a significant hour," said The Little Gray Bubba.

It had been an exhilarating hour, letting go like that, spewing out anger in all directions. But, like martinis, intoxication in the analyst's office is followed by depression, and now, prostrate in the bedroom of his beach house, George felt a depression so deep that he wanted to swear off mental health. Look where it got him. Look what he had to face. Dry-rot in each and every pillar of his existence: his marriage, his job, his neighbors, his very socio-religious background. He could never rise to it. He was proneness-prone. He would lie here forever.

Fifteen minutes later he was sitting at the breakfast table, smiling to the right and to the left. Three sunny faces sparkled at him, three bright pennies. His children, because they didn't know any better, glistened. His wife was tidy under her yellow hair and within her yellow bathing suit and, because she didn't know any better either, her spotless soul also glistened out of her eyes, blue as laundered denim.

Ellie poured coffee for him and cut French toast for Nicky, who was three.

"You are a toaster," said Nicky.

"You are a coffee pot," said Ellie.

"You are a refrigerator," said Nicky.

Nicky threw himself backward in hilarity. Ellie caught up his glass of milk. Ellie listened to Susan who was five and planning to make poison with the Kripps children. Ellie said to George, "The game's off. Bob Wass came by. His kids are coming down with something and the Langbourne's have guests and, you know. Since that man Rudd, it's just too much trouble."

George didn't even bother to react. You couldn't win.

"You are a sugar bowl," said Nicky.

"You are a blueberry," said Ellie.

"You are a paper napkin," said Nicky.

"Don't eat the poison," said Ellie to Susan.

"My God," said George to Ellie, "can't you manage to be just a *little* bit morose in the morning?"

As Ellie stared at him, a lot went on in those two blue eyes. First she was startled; then affronted; then she blinked, click!—as though she tripped the shutter over a lens. Now her eyes were bland, now she was on top of everything again, now she was ready to soothe, cajole, manage. She was always clicking that shutter at the children. Now she had clicked it at him. He stood up, flung his napkin on the table and strode out of the house.

Ellie. He was so prone and Ellie was so vertical. Just give her a problem and watch her stand up to it. Give her a special day, Christmas, Chanukah, a birthday, the first snowfall, the first budding of the forsythia, and watch her sashay. Give her sadness and watch her weep. Give her injustice and watch her rage. Give her something lovable, and she comes all over tender. All the appropriate emotions, as Monsieur le Docteur would say, spontaneously experienced. But the thing is, you can't go to somebody, your analyst, your bosom pal, another woman, and say, "Have I got problems! My wife is perfect; and what is worse, she understands me."

With the sun curling around his body, with his bare feet sinking into the warmth of the concrete, George was plodding up the walk toward the dunes, when who should he see coming toward him but Himself. Immaculate. White hair sheered off square across his skull, white shirt, Madras shorts, knee socks, for Christ's sake. George, who had never spoken to him, supposed that he would pass him by with nothing more than a malevolent glance and incipient colitis. But Rudd stopped because his way was barred and it was George who was barring it.

"Good morning," George said. "My name's Pastorius. For three years now I've been playing volleyball on the beach in front of the house you've just bought. Now, really, don't you think it was a trifle high-handed, the way you had our court removed?"

"My dear Pastorius," said Rudd, who had little raisin eyes, "now, really, don't you think one court on one small stretch of beach is quite enough?"

"That court," said George, "belongs to groupers."

"Furthermore, sir, your . . . ah . . . apparatus was merely moved to an uninhabited part of the beach."

"It was moved to hell and gone," said George. "We've all got babies and small children. Have you ever trekked half a mile

through sand carrying babies and beach chairs and towels and
orange juice and zwieback and extra sun suits and pails and buckets
and cigarettes and lighters and suntan oil and the morning *Times?*"

"You're flogging the wrong horse," said Rudd. "What you've got
to watch out for is the new element. I sold my house in Eel Beach
because of the new element, and now I find they're moving in
here. You watch out, or you're going to have pretzel stands on the
beach."

Rudd bowed and walked on, and George walked on, too, and
then sat down on the top dune step because he was shaking in
every extremity. He had felt angry and he had squawked— The
Good Gray Nuthatch was going to be proud of him for that.
Why then did he feel so vanquished? Pretzel stands. Was a fear
of pretzel stands anti-Semitic? George had seen pretzel stands only
on the Lower East Side, but were there, for instance, pretzel stands
at Coney Island? Was Rudd being only anti-poor people? In either
case, George thought, he should have socked him.

For not being much of a Jew, George was always astonished at
his Jewishness. He had been raised in a small town where they had
never seen a Jew, and one afternoon in Billy Cochran's garage some
of George's friends had asked him please to pull down his pants
so they could see one. Being a momentary object of interest had
been pleasant, like having your arm in a cast, or being the first
boy to get a BB gun. He had never once been hurt. Perhaps that
was why he thought he could see how intricate a thing, for a Jew,
anti-Semitism was. He did not, for example, want to see storm
trooper's boots under every bed; but on the other hand, he damn
well didn't want to take any anti-thing lying down.

He wondered how his friends would react to pretzel stands. His
Jewish friends were all pretty distant from the patterns of their
parents and grandparents—before her marriage, for instance, Sophie
Kripps had agreed to a *mikva* in order to please Seymour's grand-
mother and had then spent an enjoyable afternoon in a steam room
at Elizabeth Arden—but they didn't take anti-things lying down.
Same with his Gentile friends; they also sent money to Martin
Luther King and CORE and SNCC, and they also recognized anti-
Semitism where it appeared in English detective novels and some
of them even wrote letters about it. He wondered how Ellie would
react. Ellie was a Congregationalist from Colorado. She used more
Yiddish words than George, although that was partly because she

was still in love with New York City and wanted to master the argot: she *schlepped* groceries, she had *mishigas*, she said so-and-so was *meshugge*, she bought little *schmatos* from Bonwit Teller. But when Susan came home from nursery school one day and said she hated Jews because they fought against us in the Civil War, it was Ellie who set her straight and said, to clinch matters, "Why, Daddy's a Jew," (and George had held his breath until he was sure that for Susan it did clinch matters). After that, it was Ellie who would exclaim, "What a treat! Ham sandwiches on Jewish rye *and* a Jewish pickle." When the two holidays overlapped, it was Ellie who bought the Christmas tree and the menorah. And last year when George's older sister, who had moved to the suburbs and become religious, invited them to a seder, it was Ellie who had removed the little booklet from the bottle of Manischewitz wine, had studied it, and then, wide-eyed, had related the story of Passover to their children.

Pretzel stands. Life was so foggy.

He became aware that someone had sat next to him, and when George, a tall man, looked down beside him and saw only creases, he thought he was looking at a naked young woman.

"What's the matter?" said the girl whom everybody called Brandy-wine. "You are glowering. I like men who glower."

"I am angry," said George. "I am fit to be tied and I don't have a cigarette."

She fished out cigarettes and matches. In George's hand, the pack of cigarettes was at body heat, and so was the book of matches.

"You're married, aren't you," she said.

"Yes," said George.

"I could tell. If I didn't like you, you wouldn't be married. Do you believe in things?"

"Certainly not," said George.

"That's why I'm in group," she said. "My parents said I would have to believe in things, or I couldn't stay in New York. Actually, they just *say* believing in things. Actually, they want me to get married and get off their hands. All the people in group think just like my parents. They think I ought to start believing in things and stop liking married men. Screw them. I mean, who do they think they are, wanting me to agree with a bunch of nuts? I mean, they wouldn't be in group, would they, if they weren't a bunch of nuts?"

"Certainly not," said George.

When the sun was out Brandywine wore the same bikini day after day, and when the sun went down she wore the same blue jeans and the same polo shirt with the same stain on it. Her hair was long and straight and black and sometimes she braided it in a pigtail down her back and sometimes she wrapped an elastic band around it at the nape of her neck and let it hang down her back. She wore no make-up and she never smiled. The thing about her, of course, was the boobs. She used George's walk to go to and from the beach and when she was coming off the beach, say, Bob Wass, whose house was nearest the dunes, would signal diagonally across the walk to Seymour Kripps, whose house was in the middle of the block, and Seymour Kripps would signal across to George, whose house was farther up the block. When Brandywine was going *to* the beach, the signal would zigzag back in the other direction. That way, they were all alerted. They liked to watch them shimmer when she walked. Brandywine walked as if she didn't care a damn whether she had them or not. She walked as if she didn't care damn-all for anything.

"Screw them," said Brandywine, who had been brooding.

She was hailed now by a knot of men on the groupers' volleyball court. Groupers were unmarried persons who grouped together to rent houses for the summer. On the island, the term had nothing to do with therapy. The groupers on the court were hard-bellied young men who spent their weekends drinking beer, playing volleyball and attempting to coalesce with the households of female groupers. They wore a lot of Ace bandages and now and then adhesive tents over broken noses.

"Come on, Heathcliff," said Brandywine, "let's do the volleyball bit."

Brandywine played well and with a single mind. She never cracked a smile, she never opened her mouth, she never took her eye from the ball. She never bothered to pull fabric down or hoist it up, but they never sprang out. When she served, bending in a kind of curtsy, a mass sigh would accompany the ball over the net. George played faultlessly. His serves were unreturnable, his set-ups were perfect, and on the net he even slammed a ball dead at the feet of Bull Somebody or other. After the game, they all dashed across the sand and dove into the sea, and as George knifed up through the surf, he felt hard-bellied.

"You were very good, Heathcliff." Her glum face was striped with wet black hair. Her arms were outstretched on the water as if she were walking on a submerged tight rope. Buoyant, they were shimmering now, and gleaming when the ocean slid over their roundness.

"Come see where I live, Heathcliff."

"Look," said George, "why don't you give these guys a try? I mean, it'll be something different, a new thrill."

Brandywine regarded the young men who were treading water in a circle around her.

"Screw them," she said finally. "I wouldn't want it to get back to group."

George returned to his house where Ellie, morose, was washing lettuce in the sink. "Look," he said, "I'll paint that wicker chair for you today." Ellie turned and when she put her arms around his neck, she hung her wrists over his shoulders so that she wouldn't drip on him.

That evening everybody came to their house, the Langbournes and their guests, the Vinsons, the Wasses, the Krippses, the Fords. They were as usual, the vodka and tonic was as usual, the evening was as usual. Somebody suggested charades and everybody agreed, but they never got around to it. Dick Langbourne told a funny story about the taping of a documentary in the south. Freddy Ford, who was an actor's agent, imitated one of his clients, who, Freddy said, was a southern gentleman and a drunk, at a tryout: "Tomorra, and tomorra, and tomorra. . . ." Everybody rocked with laughter. "Out, out li'l ol' bitty candle! Life's but a walkin' shadda. . . ."

George padded back and forth, back and forth, finding it extraordinary that they could sit there, chortling, while all around them life was seeping away, like rain soaking into the sand and dissipating in black, buried channels.

Someone made Sophie Kripps do her Yiddish commercial: "*Hellka-Seltzer! Hellka-Seltzer, a fargunigen! Me nempt ain tablett, laikt es arein in vasser zhoozhit es. Herr nor vie se zhoosit—zhoo-o-o-ozh!*"

"That's how I feel," said Ellie, "*zhooo-o-o-ozh!*"

"Sinners!"

It was incredible that the voice was his, that the cigarette in his hand was steady—he, who had never once attempted to capture the attention of a roomful of people. George looked at those friendly, surprised, anticipatory faces, and he sort of hated them.

"Yes, we are all sinners, sinners all. And why are we sinners? Because an injustice has been done and we have sat back and took it."

"Taken it."

"We have taken it, when we should have risen in the majesty of our wrath. We have kept our anger within us, it is festering within us, and that's a sin, brothers, that's a sin."

"Hallelujah!"

"Who has wronged us? Who is the immaculate bastard who has deprived us of the pursuit of happiness? My children, his name is Rudd."

"Ha, ha."

"His name is Rudd, this high-handed insolent creep. He—" George was about to denounce him as an anti-Semite, but it struck him that the crime was so nasty that the denunciation, if untrue, would be even nastier—"he drinks hot lemon juice for breakfast."

"My God, hot lemon juice."

"Now, brothers and sisters, the time has come to rise up. Now. This night. We must right the wrong. We must move the world. Do you hear me?"

"We hear you."

"Do you hate immaculate bastards?"

"We hate immaculate bastards."

"Do you wax wroth?"

"We wax wroth."

"Then I say to you, arise! Arise, and go forth in anger."

The women removed their sandals, the men rolled up their trouser legs; when he saw that they meant to do it, he sort of loved them.

Outside they were boxed in at first by the blackness but in time the night expanded under a sky peppery with stars. On the beach, the cold sand felt like crushed grapes to George's bare feet. The dark hulk of the dunes stalked along with him on the right, the white ruffle of the surf slithered along with him on the left. Behind him he heard giggles and oaths and he experienced a bubbly feeling which he suspected was glee.

It took no time at all to unfasten the net, dig out the four-by-fours and transport them back along the beach. It took no time to dig new holes in front of the Rudd house, set in the posts, tamp the sand, refasten the net. A noble sight, it was, standing straight and tall against the universe. If a couple of four-by-fours and a net with a tear in it was going to be his monument, so be it. It was a symbol, finky, but a symbol.

The beam from a flashlight played up one post, across the net, down the other post, and came to rest on George.

"What's going on here?" said the voice of Rudd.

"Get that thing out of my eyes," said George.

The beam remained and George felt trapped and exposed, like those dreams of being naked in the Chase Manhattan bank.

"I said, get that thing out of my eyes."

The beam stayed fixed. With one hand George slapped the flashlight down and with the other he socked Rudd in the jaw. The flashlight landed at his feet and George picked it up. In white pajamas and seersucker robe, Rudd lay flat on his back, without a wrinkle, like a fallen Weber & Heilbroner dummy. George sent the flashlight spinning toward the ocean, end over end.

In the sudden darkness and the sudden stillness, everything seemed to have stopped. "Go to your homes," George said, "this night's work is done." Then he bent over Rudd. "Come on, come on," he said, "get up. I want to talk to you."

A soothing hand was laid on his arm. "Now, George," said Ellie, "I think it's time for us to go home."

George shook off her hand. "Git."

The word spiraled through the dimness like a four-letter word. Ellie stiffened and then turned on her heel.

George helped Rudd get to his feet. Rudd stood for a moment, holding his jaw and jiggling. "Sand in my pajamas."

Feeling that chumminess that a persecutor is supposed to feel for his victim, George took Rudd's arm. "Look," he said, "I want to ask you something. Are you anti-Semitic?"

"Hate sand in my pajamas. Are you Jewish?"

"Yes."

"Then I am now."

George withdrew his arm. "Why didn't you sock me back?"

"Because I am familiar with your personality structure. I work with the city's troubled teen-agers."

George stood very still while the flickering white figure walked across the sand and up the dune steps. Then he felt two soft nuzzlings in his back. Then his hand was taken and he followed where he was led. In silence they walked along the edge of the black ocean, the water every now and then coiling around their ankles like snakes.

"Are you one of the city's troubled teen-agers?"

"No," said Brandywine.

"Then you haven't come in contact with a man named Rudd."

"No," said Brandywine. "Is he married?"

"O God," said George.

George had not known that a cottage like Brandywine's existed on the island. He wondered if the property owners association knew it existed. There were not even travel posters on the rough wood walls which showed tarpaper through the knotholes. There was a bed that seemed to be covered with burlap bags. There were a lot of cats everywhere, one on the bed, one on the table, one on a shelf, one on a chair, all hunched up and looking at him through half-closed eyes.

"I don't know where they all come from," said Brandywine. "I feed them TV dinners." She took off her polo shirt. "I know my face isn't beautiful—"

George flung himself on them. Brandywine edged him over and onto the bed. After a while George shifted from one to the other. After a while he happened to open his eyes. A few inches from his nose he saw Brandywine's black hair spread over the burlap and on the black hair he saw something very small and coppery.

He raised his mouth an inch or two. "I think I see a flea," he said.

"Oh yes," said Brandywine.

Adulteries are wrecked by such small things. Outside, having stuffed his shirt into a garbage can and started for home, having stopped and retraced his steps to the garbage can, having removed his Bermuda shorts and his underwear shorts, he then raced to the ocean and plunged in. All at once he was feeling good again. The water was so soft and so sweet that it seemed he was floating in the star-filled air. When at length he emerged, naked as the day he was born, and not unconscious of the fact that man had started from the sea, he felt that this night need not be lost to him after all. He sped across the sand and up the walk to his house, pausing only long enough to urinate on Rudd's property.

In his living room Ellie was sitting, just sitting. He swung a chair up to the deal table which he had sanded and oiled for Ellie and which served as a desk. He took a sheet of letter paper.

"You're not dripping on the Naugahyde," Ellie cried, "you're dripping on the real leather!"

George reached over and dried his hands on the yellow linen curtains and Ellie ran from the room.

"I do not intend to keep any further appointments with you," George wrote. He signed his name, folded the paper, slipped it into the envelope. Then he slipped it out of the envelope, unfolded it and added, "this week."

On another sheet of paper he started to tell his boss what he could do with his job, when he remembered that the mail would not go out till noontime on Monday. He reached for the telephone and when he got the Western Union operator, he gave her his boss's name and address. "No," said George, "change that. Make it Secretary of Defense, Washington, D.C." "What is the message," said the operator. "It won't do. Pastorius," said George.

He hung up. He tore the letter to the analyst in half. He slumped in the chair. The yellow linen curtains raised, letting the empty night into the room. His nerve ends quivered with chill and he was very tired. He thought of sleeping in the living room on the built-in sofa, but the fabric was scratchy and the idea was even more cheerless than what awaited him in his bed. He slogged into the dark bedroom and inserted himself between the sheets.

When Ellie spoke, her voice was muffled. "I don't understand you."

"What was that?" he asked, holding his breath.

"I just don't understand you any more!"

He lay for a moment savoring the recovered night. Then, growling deep in his throat, he reached for her.

CONRAD KNICKERBOCKER, who died in 1966, was born in Berlin in 1929, and graduated from Harvard in 1950. Although he was best known for his reviews and criticism, he was also the author of a remarkable biographical study of Malcolm Lowry in the *Paris Review*, and of short stories that were published in the *Kenyon Review*, *Esquire*, and Bruce Jay Friedman's anthology, *Black Humor*. At the time of his death he was a regular book reviewer for the New York *Times*.

Diseases of the Heart

MANY years ago a Filipino intern sat down at the hospital bedside of Charlie Armbruster the advertising man and asked, "How much each day you drink?"

Looking into the black, bottomless eyes of the young doctor in white who seemed so anxious to begin a cure of the soul, Charlie replied, "Well, um, actually, quite a bit lately. Yes." He could not remember whether Filipino interns meant he was in a good hospital or a bad hospital.

"Every day? Not so good, every day," The intern frowned at the admission sheet in a metal clipboard. Charlie felt his hands trembling as they lay at his sides. His internal medicine man had assured him that he would be admitted with the diagnosis of organic mid-brain disfunction. That way there would be no stigma. They would pump him full of sparine and niacin and maybe the shakes would be reversible and maybe not, but he would have to quit drinking, that's for sure. "Your nerves don't have any lining left on them. You're demyelinated, boy," the fat internist, sighing and cleaning his fingernails, had told him.

Charlie spent two weeks in that hospital. A sheriff's deputy served him the divorce papers, and his psychiatrist came to see him once to tell him that he had to build a new life. Shirley Myre's husband also showed up and sat close to the hospital bed. No hard feelings,

Duane Myre had said, but kept opening and closing a small pen-knife with a blade just long enough, Charlie estimated, to puncture the peritoneum. Shirley had returned to the fold and was now the perfect mother, which meant, no doubt, that after work she and Duane were back at it in the bathroom to get away from the kids, Duane's cigar parked in the soap dish. In the hospital, Charlie dreamed that Shirley was kneeling over him, while outside the car window Orion gleamed cruelly in the winter sky. He would awaken then, the sweat cold on his neck, and remember with panic the tele-phone conversations they had toward the end after Duane became suspicious. They breathed clouds of moisture into the receivers.

"Now I am touching you there," he would say.

"Yes, yes," she would answer.

"Now I'm———," he said.

"—."

"—!"

After he hung up, he would go over to the window of his office and look through the Venetian blinds. He was always sure someone had been watching, twenty stories up.

The big blowup ended the telephone conversations and every-thing else. Charlie's wife Isobel had flown down to see her parents in Topeka, and Charlie took Duane and Shirley to a bad, small Italian place on Rush Street, since part of the whole Shirley business had been putting it over on Duane, the dumbest, lardiest insurance agent west of the Hudson. Then they had gone to one of those fake key clubs and Charlie felt up Shirley on the dance floor while Duane sat and drank sixteen bottles of beer. At 3.15 in the morning, parked in front of the Myre apartment on North Sheffield Avenue back of the ball park, Charlie and Shirley had clutched and fumbled while Duane wobbled at the apartment house door, stabbing at it with a key.

Shirley had stuck her tongue in Charlie's ear and groaned, "Oh, God, let's go, *now*." For months, parked in the dark up in Evanston, huddled under a blanket in the back seat, they had talked of just cutting out, going to New York and starting over. Charlie had begun to feel self-righteous at 3.15 in the morning, that frigid bitch Isobel and her gunboat mother always blabbering about pioneer Kansas stock. He and Shirley finally disentangled and went into the apart-ment. Duane sat on the sofa waiting, his hand neatly placed on his knees, his eyes glittering.

"Let's have a nightcap, folks," Charlie said, smiling the smile he usually saved for clients. He went to the can, and heard it—whop! —and Shirley, softly to Duane, "You bastard."

Charlie came out zipping up his fly and said, "You can't do that. I love her," and gasped with relief after all the months of sneaking around. He opened a can of Hamm's and drank it in one swallow, happily, waiting to be shot. But Duane just sat there, his eyes shining, and Charlie made a long speech, and Duane, the bonehead, *agreed*, yes, yes, he had been a terrible husband. The upshot was that Shirley said, "You can't leave me here like this," and Charlie took her home. They woke up late the next morning with terrible hangovers and Charlie went into a panic, expecting Isobel's key in the lock at any moment. Shirley lay there crying without a sound— she never made a sound even in the back seat—until he could get her dressed and into a cab. "Let's think this thing over," he had said. She went back to North Sheffield Avenue.

The next day was Monday. He fixed himself two huge Bloody Marys to get to work. He sat in his office sweating, staring at a florid layout, and with a vodka-and-meprobamate lunch, made it until 4.00 o'clock. Shirley called. "He went to work today, but I think he's going to kill us." Then she hung up.

Charlie drank a bottle of Scotch in his apartment that night, listening to Frank Sinatra sing "I Let a Song Go Out of My Heart" over and over again on the phonograph. The next day he went to the bank and closed out his account, $817 in cash. At the office, four telephone messages were waiting, three from the client and one from Shirley. He called her, and she said, "He has promised to kill us for sure." Charlie told his secretary a family crisis had come up and he had to leave immediately for Fort Smith, Arkansas. He called Isobel in Topeka and told her she'd better stay there awhile. She said that was fine; she planned to stay there permanently and he would be hearing from her lawyer. He went to his apartment and got his clothes and picked up Shirley with her clothes and a table radio. They roared east through Chicago's atomic night. He called his psychiatrist from Evansville, Indiana, and the doctor said something about the Mann Act. They drove back to Chicago in silence, sipping from half-pints of Scotch. In a roadhouse near Gary, he discovered that she had actually never had a dry martini. Sometimes she had said, "They *was* . . ."

That was it, the big blowup. Shirley went home to Duane and

Charlie stayed drunk for six weeks in a small hotel on Diversey, staring at a cosmic afterbirth pattern on the wall. Finally he called an uncle in Dalhart, Texas, the only remaining member of his family who would speak to him. The old man wired him $300, to be paid back at six per cent interest from Charlie's tiny share in two family gas wells, and he went to the doctor. He had begun to hear organ music outside the hotel window at night.

In the hospital Charlie read two novels a day and occasionally flexed his wrists to see if the shakes were improving. He could never get beyond the first line of the Lord's Prayer, *which* art in heaven, or *who* art in heaven? At first he shared the hospital room with the owner of a Greek candy kitchen who lay there muttering all day. When the confectioner went home, they wheeled in a large man with a handsome, gray, ruined face and set up a screen and oxygen equipment.

A woman showed up and dabbed at her nose, slumped next to the man's bed. "Is it the heart?" she kept asking. "Is it the heart? I had to borrow the taxi fare over here from the girls at the office."

"Oh, God," the man said, and threw his forearm over his eyes.

At night the man snored and broke wind in huge, gut-wrenching bursts, the explosions of a being in grave distress. He was on only 1000 calories a day; yet he shattered and roared, floating on the thin tides of infarcted sleep. Charlie thought of gales and thunder. Was this the true sound of the heart's anguish?

He lay very still when the interns pushed the big niacin needle into his vein, and wished he would die. He listened for the brisk tap of Shirley's heels in the hall outside signaling that she had come to take him away, but the only visitor to the room was the woman who dabbed at her nose and worried about Blue Cross.

"I told that deputy you would jump out of the window if he served that paper on you in here, but you didn't," the fat internist said to him one day. "Now it's time for you to get off your ass and go to work. Quit drinking. Call the AAs."

Charlie read the interns' bulletin board on the way out of the hospital and, from it, located a one-room basement apartment in an older building up near Lincoln Park. He started going to AA meetings, sitting quietly in the back of the room, his hands neatly on his knees, and, by God, didn't take a drink. He landed a temporary job as copywriter in a small shop, and through a screwy piece of luck developed the "Lion's Roar" campaign that put Simpson Oil, then a regional chain, on the map. Little stories about him began appearing in *Advertising Age*. Soon he was getting offers from New York. At first he was afraid to think about them, hanging on to his basement apartment and the AA meetings. "Don't let yourself feel anything at first," his alcoholic counselors told him.

When he had been sober a year, it became his turn to speak. "Think," he told the crowd after they had yelled "Hi, Charlie" to him. "Easy does it. First things first," he told them. They clapped and gave him a birthday cake with one candle on it. He found he enjoyed speaking at the meetings. He began to tell the tale of the big blowup, embellishing the call to the psychiatrist and the Mann Act part. They always laughed. At first he told them about the hospital, but as time went on and he became more confident, and the New York offers kept coming in, he condensed that part until it was as if he had never been in the hospital at all. He liked being in a room full of smiling, sober people, prosperous and discreet. Especially he liked knowing that a flaw ran through each one of them from top to bottom. He began to give counsel himself, urging the new members not to permit themselves to feel anything at first.

The big offer came, copywriter on the Toedman Socktane account; Hunsecker, Kadish, Robinson; $18,000 and all the gasoline he could use. "They got good AA in New York, Charlie," the old-timers wheezed over coffee after the meetings. "You can do it, kid. Remember, a day at a time."

"Yeah," Charlie said. "Except the days in New York are longer than other days." They laughed and punched each other on the arm, and for the first time in a long time he thought about a drink. It passed. He found a little apartment with a terrace on East 65th between Lexington and Park. He spent a lot of time prowling for antique pieces. He wanted the place to look 1920 Moderne, in memory of nothing.

At work he stayed to himself and hammered away. They began to call him Ramrod. Instead of griping about creativity with the copywriters in bars, he sided with the research specialists and the account people. He bore down hard on facts and figures. "You're underreached in twenty-three markets, Mr. Cibulski," he would tell the Toedman advertising manager on long distance to Ponca City, Oklahoma. Budgets, reach, markets. Hunsecker, Kadish gave him a $2000 raise. Kadish, who had a Bentley, stopped him in the hall one day and asked him if he was interested in account work. "Hell, yes, Mr. K.," Charlie said.

"You're on, boy," Kadish said and punched him on the arm. He became account executive on Socktane. He heard talk that he was in line for account supervisor. They gave him an office with a view that extended far uptown.

At an AA meeting on East 90th Street, he met a girl who used to drink a quart of rum and take six doridens a day. She had fine blond hair and a year-around tan and her face had no lines, none at all. After an AA meeting one night, he took her to his apartment. She admired the framed photograph of Amos 'n' Andy and his copies of *The Dial* on the coffee table. He left only the Tiffany lamp burning. While they were seated on the sofa drinking espresso, he kissed her on the ear. Her head fell back and her knees relaxed. "Oh, yes, Charlie," she said.

He took off his $200 suit and hung it up. As he lay down beside her, somebody began ringing the doorbell. They said nothing, straining on their elbows, until the ringing stopped. Charlie found that a calling card had been shoved under the door. It said Avon. "It must be a joke," he said, but he no longer knew any jokers.

He lay down again and the telephone rang. It was Isobel, his ex-wife, calling long distance. She was drunk. "Charlie," she said, "I just called to tell you you're a goddamned dirty son of a bitch." She hung up. The girl got dressed and went home. Later he heard that she stayed sober by inducing her AA lovers to start drinking again.

At twilight on the forty-sixth floor, after the last secretary had gone home and no heels clicked in the halls, he drank coffee and stared across the stone frontiers of the island, watching the lights as they came on all the way to the horizon, wondering how fragments of newspaper headlines managed to reach his altitude on the thermal winds of New York. He did his best work then, when he could hear the full electric hum of the building. At that time, as scraps of newspaper blew past his window, the sensation of floating came to him, a feeling that he was drifting far away toward some sunset. He used to feel that way after a pint of Scotch in the Shirley Myre days.

Working in these twilights, he completed a television presentation, the big one, for Toedman. In his old age, Eleazar Ralph Toedman wanted to save the world. Oil and service stations had not been enough. This was to be a dramatic series on the origins of capitalism and the free enterprise system: "Freedom's Fighters, presented by the Toedman Corporation," great moments in the lives of Lorenzo di Medici, John Calvin, Nathan Rothschild, Jay Gould, John D. Rockefeller, Andrew Carnegie, Henry Ford, and other "pioneering giants whose vision enabled America to reach the pinnacle of greatness." The network had enough confidence in the idea to bankroll a $200,000 pilot made in Italy. The message was that without Lorenzo's capitalistic insight, Michelangelo would not have made it. That way you got in culture and money both. Toedman was supposed to be so excited about the idea that he was flying in for the presentation. He almost never came to anyone; they came to him.

On the day of the presentation, Charlie decided to walk to work in order to encourage blood circulation. Waiting for a light on Park, he noticed that on the opposite corner a panhandler had worked his way uptown and was pacing unsteadily back and forth tipping his baseball cap to passers-by. The panhandler looked like Duane Myre, grizzled, a burnt-out cigar butt clenched in the corner of his mouth, fatter, but somehow more shrunken, and now minus an arm, the stub flapping and waving from the sleeve of a filthy blue sports shirt. A cab discharged an elderly lady at Charlie's corner, and he got in and rode the rest of the way.

Kadish and Charlie waited in front of their office building for Toedman's limousine. The old man had flown in via his Jetstar that morning and was coming straight to the agency. The white Cadillac pulled up at last, bearing its small blue fender flags emblazoned with their phony medieval capital Ts. Son and the old man were in the back seat. Son was E. R. Toedman, Jr., a thin-eyed, computerized young man who kept his father from spending too much in behalf of freedom. Willard, the driver-bodyguard, and Son helped the old man from the car. Even though it was a warm day, Toedman was wearing his long black greatcoat with the sable collar and lining.

The old man aimed his famous pale-blue stare at Kadish and Charlie and finally said, "How do." Those were his last words until they were upstairs in the agency auditorium on the forty-sixth floor. Meredith Walters, known as Old Slick, executive vice-president of the network, and a couple of aides were there, but they kept very quiet. Charlie went to the front and began to talk about the program concept and potential audience, referring to charts on an easel.

"No charts," the old man said. "Let's see the show."

Charlie signaled the projectionist and the lights went out. After about five minutes of the pilot, the projector's beam glinted on something in Toedman's hand. It was a flask. The old man was at it again. Cibulski had not said anything about that. A fist began to form in Charlie's solar plexus. The flask glinted again and again.

"God, look at the boobies on that girl," the old man said. "Gawd, luk et thuh *buh*-bees 'n thet gel, hawg fat!" He shook the flask and handed it to Willard. The film ended. The old man stood up and faced toward them, Willard at his side.

"That was a *rough* show," he said. "Awful rough."

They went to the agency dining room for real Oklahoma steaks. "Where are the drinks?" the old man asked. Kadish, whose face now had locked into a half-smile, nodded to the waiter, who opened the bar credenza. For an hour they stood there while the old man drank martini after martini from a highball glass filled with ice. At last they got him to the table.

"My friend Judge Leonard in San Angelo was telling me they got a rape case for damages down there," the old man said. "Seems this mutt got to this fancy poodle owned by a high-toned old widow woman. The widow woman is suing the mutt's owner. Dog rape, what do you think of that? Dawg raip!" he yelled. He fell forward so that his face almost touched the Vichyssoise and began to snore. Son finished his soup and ate his steak in silence while his father slept.

"Dad is tired," Son finally said after he had lined up his knife and fork. "We'd better get him back to the apartment." He and Willard took Toedman by the elbows. In the elevator, the old man pulled himself erect, and by the time they reached the street he was moving under his own power.

A 1948 Chevrolet two-door was double-parked in front of the building, blocking the white Cadillac at the curb. The Chevrolet's door was open and a man's legs dangled from the seat. A few people had gathered around the old car.

"Take care of that, will you, Charlie," Kadish said. Charlie and Willard went over to the Chevrolet. In its rear window was a stuffed tiger, a plastic hula girl, a miniature stop light, and an illuminated sign that was blinking on and off. It said, CAUTION: ELECTRUM DE-LIVERIES. An old man, lean and deeply tanned, with a great head of white hair, was lying in the front seat, gasping in long shudders. He appeared to Charlie to have come a long distance.

"Get me a little brandy and strychnine, son," the man said in a hoarse whisper.

"You'll be all right," Charlie said. He depressed the clutch and shifted the gear to neutral. He and Willard pushed the car a dozen feet so that the Cadillac could move.

On the curb, Toedman, his arm around Son's shoulder, swayed slightly. Kadish held out his hand. Toedman ignored it and pointed a huge, accusing finger toward Charlie.

"You, boy," the old man said, "you're a flat tire. Down in Ponca City, we'd string you up by the pecker if we could find it. Do you know what we'd call you down in Ponca City? We'd call you a piss-ant." He and Son got into the back seat, and the old man moved the power window down. He caught them all in his Dutch-blue Eisenhower stare. "Pissant," he said, and the white limousine pulled away, moving smoothly, its flags rippling, past the Chevrolet.

Charlie's eyes had filled with sweat, and the four glasses of to-mato juice he had drunk before lunch had begun to turn to burning clay in his stomach. For a moment, he thought he saw Duane Myre strolling across the street, tipping his baseball cap to the crowd, the rum-and-doriden girl clutching the stub of his arm, laughing and gay.

"You look terrible, Charlie," Kadish said, the half-smile still locked on his face. "You'd better go home and lie down. We'll talk about this tomorrow." Charlie nodded to them all. Meredith Walters and his aides had already turned and were walking away, an elegant little cadre amid the Nielsened slobs, their pinstripe backs totally indiffer-ent.

A cop was leaning into the Chevrolet, and Charlie walked in the opposite direction. If the presentation had worked out, he had planned to buy a good used Aston-Martin 2+2 and take blond girls for long rides in Pennsylvania on the weekends. He caught a cab, wondering if newspaper headlines and old fragments of *Advertising Age* were drifting high overhead in that bright sun. When he felt an iron band clang shut around his chest, he slipped to his knees on the floor of the taxi. The gas howled through his intestines, and suddenly he remembered the gray-faced man lying amid tubes and oxygen in his bed those years ago, and the wife who worried about fare to the hospital. It all came back. He remembered Shirley Myre's tongue in his ear. He remembered the roars of the man's body in its wounded sleep. He whimpered. The entire lower half of his body seemed to be turning to gas. As the terrible eructations began, he screamed, "Take me to P. J. Clarke's. Take me to the Gordian Knot. Take me to the Four Seasons. Take me to Malachy's."

"Mal— Mal—" he barked, clutching his stomach. All the lights on Park turned green, and the cab moved gently forward, floating in the twilight that now perpetually bathes that avenue.

ROBIE MACAULEY has been editor of *The Kenyon Review* since 1959. He is the author of a novel, *The Disguises of Love*, and a collection of stories, *The End of Pity*. This is his third appearance in the O. Henry collection.

Dressed in Shade

Accordding to the account of Victor Belding, our Branch Manager in London, he was having dinner with his family about 8:15 one evening when he was called to the telephone to speak to a certain man. He got up violently and nearly knocked over his chair.

"Travis," he almost shouted into the phone, "thank God!"

"Worried!" Belding said. "Jesus Christ, man, haven't you seen the papers?" He shoved the telephone aside and sat down on its frail table.

"Well, you ought to. There was a nasty prang. Yours, in fact—that Comet we thought you were on crashed before it got to Khartoum. No survivors reported. We've been trying all day to verify whether you were actually aboard."

"What incredible luck. You actually got as far as the airport then? Will you come 'round and have a drink after dinner?"

"I see. All right, first thing in the morning at the office, then. Yes, of course, any of the papers. It's great to know you're safe after all. Good night, Travis."

At 10:00 the next morning, Belding said to his secretary, "Yes, before now. But I expect he's tired and has overslept. Remind me, will you."

At 11:00 he said, "Call the Regency Hotel and see if he's left yet. I have that lunch appointment at 12:30."

At 1:40 he said, "You've rung his room? That's not like him. Call the desk and if he's still there ask them to take a message up."

At 2:00 he said, "Good Lord! I hope they've had sense enough to call a doctor. Tell Parker to—no, I'll go myself."

The manager himself was sitting at the desk, drumming his fingers on it and talking to the clerk in harsh undertones. But Belding is a very quick reader of such scenes and knows how to command them. (There is the hawk face with the black mustache, the military stride, the excellent tailoring, the Tidewater accent, the fine sense of when to be rude—Belding is the result of formidable craftsmanship.) The manager's aim was confused.

"Mr. Travis has been very ill," said Belding, as if rejecting some dangerous nonsense that was about to be advanced. "I'll see him at once."

"I'm afraid he still is, sir." The manager was accepting the new formula though it was sour in his mouth. The clerk was attacked by a coughing fit that might have started as a laugh. "There has been a certain amount of damage to the room," the manager said in a tone of monstrous understatement.

"To hell with the room," Belding said in a voice loud enough to startle two ladies and an Indian gentleman in a snow-white turban who were passing through the lobby. "Where's the doctor? Where is Travis?"

"Yes, sir. Sorry, sir," said the manager in disorder. "Don't just stand there. Take Mr. Belding up at once."

In the elevator, the clerk said, "He was wild when he found out. You should have seen the bloody man!" Then he recollected himself. "Mr. Travis was quite all right when he arrived last night. He sent out for a newspaper and went to bed early. When you called today, the porter went up with the message and he thought he heard a small moan so he let himself in. Mr. Travis was in a shocking state."

Belding could get a glimpse of the shocking state through the open door of a room where a maid was busily cleaning up. Travis had been moved to another three doors down. The doctor let them in.

Travis was lying in bed asleep. He breathed with a heavy rasp and his face was the color of milkweed. "Acute alcoholic poisoning," said the doctor. "He must have drunk about a pint and a half of brandy very quickly. I've used a stomach pump and have given him a bromide—but he should be taken to hospital anyway."

Belding arranged for that. He paid here and tipped well there. The hotel was soothed; clerk, maid, and porter were smiling and the tone about Mr. Travis changed quickly. Now he was an unfortunate gentleman who had met with an accident. The manager himself supervised the storage of Travis' larger bags and the packing of a smaller one for the hospital. Belding left amid repeated sentiments of hope for Mr. Travis' early recovery. He was carrying Travis' attaché case under his arm and for the first time allowing himself to look perplexed.

There are certain things about this part that are recorded facts, known islands which must be arrived at, however, across misty and uncharted seas of supposition. Thomas Travis, who was a confidential courier for a large American investment firm with a good many international interests, left his hotel room early one June evening last year. That is one of the footholds of truth in this hypothetical scene. He was about to fly from Lat. 1.17 S. Long. 26.50 E—white surrounded by black on a field of green—to Lat. 51.28 N. Long. 0.27 W—gray on gray—where he would remain for two days, then on to Lat. 40.49 N. Long. 73.37 W—steel color, glass color, dust color. We know that something delayed his cab on the way to the airport.

It is not at all far-fetched to imagine the evening as clear and gentle when he climbed into his cab and that he sat back with that mixture of tension and relief peculiar to airport transits. I have sat in that same taxi or its brother and I know the feel of the scabby leatherette upholstery, the loose spring under it that sticks one exactly in the point of the left buttock, the flattened cigarette ends underfoot. And there is no real proof—but at that time in that climate likely enough—of a sudden change in the sky, which suddenly began to ripen into a huge dark fruit and then burst with a tropical deluge. Or that the driver cursing (in Gikuyu? in Hindi?) bulled slowly ahead into the wall of water; or that they arrived at last under a temperate and gently-clearing sky. It is true that Travis, knowing himself hopelessly late, ran across the lobby to the BOAC counter and found that he was too early.

He must have stood in front of the ticket counter and heard the airline's regrets with that dismal anti-climactic feeling familiar to all travellers by plane. The Cairo-Rome-Paris-London jet had been delayed by mechanical trouble for at least three hours; the scheduled takeoff time was now 1:30 a.m.

He must have stowed his luggage at the proper entry gate (where I see a blonde Lufthansa girl so deeply engaged in conversation with the pocked Arab BOAC man that he barely acknowledges Travis' question, nods in a bored way). Travis must have turned to face the vast emptiness of that airport, the vast emptiness of three hours ahead.

Like courtrooms, like operating rooms, like any station between one existence and the next, airports have almost no local identity—this one no more than any other. Still, at a late hour, with almost no one around, it does take on a surreal air of having a kind of geography. The desert floor of tile is lighted by a high distant glare without illumination and long empty canyons stretch away. After the first tour, one finds that it is built in the form of a hollow square and that imprisoned in the very center behind walls of glass—like a captured piece of Africa—is a green-drenched court-yard garden. But these idle speculations are mine, not Travis'; he would very shortly have found his way to the bar.

You walk down the long row of entrance gates on your left and arrive finally at the first turning. On the right then the wall has some shopfronts—chemist's, curio, book—but they are closed at this hour and, in any case, Travis would have no need for Lux, Pond's, Agatha Christie, Ian Fleming, or a fake-ebony carving of an old Masai man leaning on a stick. On your left are counters and gates for incoming passengers, then the plate glass wall of the garden and finally at the distant end of the corridor, ascending stairs.

When you arrive there, you find a portable wooden signboard with a legend in square white letters: Waving Base.

At the top of the stairs there is an iron turnstile and another sign saying that you are supposed to pay 6d. for entrance, but there is nobody to take it. As you enter, you notice the service bar to the right which, at Travis' hour, would be closed. In front stretches the wide deck that overlooks the field—the Waving Base explaining itself—and at its edge the railing from which arriving faces are seen to advance, become familiar ones of friend or family; or departing faces recede, become part of the crowd, become a thought on an aircraft rapidly dwindling into the pale sky.

It is quite logical to make this a misty night, the air still full of a damp indecision that the rain had not settled, only added to. There is a blare of light down in front of the building and uniform spots of it along the runway, but up here it is all part light and broken pieces of reflection from the scattered pools on the deck.

Travis, I think, kept steadily on to the left until he reached the doorway at the far end and turned in to the bar. The bar is not much, not a real bar, but more of a cocktail lounge with half-comfortable sofas, coffee tables, and again that cheerless twilight which makes it impossible to read for very long and yet impossible to doze. I am convinced that there was one other person in the bar, a girl.

I shall not let Travis notice her for at least ten minutes, because that would seem to be a most realistic guess. He had in the course of time developed a habitual insulation against strangers, a way of excluding other human presences without any effort—unless some necessity made him engage with one of them for a moment. Travis lived in a world of strangers and he was an eternal stranger himself wherever he went. He lived, always momentarily, in cities he never saw except for the rooms in their hotels. He lived briefly in offices where he conducted a set piece of business and departed, in the seats of airport busses, in airport terminals, on planes passing over continents he saw only from 8000 feet up, in passenger bars and restaurants. In all of these places he set up his own small temporary camp alone, trading words or things for his local needs, but admitting no one inside the perimeter. There are some odd bits of information about him: he had seen only two moving pictures in his whole life. Was there too much of humanity even on the screen? He listened to music whenever he could, and once he admitted to somebody that he had a taste for Stravinsky and Bartók. The pleasure of breathing purely abstract air?

He read constantly—in the grammars of various foreign languages. And apparently he did all the exercises at the ends of chapters as some people do crossword puzzles. He spoke three or four languages usefully well, but that was not it; nor did he have any interest in literature. He neither wanted to bargain in Swahili nor read Camoëns in the original. I am convinced that it was simply a way of feeding the ravenous solitary beast, his memory.

The seats were not comfortable; the light was bad; Travis was no serious drinker. He had to notice the girl in time, though she was probably no more than a series of details registered on his retina. I have never seen her, but I see her more definitely than he did, sitting there with her drink, perhaps no more than twenty feet away. I see her instantly but for the length of an impression only. She is the kind of girl born only to vanish almost at once—the girl glimpsed through the steamy glass of a restaurant window on a winter day, on the deck of a passing boat, or perhaps for a moment on a rainy street. A waiter barges in; the boat turns; or she is lost around the next corner. But the way she looks and her one gesture speak so eloquently that it takes hours or perhaps days to undo her from recollection. How can you explain your impression—your totally convincing impression—that under the full black raincoat stretching from neck to knee she was quite naked? How can you explain that hers was not simply a pretty face nor simply a beautiful face but something that flowers startlingly in the shadow and makes your heart catch? She had, this one, hair of that light red-gold color; she was slender and seemed very young, no more than twenty-three or -four. Placed at her feet was a small traveling bag of some indistinct color. Now I have seen her, but can I be absolutely sure that Travis has? When he looked up again from his drink, she was gone.

Travis then paid for his scotch and arose to take a tour around the deck of the Waving Base before—as seems most likely—going down again to find out whether there was any news about his departure time. The place was deserted. He walked slowly across it to the far railing and looked down onto the field. Probably he saw the darkened shapes of a plane or two—very likely one of the East Africa airways' DC-3's was lying deserted there and at some distance down the tarmac was the floodlit Comet with overalled figures passing to and fro.

The logic of boredom leads one gradually along the railing to the far corner of the restaurant-side where it is possible to look down and see an ingenious sign mounted on a white post in the glare of floodlights. In every appropriate direction pointed signboards bristle from this post and each one bears the name of a city and its distance from this spot: Paris 4700, Tehran 2600, Hong Kong 5500. Moscow, San Francisco, London, Tel Aviv, Canton, Sydney—and all the other great cities of the world are given their distances. I mention this only because it is exactly the kind of information that Travis, leaning over the railing in a boredom so usual that he was hardly aware it existed, would be bound to memorize. To know what he had come to consider amusing is to know the saddest and most gloomy thing about his life.

He must have rested there for some little time, printing those statistics for mental storage, but finally he must have straightened

up to go—and just at that moment heard the voice of the girl calling, "Monsieur, Monsieur; Vous êtes M. Travees, n'est ce pas?"

He turned, no doubt, and saw her coming lightly across the platform toward him, dressed in shade, the white outlines of the face
and hands independent in the air—until he focused and realized
that the black raincoat was almost the same depth of no-color as
the gray of the deck. When she came nearer it appeared more
distinct and took on a few silky reflections in its folds, on her
shoulders, from the light below. He said slowly, "Bien sûr—mais de
quoi s'agit-il?"

She stopped about eight feet away from him and gave a little
smile; it was the smile of a child who apologizes first for what she
is about to demand. "Mademoiselle?" he said.

Still speaking in her own language, she said, "I have learned
your name from the man at the BOAC ticket counter."

"He has remembered it precisely," Travis answered and waited.

"Monsieur, he has said that you are on this delayed flight going
to Paris."

"That's true. Why do you ask?"

"I do not have a place on the plane; I am waiting on stand-by."
The persuasive tone was on the edge of anxiety now that she had
come to it. "I *must* be on that plane. Please understand me,
M. Travees; it is absolutely necessary that I be in Paris tomorrow
morning." And, probably not at all as she had planned it, her
voice changing in her throat from suasion into a naked plea, "You
must give me your reservation."

"Mademoiselle, impossible. I have important business in London tomorrow. In any case, it's quite likely there will be a cancellation."

"The BOAC says there are no cancellations. Monsieur, it is a
life and death matter."

Travis most likely felt tremendously puzzled and annoyed at having to stand in the dark and carry on this urgent, absurd debate;
it was a chilly feeling as if voices in his own conscience were
speaking aloud in the gloom. To take her inside would be an in-
vitation to hear her story, which he did not want to hear. On the
other hand, it seemed to him that she would never understand
that he meant no unless he said it to her face.

So, finally, he led her back into the bar and they sat down again
where he had sat and were brought two more scotches. He would

listen patiently; then he would refuse in a polite but absolute way. How does one phrase that? He would tell her no more than he had before.

"If, as you say, mademoiselle, this is a matter of life and death, the proper course is to approach the airline. Explain your trouble and they will undoubtedly be able to make provision for you. I am sure they can do something for a case of distress." Then he took one step backward. "If it's a matter of making it clear, I'll be willing to translate for you." In all this what really bothers me is the question: did Travis ever *see* the girl, actually look her in the face? Because if I am right in describing her as the one who is always defined just in a flash, just in the penultimate moment before she disappears, Travis could have seen more than any other man ever has. But there is no evidence that he did or didn't. His one recorded word is shapeless: she was "pretty."

"I was lying to you, monsieur." She did not cry, but suddenly she began to shiver. She put her elbows on her knees and her face in her hands and he could see the tremors start from her shoulders underneath the black coat and—through the stiff sofa—could feel them throbbing in her body. It was as if she had been dragged from the water through a hole in the ice and thrown there on the seat beside him. Travis was alarmed. He started up automatically with some idea of throwing his coat around her, then stopped himself. He noticed that she had not touched the scotch. "Drink something, mademoiselle!" She shook her head and leaned farther forward as if trying to master it. The shuddering stopped.

When she spoke again she said, "In fact, it's a very ordinary thing. It would not impress the airline. I am the only one to whom it makes a difference. I am sorry to have disturbed you over it, monsieur." If this was art, it was old. But it was superb—the silent hysteria that ended in the flat hopelessness of her voice.

By my inference, it was at this point that something strangely human began to happen inside the gray isolation of Thomas Travis. There was a quickening of senses; long-closed circuits began to come to life. There was a communication of pain so intimate and so intense that it bewildered him. The demand that a moment ago had been perfectly simple and deniable had quickly become so total that he could not imagine what it might be.

Finally he said, "Tell me what it is." She shook her head.

Of course a minute or two later she did, still in the same voice, as I hear her. "It is only this. My fiancé has been in the army in Algeria for two years. Once he was reported as killed and I resigned myself to it and came here. But the report was not true—he has been found, released, and now he is coming home again. I was to meet him in Paris tomorrow. The cable came too late for me to book a seat on the plane tonight.

"I didn't want to ask a stranger for his place, but then I saw you. You were alone and I had the feeling that it was not essential for you to be aboard that flight. I hadn't the courage to ask you at first, but then when I saw you standing all alone by the railing, I suddenly did." There were, undoubtedly, a few other, inconsequential things she added about her haste, her hopes. Then she said, "I have waited for this plane for two years."

I am simply arguing all of this as possible; it was up to Travis to disbelieve. If she were indeed of "the kind born only to vanish," a visual flash in the drabness of the day, it was completely unnatural for her to persist in this way. Some remote outpost of Travis' consciousness should have been trying to get through with a warning signal: *impossible*. She is not of an essence that reappears, becomes a real woman, sits down at a table with you, tells you a history, importunes you for something. Her only power is to strike the eyes suddenly and to elude, leaving you to trudge on toward your obligations, with the knowledge that you cannot change your life.

When Travis came back to the ticket counter, he was alone. He explained to the clerk that he had decided to give up his reservation to another passenger, the young Frenchwoman, and inquired if there were still any chance of getting a seat on the plane. The clerk consulted his lists and said that it was extremely doubtful. Travis took a reservation on a plane that left at midmorning, collected his bags, and took a cab back to the New Stanley.

Once in his hotel room, he went to bed without bothering to unpack. There is just one more thing about her—sometime, a moment or two before he had left the girl, she had quite unexpectedly kissed him. He had barely time to take the gesture in, but the kiss burned on his cheek for a long time, like a cautery of ice. That night there was a violent electrical storm over the central Sudan.

Belding has told me that his perplexity deepened in the course of the next eighteen hours after he left the hotel, especially when he was trying to phrase a cable to New York explaining Travis' delay. He was too busy to worry much over him, but Belding was sensitive to possible criticism. He did not want it said that he'd simply shipped Travis on to New York without any reasonable account of the trouble.

He finally decided to call Silenski. "Professional—well, semi," he said on the phone. "Just an informal talk about a personnel problem here; in your line, I guess. Lunch at Wilton's?" He'd known Silenski casually for several years and always thought of his line as mumbo-jumbo but then one day Belding had played tennis against him. Silenski was slow, but he played a remarkably intelligent game. Halfway through the first set, he'd caught Belding's three subtle weaknesses and from then on told him exactly what he was going to do wrong before he did it. Belding was infuriated, then impressed. It struck him that not all psychiatrists must be fools. In this odd way they had become friends.

"A pint and a half of brandy very quickly?" asked Silenski. "And ordinarily a light drinker, a moderate man who'd need extraordinary compulsion to try to kill himself like that?" Silenski had a mild blob of a face, very useful because it was so disarming, but that was somewhat spoiled by two thunderclouds of eyebrows that overcast it like a scenic mistake.

"Why? There might be any of a dozen reasons why. You see, Belding, I don't have second sight. All I have to work with is dull patience." He laughed. "Sorry, sorry. A squalid vice. But the truth is that I must nearly settle down to live with an emotional problem before anything begins to mean anything.

"Otherwise—just guessing games. All right then; here is your confidential courier who travels all over the world with your firm's important communications. Long record of reliability. Has been in trouble spots everywhere without ever getting nervous. No record of any neurotic difficulty. A widower with no family problems as far as we know. Personality withdrawn, steady, mediocre, unimaginative. Suddenly he misses a plane disaster and a day later drinks himself into a coma and almost to death. Pardon the crude condensation of your story.

"It's like something from the newspaper. Now I know most of the major but unimportant facts. Well, at any rate. Tell me something of this 'courier' business. What does it mean and what does he do? How did he come to it?

"—excuse me, but that term 'photographic memory' is almost always used loosely. There are degrees—some people have quite good memories, some have excellent. But literal recall of the kind you're suggesting is extremely rare.

"Oh, I see. That's most interesting—a rote memory of that sort. So he has the power to remember and reproduce these long confidential memoranda with absolute accuracy. I won't ask you to explain—I can assume that even coded cables are vulnerable to leaks. And I can guess that there must be some very sensitive areas, especially in your dealings with governments.

"Yes, of course. The written documents too. The post being what it is. Now I realize his importance in your scheme of things. That's just tangential, you understand. Not much to do with the main question—which is the sources and mechanism of his acute anxiety attack.

"No, I couldn't even think of offering a prognosis. All we know is that a certain stimulus—possibly his narrow escape—was followed by a relatively disproportionate reaction, a self-destructive reaction.

"I doubt whether one interview would tell me very much; I haven't the time, anyway. You should, of course, send him to a good man when he gets back to New York.

"Well, in that case I'll give you a few questions to slip in when you do. I shouldn't try to probe too much if I were you. Might have a bad effect at this point.

"Yes, a tape-recording might be useful. Of course I'll be willing to listen and tell you if it sheds any light. Call me again when you're ready."

*　*　*

Silenski came to Belding's office a week later. Travis? Well, Travis was perfectly fit again, Belding said. At least the hospital had discharged him as completely recovered. In good spirits as far as Travis was ever in good spirits; and no sign of nerves or strain. But Belding was worried—the interview had been a very odd one.

It had begun with Travis speaking uninterruptedly for forty-five minutes. He repeated the whole of the Johannesburg memo he'd been scheduled to bring Belding. He repeated the entire text of a 1958 Manila memorandum. He had then asked Belding to take down the *Encyclopaedia Britannica* volume MUSHR to OZON and had launched into a word for word recital of the biography of Napoleon Bonaparte, which he'd read just once, on August 29th, 1947. He would have gone through the entire twenty-one columns of it if Belding had not stopped him. "I was completely routed at Austerlitz," Belding explained. "But things got even stranger after that. Hear for yourself—I'll start the tape at this point."

. . . much better, Mr. Belding, now that I've proved that. Good, very good; now I want to ask you a few questions about this trouble of yours, get to the bottom of it if we can. All right? Why, yes. It was just one of those strange things. It hit me all of a sudden, you might say. It isn't like me at all and of course I won't let it happen again.

Well, to begin at the beginning, you missed taking your plane. Incredible good luck; how did it happen, anyway? Oh yes; nothing unusual about that, though. I left my hotel in plenty of time that evening but the taxi was delayed on the way to the airport. When we got there, I ran in to the ticket counter thinking I'd surely missed the plane, but as luck would have it that flight was held up by mechanical trouble. You decided to give it up and come on a later one? Well, no, I didn't decide that right away. I wanted to get here as close to schedule as possible. I left my baggage at the gate and walked around the airport for a while. I had at least three hours to wait. I finally went up to the bar to have a drink and while away the time reading.

The light was terrible in there, though. I felt restless so I took a walk outside—there's a deck overlooking the field they call The Waving Base. Funny name for it. While I was out there, I debated with myself whether or not to go on that flight. Then I came back into the bar and argued it out some more. You mean to say that you had some sort of a premonition about getting aboard that one? I've tried to recollect that, but it's just hazy. I suppose there was something of the sort. I finally decided against—I'd get the morning flight if I could. Then you changed the reservation and went back to your hotel? That's right. I remember one sort of strange thing—it felt as if my right cheek had a frozen spot on it, numb. I was rubbing it in the taxi. I got the flight next morning without a hitch.

You called me first thing when you got here? Yes, from the terminal at Cromwell Road. Were you shocked when I told you the other jet had gone down? Well, surprised of course. Maybe the papers they put on in Paris had the news but I never read newspapers on planes. I thought, a narrow shave, grace of God, and so on. But you weren't bowled over? I was very much surprised.

Have you ever been in a plane crash? No. Or been close to one? No, not physically. Had a friend or relative killed that way? No. Do planes make you nervous? Flying doesn't bother me. I often go to sleep during a takeoff or landing.

Right. So then you went to the Regency and took a room. What did you do that evening? Nothing special. I had dinner, sent for a paper, read the story about the accident, and went to bed about 10:45. You felt perfectly calm? Yes, certainly. Did you have anything to drink before you went to bed? Yes, I had a glass of milk with dinner and a glass of water before I went to bed.

I was expecting you at the office first thing in the morning. I remember, but I had trouble sleeping and when I finally did doze off, I overslept and didn't actually wake up until 11:30. What kept you awake? Well, sometimes I have these muscle cramps. I wake up with a pain in my foot and after I get that unkinked and go back to sleep, it's the other leg, and so on. As I said, I was worn out when I finally did get some rest. Then I woke up late.

What happened when you woke up? I sat there in bed just as if I were dazed. I was feeling terrible. The first thing I saw was the newspaper I'd been reading the night before and I picked that up and read the account of the accident all over again. It hit me for the first time that people—even someone I might have talked with—had been smashed to death in the wreckage. I began to shudder. It started in my shoulders and ran through my whole body, one spasm after another and I couldn't control it. I felt as cold as if I'd been frozen in icy water. And when it finally stopped, I knew just as clear as day that I was losing my mind. Anyway, I was convinced of it at the moment.

A delayed reaction to the news? Oh, no. I'd got over that. It was my second thought. I was sure I was losing my memory. I don't follow that, Travis. There's a big jump I don't understand. What did you read in the paper that made you think you were losing your memory? Oh, it wasn't anything that direct—just something associated. Associated with plane crashes? Yes, in a way; eventually, I suppose. But much more with the idea of missing a plane that way. You know I told you I'd had a very uneasy night. Well, just as I woke up or half-woke up—this wasn't a dream—I had the sensation of seeing a door open. I had the impression that I'd been living in a house for years and that somewhere in the course of time I'd forgotten where one of the rooms was. I must have passed by it twenty times a day without realizing it's there. Then one night I find myself in front of the door and it begins to open—

—Did you have any fever, Travis? No, I'm quite sure I didn't. Well, I always associate that kind of thing with a high fever. I'm sure it's much better for you to forget all this nightmare business about hidden rooms and creaking doors.

But it didn't creak! It was just the fact it was there—oh, I guess you're right, Mr. Belding—stick to facts. They don't add up to much, though—

—It just occurred to me, Travis; have you ever had fits of any kind? No, never. Sorry, carry on.

I don't think you quite understand what this meant to me. An awful thing—very hard to explain. I'm not a very capable kind of person. That is, there's only this one single talent I've ever had; no advantages, no family. I was an orphan kid brought up in the slums of Pittsburgh, then Detroit, by my aunt. She used to say that the Depression started back in 1918 for us—that was when my uncle was killed in the war. She worked in a bindery. A boiled potato and a cup of vegetable soup was a good dinner in those days. I remember going to school with nothing on my feet but my uncle's old rubbers stuffed with newspaper.

I'm sorry to hear it, Travis, but getting back to the point—— This *is* the point. I'm trying to explain so you'll understand. All right, all right. Go ahead then.

Another thing my aunt used to say was that God remembered me at the last minute and cast me a crumb. He darn near forgot, though—I was squat, homely, near-sighted, unhealthy, shy, unfriendly, awkward, and dull. I had this one thing, though. She was smart enough to notice it when I first came to her, when I was about three, and she made me work on it. I remember how I used to show off in school—read five pages of the textbook, close it, and recite it back to the teacher without a mistake. Anyway, it got me a scholarship to college and I worked my way through. It got me a job. It even got my name mentioned in a couple of psychology monographs. I've always thought of the thing as "It," something kind of separate from me. When I woke up that morning I was terrified it had left me. Don't you see?

I'm afraid I don't see. That is, I'm quite sympathetic with your feelings, Travis, but I wish you'd manage to tell me whatever it was, the important thing you thought you'd forgotten? I had the *impression* it was important, but it wasn't really. The important thing was that I couldn't remember.

But you were in fact remembering something, weren't you, Travis? In a very funny way, yes. In a sort of agonizing way. You see, when I want to remember something it's just like clear print, black and white, no blurred edges. This was like floundering around in the fog.

I'm standing at a tobacco counter and I have just bought something. That's all I know. I was trying desperately to recall when and where. I was casting around for clues and so I tried to concentrate on what the clerk had just handed me.

It is a small box of Suerdieck cigars from Bahia, Brazil. That was something, anyway, though I can't remember ever smoking those cigars. I thought I might have been buying a present for somebody. I tried to see some of the surroundings, but it was very hard.

It is a crowded place and people are passing by all around me, but nothing is familiar and there is nothing to identify it—yet I have the feeling that I am waiting for something. Then a voice through a loud speaker begins in Portuguese. It is announcing a flight to Montevideo and Buenos Aires and I know instinctively that isn't my flight.

I deduced in a kind of logical way that this must be Galléo airport at Rio, because I've been there several times, but I couldn't place this particular memory at all.

Then it seems that I've sat down at a table and I'm drinking a cup of coffee. I am—I don't know how—in the midst of a conversation. With a young woman, a pretty girl. I know that I have never seen her before. She's wearing a black raincoat of some silky kind of stuff. She has red hair and a very white complexion—in fact, she's quite pretty.

But I couldn't hear what we were saying. There was no sound of voices at all in my memory at first and I concentrated so hard that my head ached. Finally I began to hear some of the words, though again it was like groping around.

The girl is evidently trying to persuade me of something. She is speaking French. The word "Paris" comes into it. She puts her hands over her face for a minute and I feel very strange. Then she seems to be confessing to me that she hasn't been quite telling the truth, that she didn't mean to "pigeonner" me. She's in love with a man who has just come back from the war in Algeria and she wants to be in Paris tomorrow to meet him. I can't understand why I'm so—affected. It's as if I feel all that she says very painfully, though it isn't so much her words.

One of the strangest things about this is that I couldn't at all remember what I said to her, how I answered. I can just remember how I felt. The next thing is when I've taken out my airline tickets and I seem to be agreeing to what she asks. After that, later, they are calling my flight. The girl kisses me very quickly on the cheek and then she is going to the entry gate and I am staying behind, watching her go.

It's morning. The sun is shining through the windows of my room and the curtains are moving in the breeze. I turn on the radio and go into the bathroom to shave. A voice is broadcasting the news, in Portuguese, and I half-listen. I hear the words "avião transatlantico," "a busca," then "o desastre." It's my plane—the Lineas Aereas Argentinas flight last night, lost over the ocean before it reached Dakar. I don't remember anything else.

Belding's report of the Travis matter was an admirable one. It contained all that he had observed, a transcript of the tape, and a section incorporating Silenski's opinions. All of this came, eventually, to my desk; and I have read it carefully and speculated about it. With the death of Travis, however, the whole thing was transformed from a rather sticky personnel problem into a curious anecdote. That anecdote has had a good many distortions in the course of its wandering, and a few strange versions of it have come back to me. At a cocktail party not long ago, for instance, I overheard a woman talking about psychic experiences and citing the story of two "salesmen" she had heard of. They were going to board a night flight for Europe when a mysterious woman in black barred their way and warned them that they would be killed if they took that plane. One of the men was so shaken that he decided to wait over for a later flight. His friend indignantly rejected the warning and took the plane which, predictably, did crash. No trace was ever found of the woman, however.

The file on Travis was, of course, retired, though I have kept it. Dr. Silenski's remarks—which were concise and put in non-technical terms for the most part—have been accepted as the best explanation of the whole affair, even though Silenski at the beginning warns that his is no more than a preliminary suggestion about the case.

He begins by saying that he feels that Travis may be experiencing a "retroactive amnesia," that is, an inability to recall the events coming just prior to his experience of a considerable shock. He goes on to say that the definition more properly could be called "retrogressive" because Travis apparently was now able to recall a good deal of the material just prior to the crucial event occurring in Brazil several years ago.

Silenski then goes on to speculate as to whether that recollection is one of actual events or whether it might be distorted by a traumatic element. (I interpolate. Our records show that Travis was in fact in Rio de Janeiro in the fall of 1956. A Paris-bound plane from Rio disappeared in the South Atlantic at the time.) He suggests, further, that Travis may have an increasing phobia associated with flying and also closely associated with fears of a loss of memory. Silenski thinks it possible that the pattern of contriving to miss a plane or—as in the recent case—of being forced to wait and then withdrawing is a recurrent one. He is inclined to suspect that the "memory" of a woman who somehow contrives to delay the conscientiously-punctual Travis is illusory, though he does not at this point wish to make any guesses as to why the mechanism assumes this particular form. The coincidental fact that Travis has—apparently—been fortunate enough to avoid two air disasters may complicate the treatment, although it should be possible to make him realize that there is nothing uncommon in two such incidents in the course of some fifteen years of air travel.

He says, in answer to a question of Belding's, that he sees no real danger in Travis' being allowed to return to New York by air —Travis himself has requested it. He thinks that Belding should accompany him to the plane and that Travis should be met by a responsible person at Idlewild. He ends by recommending immediate psychiatric attention.

This eccentric little history of Thomas Travis ends in anti-climax. Belding got in touch with a friend of his, a Pan-Am official, and made all the arrangements about getting Travis aboard the plane; then he made a successful appeal to the Immigration and Customs officials. He took Travis to the plane himself and stayed with him through all the pre-flight formalities, even taking the bus that transports passengers across the field to the plane. He was there to reassure until the moment Travis stepped off the ramp through the plane's doorway—and he must have turned back with a great sigh of relief when that was done. Travis seemed cheerful and calm through all of this. He had obediently taken two tranquillizers and had another tucked away in his coat pocket. At one point while they were waiting, he recited the various airline distances between Nairobi and about twenty other cities of the world. This little demonstration of memory seemed to please him. At the last, he shook hands with Belding and thanked him for all his help, then he made his way up the steps in the morning sunlight, turned, half-smiled, and entered.

The plane had few passengers and it seems that Travis had two seats to himself. The flight was eventless and it arrived over New York only a minute or two off schedule. There were the usual warnings and the big jet settled into its approach. Then it touched down. Travis must have been dozing and perhaps woke at that moment a little astonished and confused. He seems to have unfastened his seat belt and started out into the aisle a second or two after the wheels touched. At that moment the plane bucked—it may have hit some small obstruction or it may simply have bounced a little in landing. Travis pitched forward, hit the seat ahead of him, and fell in the aisle. He was taken off a few minutes later and rushed to the hospital, but he died en route. His neck had been broken.

"A silly way to die," Belding said to me in September. We were in the bar of a restaurant on 51st Street, called The Portingale. He was over here for a conference and I was taking him to dinner. "A silly man, too." Belding had drunk three and it hadn't improved his mood. "*Nil nisi* and all, but I really couldn't stand the little clod." I said something about the reports not showing it; I thought it was a sad and pointless little story and I felt sorry for Travis.

"Perhaps I did, too," Belding said, "but he made my flesh creep."

"How?"

"He carried the air of the graveyard around with him. You look surprised. I know—the busy little mechanical man who never had a thought of his own. Just worried that one of his springs had broken. Silenski summed it all up rather neatly, didn't you think?"

I said that Dr. Silenski's opinion—insofar as anybody had cared by the time it got here—had been accepted as the truth of the matter.

"I thought so myself," Belding said in a remote way. "But then afterward I was the one who packed him off on his last airplane."

I said that it was just an accident. It might have happened on a ship as easily. Belding was silent through the next drink. Then he began to talk.

Belding had called for Travis that morning at the hotel and had taken him to London airport. "He talked all the way down. You have no idea of how many unimportant things the man could remember. I was sick of the whole Travis business by that time.

"I'd cleared everything with the authorities so that I could stick with him until he boarded—not easy. Well, we got there, got upstairs and through the formalities, and then we had to wait in that departure lounge that overlooks the field. We were a little early. Nothing to do but let Travis talk on.

"It was one of those changeable mornings—very yellow sunshine one minute and then clouded over and almost dark the next. We walked around for a few minutes and finally we sat down."

He stopped. "What do you think Travis' trouble was—that he couldn't remember enough or that he remembered too much?"

I said that I hadn't a theory.

"Good. Well, we were placed this way. Travis was sitting on a chair facing me. It was on a small sofa, looking in the direction of the windows on the corridor. The corridor has windows on the other side through which you can see the field. Along that wall is a row of seats—all empty when we first sat down. Then a few people began to drift into the passenger lounge.

"I'd been listening to Travis go on about the distances between Nairobi and a lot of other cities—he remembered all the figures, it seems—when I suddenly had a sensation of something cold on my face. There was somebody sitting in one of the seats by the wall.

"Do you really want to hear all this?" Yes, I said. "I can hardly stand it myself," Belding said. "You'll think I'm hysterical." I said I wouldn't. "I won't fuzz it up, though. So go ahead if you want to. It's very simple. She was sitting there." I knew what he meant, but I wanted to pretend that I didn't. "Who?"

"All right—forget the 'she.' There was a girl sitting there, a remarkably lovely girl who'd been invented only a week before in the delirium of somebody just about off his rocker. She had a very white face, very dark eyes, hair that sort of delicate red-gold color, and very exciting lines all the way down." Belding said, "Oh, Christ.

"I saw her. She was still wearing the black raincoat.

"She was looking straight at Travis' back, hands folded in her lap, a little bag by her feet. I had the absolutely certain feeling that the moment I left she was going to get up, come over, and sit down to talk with Travis.

"I'm not neurotic. I don't have hallucinations. I didn't even believe in most of that nightmare Travis was telling. But there she was, and I saw her.

"The sunlight was shining on that red hair. I think she was looking anxious—but in a very young and innocent way. I expected her to move toward us at any moment.

"Would you have panicked? Well, I did. Just then I saw Travis' head slowly begin to turn in her direction. He'd stopped talking. I gave her one heavy frown and jumped up. I yanked Travis to his feet and set off with him at a good fast walk down to the other end of the lounge, where the bar is. I was jabbering God-knows-what and trying to steer him. I think I must've looked demented. That's all. There isn't any more to it." Belding was a little shaky with his drink, though not as much as you might expect.

I asked about the actual departure. Had the girl been seen again?

"I stuck with Travis like a swarm of mad bees for the next ten minutes. Luckily they called the flight then. The girl wasn't in the crowd at the door; nor on the ramp as we went down. She wasn't in the bus that takes you out to the plane, either. Travis shook hands with me and thanked me. He seemed unusually happy to be going at last. Just before he got in the plane, he stopped and smiled at me. I was standing there sweating. I told you that was all."

ALLEN WHEELIS was born in Louisiana and grew up in San Antonio, Texas. Following his graduation from the University of Texas he did graduate work in Economics and directed the Little Theatre in Austin, Texas. He is a graduate of the Columbia University College of Physicians and Surgeons and the New York Psychoanalytic Institute and has served as a Fellow of the Menninger Foundation School of Psychiatry. Dr. Wheelis lives in San Francisco with his wife and three children. He has written for professional journals as well as *The New Yorker* and *Commentary*. He is the author of a novel, *The Seeker*, and a collection of stories and essays, *The Illusionless Man*.

Sea-Girls

SOMETHING is moving inside him. What? Like a hand feeling its way in darkness. He struggles up from sleep. Perhaps a trailing dream. The vision fades as he tries to see: the action continues but the actors have fled, the stage is empty. He opens his eyes; the movement ends.

Six-thirty, another half hour to sleep. Before him the back of Hilda's head, one curl standing out on the nape, below it some wispy black hair, the shadow of a midline groove disappearing under her gown. He moves closer, arm over her waist, is dozing off when he hears a whisper, low, husky—the image of curved lips moving at his ear. He looks at his wife, who is asleep, then realizes the sound comes from the next room where Anneli, his daughter, is watching television. Dawn; the shades are drawn, the room filled with a vague gray light, like a mist; above him, at the juncture of wall and ceiling, he can just make out the molding, curving around the room and out of sight. In the distance the falling note of a foghorn, unnnmm-unh: not a warning but defeat. He thinks of ghostly ships moving in the fog and remembers something that happened thirty years ago.

He stood barefooted in smooth red pebbles, blue jeans rolled up over white legs and bony knees, looked up the beach that stretched straight away for miles in a smoking, turbulent, yet windless haze. The water was an oily greenish gray, made a hushed lapping at his feet; a few yards offshore a wall of fog boiled silently, moved slowly closer. On a dune his mother was spreading a tablecloth; his grandmother bent over a basket, exposing twitching cords behind her knees, wrinkled brown thighs. His little sister was playing in the tall grass, his father leaned against a rock reading a book. Overhead the sun was a roiled eye, shimmered and turned in a high milky overcast, glared down a thin vibrant light which picked out colors, isolated them, concentrated them as if to the point of bursting. The bald spot on his father's head glowed with bonelike whiteness, the red-checked tablecloth was in flames, the white hair falling over his grandmother's face was phosphorescent. He stared. The leaping yellow of the long curving blades of sea grass struck at his eye like swords; he turned away.

The fogbank now had reached the shore; he walked along the edge, picked up a sand dollar, ricocheted it into the murk—and heard a woman laugh, not loud, but utterly clear and very close. He peered, shocked, into the fog—had he hit someone?—listened now in an unnatural stillness, vaguely aware that a moment before there had been the sound of cars on the highway, a distant plane, foghorn, and a barking dog, but now, strangely, nothing, and the harder he listened the more impenetrable the silence became. He looked back, could see no one; the dune was out of sight. Now again the laughter, a happy silvery sound with a strangely questioning, tapering incompleteness, as if interrupted by an ambiguous gesture. It could come from no more than a few feet away. The fog boiled slowly, he moved back and forth, peering, thinking at any moment to see a boat. "Hello!" he called. Now another voice, a man's, the words distinct, yet he could not understand. At first he thought he didn't hear, but he did; then that the language was foreign, but it was not; yet he could not understand. The woman's voice again, but fainter now; they were moving away. He followed along the shore, seemed to get closer; called but could not make himself heard, shouted but could not interrupt; heard music, strings, laughter of a particular happiness and sympathy. He called louder, ran harder, and, believing himself close to the boat, ran into the water. Fog was all about him: "Wait!" he called. Water was at his waist, he could not see, raised his arms, groped forward. "Wait! Wait!" Water was at his neck, the voices became fainter. He found his way back, could hardly hear them now, ran along the shore, calling, "Wait! Wait!" fell in the sand.

Then his mother running, "Edward! What happened?" His father bending over him: "What's the matter, Son?" He tried to sit up, was panting; pain in his chest and in his head, his clothes wet. He fell back on the sand, turned his face to the sea. The fog had rolled back a few feet, exposing now again a strip of slate green water. Thin vibrant sunlight streamed down from an annunciation sky; he listened, could hear nothing but a motorcycle on the highway.

The alarm goes off; Hilda whines, kicks in simulated tantrum. He turns off the alarm, takes her in his arms, and she talks to him then in a special language of bed and sleep—in groans, moans, purrings, gruntings. He pets her, and the sounds become deeply approving: "I like that," they say; "I like that very much." He stops, and the sounds protest. She cuddles closer, twists, quivers, wanting his hand to move, to caress her; she's a small furry animal in a warm cave squirming among brothers and sisters—she delights him.

He loves her most at this time. Soon they will be at breakfast, she will be rushed, will scold as she brushes Anneli's hair, will look at her watch, think of her job—"I'm going to be late," she will say; "hurry the orange juice, I can't do everything"—a clear articulation then, reproach real not simulated, lines of strain appearing in her face. And he will remember this moment in bed, the cave of warmth, the snuggling bodies under the cover—only a half hour past, but a different world, another dimension, irrecoverable. But now in the gray light of dawn, slowly brightening, he has it, and smiles as he pets her; and she goes on in her strange happy animal talk, gradually increasing in complexity, in subtlety of inflection and meaning, until it overflows finally into human speech. She opens her eyes, laughs, kisses him on the nose; "Time to get up," she says.

He could never forget the voices in the fog, but he could never remember what they had said. Many times he felt at the point of knowing, it was his own language, utterly familiar and clear, yet something would slip and he couldn't understand. It was like a sentence the sense of which must wait in suspension pending a crucial predicate word; at any moment as he had listened that word might have precipitated meaning, but the voice had stopped, the word still missing, and the message was lost. Many times he went back to that beach, after school, riding his bicycle. He was there when fog covered both water and beach and the foghorns cried out their two-tone despair, unnnmm-unh, unnnmm-unh; was there in rain and wind when the sea was hammered lead; in sparkling sunshine when it was a vertiginous blue, when he could feel the roundness of the world, the ocean clinging to it like a film of ink to a ball. But he was never there again when a sheer cliff of yellowish fog came almost to the shore and the water was slate green, nor did he ever again see that kind of annunciation sky. He would stand there in all weathers, would ricochet stones and sand dollars, walk barefoot in the lace of foam, watch ships passing in the distance, until presently a friend would call, and, throwing a last stone at the elusive door, he would turn away.

He goes down to the kitchen. Anneli is lacing her shoe, Hilda is making coffee. He prepares breakfast for Whisky, the dog, goes out to the back yard to get him. Ten months old, sleek black, seventy pounds of wild playfulness, Whisky leaps, puts his head down, rolls his eyes, crouches, springs into the air, dodges, runs away, charges, growls, yelps, all with explosive exuberance like a burst of laughter. As the door is opened he streaks through, a twist of black fur, dashes through the house, claws rattling on the polished floor, slides into the kitchen. A sniff at his food but doesn't eat, must greet everyone first, nuzzles Anneli, takes her other shoe, jumps up at Hilda, surrenders the shoe after a struggle; turns to his breakfast, laps it up noisily. All happiness and sociability then, milk dripping from his mouth, he starts to nuzzle Anneli; and as Hilda tries to wipe his mouth he seizes the paper towel and runs. He bounds about the room, nudging everybody, saying hello to everybody, ducking, avoiding capture, holding the paper, tossing his head proudly high, circling under the table, between the chairs, around and around, then changing his course to a figure eight, wagging his tail, smiling, banging the table, lifting his head every few moments, sniffing, whiskers back— and it seems to Edward that the kitchen is a pool of water, shimmering, greenish, transparent water, waist-deep, and Whisky is a seal with a fish in his mouth, surfacing to snort and breathe and declare an invincible joy.

Anneli is eating a boiled egg; Hilda stands behind her brushing the black hair, Anneli twisting about to watch Whisky. "Hold still," Hilda says, pulling Anneli's head back. "Ouch!" Anneli says. Whisky circles and snorts, swims powerfully through the subtle water, nuzzles and wags his tail. Anneli turns again and a drop of egg falls on her skirt. "Now look what you've done!" Hilda says, removes the egg with a knife, "and I've no time to go cleaning you up!" looks angrily at her watch, pulls too hard on the hair; Anneli begins to cry. "Oh I can't get anything done in here! Hold still. Edward, take out the dog, can't you?"

Hilda leaves for her job, takes the car. Edward straightens the kitchen, walks Anneli to her school, catches a bus to the city.

On the bus he sits by the window, looks out, houses pass, children with school bags. Presently a girl in a yellow dress sits beside him, the skin of her knees becoming white under the pressure of nylon stockings. Pretty knees. He looks further: legs quite shapely, the impression of a slender waist, small breasts; can't be sure. Pretending interest in a passing sports car, he looks back and sees her face. Yes, a pretty girl, very red lips and long black hair. She takes a transistor radio from her handbag; he turns toward her, hoping. "Do you *mind?*" she says haughtily. "No, no, not at all," he says. She turns on the radio and he hears a snatch of waltz before she changes to a newscast.

Over the years he had listened to countless radio programs, hoping to hear again the music he had heard from the fog. Sometimes, in *Nights in the Gardens of Spain* or *Der Rosenkavalier*, it would seem about to start. At any moment, he would think, there would begin that singing upward movement in the violins, becoming faster, lighter, gayer, to a pinnacle of exhilaration, then, falling like water in a fountain, the melody he waited for; and if ever he should hear it, fully, he thought, he would never lose it. Many times it was at the tip of his tongue, in another moment he would have it. Many times he heard music that was close, would listen, compare—is that it?—no, not quite. The trouble, he gradually realized, was that he had heard, not the melody itself, but an introductory passage—a passage that had disclosed intimations, one after another, of the melody to follow, creating cumulatively a portrait of unusual happiness, arriving at last at a point of utmost expectation, of such pressure of nascent melody that the explosion could be delayed no longer, must at the very next moment cascade downward in an ecstasy of song—and at just that moment it had faded.

In all the years since, he had heard it only once—or thought he did, for he could never be certain. It was four in the morning and he was lost in the deserted wastes of the Bronx, had been playing poker with friends and had left, a loser, before the game was over;

was looking for a bus or taxi or telephone and could find none of them, nothing; wandered along empty streets, past miles of identical apartment houses, from corner to corner, street light to street light, examining the street signs, thinking surely he must come soon to one he knew. A car approached from behind; he stopped, turned, started to call, but something strange made him pause, silent. It was a black convertible with the top down, moving very slowly. A man was driving, a woman sat far over to the right, turned away from the driver. The man looked straight ahead, the woman leaned out of the car, head down, black hair falling over her left eye. A tapering white hand drooped over the car door. She wore a black dress, was beautiful but sad. They've had a fight, Edward thought. The man leaned forward, his hand to the dashboard as if to turn on the radio. The car passed slowly, the woman glancing at Edward for a moment. It was perhaps a minute later that Edward heard the theme he had heard at the beach. He ran after the car, calling, but couldn't catch it. The music faded, disappeared; he didn't know whether the car had picked up speed or the radio had been turned down. He ran for many blocks, then stood panting under a street light trying to hold in his ears the fading arrangement of notes. He couldn't quite get it, for it was that same intimation of melody rather than the melody itself, and after a while, seeing light in the east, he knew it was hopeless.

He takes an elevator to the nineteenth floor, greets Marie the switchboard operator, picks up his mail. His own office is on the twentieth floor and he has started up the spiral stairway when he sees what appears to be a statue—life size, female, perhaps of a saint. The face is lowered and turned aside, the robes fall away from the slim waist in gray marble. The impression is momentary, just enough to make him stumble: this is no statue, but a live woman—a woman in a gray silk dress, with a gray face, standing by the wall with the immobility of stone—perhaps a new client in need of direction. He is continuing up the stairs, expecting her to look at him or speak, when he is jarred a second time: this is no stranger, but Liz Talman, friend and colleague. How odd that she who is all grace and quickness of movement, expressiveness of face, should stand so still, appear so grave. "Hello there," he says. "Hello," she says slowly. "You gave me a start," he says; "are you all right?" She nods and with still a faraway look goes down the hall.

The best thing about his job is the window: a large window in a small office in a tall building, it opens onto all the world, and much of the time he stands there, looking out. Around and below him is the city: buildings, bill-boards, tanks, towers, clocks. Down the sheer cliff on the sidewalk are the people, dots without elevation, scurrying east and scurrying west; in the street the cars, rectangles without wheels, moving on invisible currents. He sees the Embarcadero, the bay, the bridges, in the distance an airport; watches ships come and go, planes arrive and depart, above all the great arching sky, and thinks that out there, somewhere, is something that concerns him, in what way he doesn't know, but something or someone to which—or to whom—he could not be indifferent; which—or who—would not be indifferent to him. Something is waiting for him—a mystery, a puzzle, and no clue—but it's out there, he thinks, not in this room. He stands, waits, is confused. Where in all this variety should he look? Is it on that freighter now leaving the harbor empty, red Plimsoll line riding high over the water? He takes from his desk a telescope, sees a sailor leaning on the rail. Is it on that Greyhound bus now winding up the ramp to the bridge? He feels baffled, sentenced for a crime unknown to him to search always for something undefinable, unattainable because he will never know what it is. He turns from the window to his desk, and his field of vision crashes down to narrow focus. His work is to read and brief state legislation which may have bearing on insurance contracts, and he knows that, whatever it is, it's not to be found in this small print. From the hallway he hears a laugh, listens: that's Marie going to the ladies' room.

Always he had listened for the laughter from the sea. On a bus, at a movie, in a grocery store, walking on the street, wherever and whenever he saw a pretty girl he would wonder about her laugh, would glance at her legs and breasts, face and hair, thinking helplessly—sometimes smiling to himself at the ridiculousness of his thought—"Pardon me, miss, would you mind laughing for me?" But if there were anything hard, suspicious, or selfish in her face or manner he would not wonder; for the laughter he had heard and wanted to hear again was of such clarity and generosity it could not come from a small or twisted heart. Many times he felt a start of recognition, thought "that's it!" then knew it was not. It *was* up to a point, then veered away—and he came finally to realize that the laughter he once had heard was unfinished, had not run its course, was interrupted by an unseen gesture, was like that introductory passage to the melody that never quite began. He did not know the ending, the destination, of the laugh, and for this reason perhaps didn't recognize it when once, later, he did in fact hear it again. He heard it, yet didn't know he had heard it until many years later. It was during a dinner with friends and he was telling of an evening in Venice five years previously. In the midst of his story he became aware of constraint in his listeners, paused; "I think you've told that before," his wife said. And later, in bed, "It *was* a lovely evening, but aren't you getting a bit of a bore about it?" Perhaps so, he thought, and felt sorry for himself becoming old and repetitious. What *was* so special about that night? he wondered, and after Hilda was asleep continued to puzzle about it.

It had been one of those marvelous evenings in September, neither cool nor warm, air of such balminess as to dissolve the sense of boundaries, of skin and clothing. The Piazza San Marco was filled with strolling couples, three bands were playing, happy people in light clothes were strolling about. One couple started dancing, others followed, soon the whole square was dancing. Edward and Hilda were happy, danced a long time. The throng became gayer. An American girl got up on one of the bandstands, danced solo, presently started to strip. The crowd cheered, there was loud singing; Hilda became tired, wanted to go home. They walked through the laughing people, and out of the square. It was but a short distance along a narrow street to their hotel; while crossing over a high bridge Hilda slipped, sprained her ankle.

He had told this story many times in the five intervening years, but now for the first time remembered having heard on that evening the laughter he had been waiting for. They were on the bridge, there was a lapping of black water; the arrogant prow of a gondola appeared beneath them, passed full into the beam of light from a restaurant window. A woman was leaning back, her long black hair touched the water, and she laughed—that was it!—and at that moment Hilda had pitched forward with a cry, he caught her just in time, bent over her, fearing the ankle was broken, helped her, half carried her, to the hotel.

He reads the small print, smokes, the ashtray fills; at 11:30 he looks up. He senses the immense world outside the window, feels the blinders that limit his vision to small print, thinks I don't want to live like this, I want something more. What? Travel? Maybe they can swing a trip to Europe next year, his mother would look after Anneli. But that's not enough. Look forward to it for months, finally it comes, a few weeks and it's over. He wants something more than respite, wants something different, something to stay. He wants —and it's not a luxury, he feels, but a right—that ordinary everyday life be the real thing. And what is the real thing? He goes to the window again. Maybe it's not out there, but inside him; not to be found but achieved, something he must do.

His gaze falls on Alcatraz. He'd like to be an architect standing in wind and salt spray before a great rock, seeing with inner vision the mighty spire he will erect. A white ship is putting out to sea. He wants to be a movie producer like Fellini, setting sail for Algiers with actors, technicians, photographers, set designers—all talking, laughing, bickering—and only he seeing, in the eye of inspiration, the marvelous unity he will fuse from warring abilities and interests. Dreams. What could he do? actually? He would like to write something like *The Little Prince*, whimsical, funny, moving, for both children and grown-ups, subtly conveying some overall view or philosophy. Last year when he had pneumonia he made a start. Should go on with it now, but has no time. Always puts it off, he thinks, always has excuses, always will regard himself as one who might have written such a book. Either you mean it or you don't, he thinks, so why not now, will never be easier. Determination blooms within him; he will begin this very day, will simply postpone other work, will write at night, weekends.

He goes to lunch, feels fine, thousands of ideas chasing around in his mind, admires the fine legs of a girl at the counter. Back in his office he gets clean paper, takes from his file the few pages he had written, reads them over, starts making corrections, feels a slow downward movement of feeling, the first intimations of a slide; tries not to notice, maybe it will go away; whistles a bit, looks around. Pictures on his desk: Anneli sitting in the sand at China Beach, Hilda at the Empire State Building, yellow sweater, hair blowing back—that was when they stayed at the St. Moritz and she had an infection of the foot, in bed three days. Clock, calendar, pictures on the wall; moments ticking, days passing, years. He looks out at the expanse of clear sky, a faded blue; it seems far away and silent, no planes. The faint sound of a typewriter, distant laughter. Then it's on him, he can't ignore it; the slide has become an avalanche. So, he thinks, might as well face it at the beginning, stand up to it, work on through it. This is what it's like to make something out of nothing. Or to try—because you can never know you'll do it till it's over. Just accept it and keep going. He continues to read and edit and correct, he makes notes, writes; an hour passes, and then he turns a corner in his mind, vaguely familiar, and comes suddenly upon such a sea of despair he can't go on.

He leans at the window, looks down. That hardness at the bottom is what's waiting for him, always at the back of his mind, behind every thought, every diversion, at the end of every hope, lies there now at the end of this shaft of air, waiting, flickering, signaling their belonging to each other. He turns back to his desk. But he never will. There's something about this, he thinks, as about everything else, ambiguous and incomplete. He has no tragic dimension. If he and that hardness were going to meet he might feel some heightened meaning, or license at least. The sidewalk is waiting, perhaps he really belongs to it, and yet he never will. So it's true, and yet not true. The hardness is not a destiny but a companion, always there outside the window, a waiting presence, a column of air extending up from the pavement to his window, unmarked but describing a fall, as clear in his mind as the beam of a searchlight. The preoccupation earns no poignance, no intensification of time; and yet the waiting presence, the beckoning hardness, is always there, defining him. Who is he? The man who did not jump. "As soon as one does not kill oneself," Camus said, "one must keep quiet about life." And he would never write that book either. He closes the folder.

The afternoon drags on; he has a headache, goes down the hall to get an aspirin and for a second time this day experiences a failure of recognition. In the men's lounge the shade is drawn, the room suffused with a strange amber light. As he enters he has the feeling that someone has just been here, then sees a stranger and stops; it is a man this time, in a gray suit with a somber ascetic face. After a moment the stranger begins to float to the left—in the mirrored door of the closet which hangs open before him.

He gets the car from the employment agency where Hilda works, goes to the bank to cash a check, stands in line. The woman ahead of him is young, has dark brown hair, a graceful neck, wears a light cotton dress. He can see the bra, sees even that it is hooked in the last holes; large bosom, probably. He steps slightly to one side: large but sags. Now she is at the window untying a dirty canvas bag, her fingernails are dirty. "Well, here we are again," she says in a nasal voice, "nice day, isn't it?" The teller is quite pretty, greenish eyes, wears glasses with gray plastic frames; has a good mouth, soft, full, but straight, a line of brown hair on the upper lip. She wears a tight dress of natural linen, breasts held up smartly, rather pointed, dress fitting smoothly under them and tapering down, it seems, to a delicate waist which, however, is hidden by the counter; he stands on tiptoe. The woman before him finishes, turns away, brushes his hand with her hip. He stares after her, trying to preserve the tingling in his hand. "Yes?" the teller says coolly. He gives her a check for fifty dollars; she stamps it, and as she reaches to replace the stamp in the holder her right breast touches the check, moves it slightly on the counter. His mouth is dry, he swallows. "How will you have it?" she says. "I . . . oh . . . five tens, please."

He takes the money, turns away, almost knocks against another woman—quite short, red hair, freckles—who has come up behind him. He starts putting the bills in his wallet, looks out over the bank. There are six, no seven, girls here, most of them young. He drops a ten-dollar bill, picks it up. No, eight: one is coming out of the vault now. Three are very pretty, all wear tight skirts. One man sits at a desk near the front, handles loans. He must be the manager, doubtless has to work late sometimes . . . show a new girl the ropes. . . .

Leaving the bank, Edward starts for his car, but turns suddenly, enters a tobacco shop. In front are general magazines; then comic books with covers showing rape, shooting, stabbing; paperback books with sexy covers—a shabby room seen from the doorway over the shoulder of a towering black figure, a busty girl shrinking in a corner, blouse and skirt in tatters. In the back of the shop is a counter, cigarettes, gum, cigars; behind it a thin man of about sixty with dry, grayish face, white hair. The man chats desultorily with a portly customer who leans on the counter. A small radio reports a ball game; the volume is low, they're not really listening. Edward turns left, past the paperbacks, to the more secluded part of the shop and there on racks from floor to ceiling are the girls. The titles speak to interests in photography, sociology, art, and the dance, but nobody is fooled: these are girlie magazines and they speak to lust. He picks one off the rack, opens it at random, and there they are: scanty clothes, no clothes, the entrancing postures. He flips briskly through the pages. The two men chat idly, as if indifferent to his presence, unaware of his interest; but he feels them to be acutely aware, they know exactly what he's looking at and why, their eyes bore holes in his back; and so we are driven, driven, driven, he thinks, till we die. He flips the pages: a slender blonde girl, naked, on hands and knees in the hay; his heart pounds, a sense of deafening noise in his head, yet utter silence, like the moment of ringing stunned quiet that follows a pistol shot. His hands tremble, he feels tremendous haste and guilt, as if he had wandered into the vault of a bank by mistake and were picking up bundles of thousand-dollar bills: he intends no theft but knows that, come upon, he would be viewed with dire suspicion. He leaves the shop without buying, walks quickly, then makes himself walk slowly, looks about, wonders if he has been seen.

In his car he thinks of the blonde, then of the man who took the pictures. That's what I would like to be, he thinks. The photographer doesn't have much money, drives an old car, telephones the girl: "We'll do a series in the country; haystacks, gingham aprons, that kind of thing. Pick you up about nine." Comes in, finds her dressed, ready; lays hands on her, feels bra, pulls strap, lets it snap back. "What's this?" he says; "didn't I tell you last time? Leaves a red mark . . . for hours. Take it off." Runs his hands lower, feels panties. "These too. You ought to know better. Gotta be ready to work." "Okay," she says, and goes in the other room. He follows, ignoring the token wish for privacy, watches her undress. "Are you shaved?" he says. She nods. "Last time there was a black shadow," he says, "took hours to clean up those negatives. Let me see." He examines her armpits, pubis. "No good. Let me do it." He shaves her, tickles her, and they have wild, bouncing intercourse; drive to the country, find a farm, get permission to use field and barn; he poses her stepping in and out of clothes by haystacks, in fields of clover, in stable and loft; intercourse again; drive back to town, she wants him to stay, he has other game in mind; "Be seeing you around!" he says.

A woman and child have entered the crosswalk. He's already into the intersection, going too fast. Could stop perhaps, but would slide. Goes on. The woman, holding the child's hand, is in the middle of the street, flinches, glowers: "Thank *you*, Mister!" she calls as he passes; "thank you *very much!*" She's right, he thinks, and he wants to stop, apologize; but the car behind is honking, and he goes on, thinking of Anneli and Hilda, of how angry he would be at a driver who treated them this way. And what about that blonde in the hay? he thinks. He has no love to give to such a girl, no devotion, loyalty, not even interest, nothing; wants her to give to him. Transient lust on his part, adoration on hers.

He stops at a bar, orders a martini, then another; begins talking to a frowsy plump woman about forty with bleary eyes, short sandy hair that stands out from her head, good figure. For many years, she tells him, she and her husband owned a small cleaning shop; one day her husband sold it without asking her. She had worked there with him for fifteen years, helped build it up, their children worked there after school; nothing great, but security, steady customers, a good living. And he sold it. Thought he could find something better, more status, make her proud of him. Now he's out of work, can't find a job; they're living on their savings, can't send the boy to college. "It was crazy," she says; "just crazy. That's the only word for it. He was out of his mind." She thinks he ought to find another cleaning business, and he's willing now, has been looking, but can't find one he can afford. She tells Edward about steam presses, insurance, cleaning fluids, leases, the big capital outlay. "We just can't afford it," she says, "don't have that kind of money." Edward buys her a drink, wishes her luck.

Hilda and Anneli are in the kitchen. Hilda frowns as he enters, pulls away as he kisses her. "Everything's cold! I work hard all day, come home, fix your dinner, and what are you doing? Out boozing around. I won't stand for it. I just won't take it!" Whisky crouches under a chair, startled by the sudden vehemence. Anneli is drawing a horse, smiles shyly as he leans over to kiss her. "I have an earache," she says. Hilda serves dinner, begins to calm down; she's worried about Anneli, has called the pediatrician. After dinner Edward takes Anneli's temperature: 100.5°. The pediatrician comes: an infection, prescribes erythromycin, will have to be home a few days. "Who will I get to stay with her?" Hilda says; "I can't miss work again." She makes three telephone calls, finds a woman to come the next day.

In bed finally, lights out, Hilda is unhappy, tearful. "This is no way to live," she says; "I'm so rushed. This morning I was impatient, rough with Anneli. Felt bad about it all day, couldn't concentrate. I hurried to buy food, come home, cook, Anneli's sick, you're out late drinking I don't know who with and . . . this is no way to live. I just hate it. I want to have some fun in life." "Things will get better," Edward says; "maybe we can go away."

ALLEN WHEELIS

"That's what you always say," Hilda says; "it's not enough. I want something more. I want to be happy." "What's the matter, baby?" "I don't know," Hilda says; "nothing. Everything. We have a good working relationship, and I mean *working*, could go on like this for years, till we drop—get up, go to work, do the job, then home, stove, housework, bed, sleep—but something's missing. You don't talk to me any more, don't really look at me, seem to be listening for something else." He pets her, strokes her hair, shoulders, back.

He lies awake after she is asleep, and when at last he too sleeps something soon disturbs him. Something moving. What is it? He wakes, opens his eyes. The room is dark, outside a sound of wind in trees, the cry of distant foghorns—unnnmm-unh. Hilda is snuggled against him, her breathing deep. Whisky sighs from the hallway rug. Edward closes his eyes, is at the threshold of a deep sleep when he feels it again: a slow movement—unhurried, unhurriable. A door. That's it. The door in which he saw his reflection that afternoon as a stranger. Somewhere inside him a door is swinging open, the noiseless movement coming now to an end; the door is open; there's nothing there.

RICHARD YATES was born in Yonkers, New York, and lives in New York City with his wife and two children. He has written for television, films, industrial and technical publications, and his short stories have appeared in *Atlantic Monthly, Paris Review, Esquire*, and others. He is the author of *Revolutionary Road* and *Eleven Kinds of Loneliness*. This is Mr. Yates' second appearance in the O. Henry collection.

A Good and Gallant Woman

O N SATURDAYS, when inspection was over and passes were issued in the Orderly Rooms, there was a stampede of escape down every company street in Camp Pickett. You could go to Lynchburg or Richmond or Washington, D.C., and if you were willing to travel for nine hours—five on the bus and four on the train—you could get to New York.

Private Robert J. Prentice made the long trip alone one windy afternoon in 1944. He was a rifle trainee, eighteen years old, and this seemed an important thing to do because it might well be the last pass he'd get before going overseas.

In the echoing swarm of Penn Station that night, feeling lost and cramped and light-headed, he shouldered his way through acres of embracing couples: men whose uniforms looked somehow more authoritative than his own, girls whose ardor was a terrible reproach to his own callowness. Once he found himself walking straight toward a girl who stood facing him in the crowd, a slender, delicate girl with long brown hair, and as he came closer her uplifted face took on the most beautiful look of welcome he had ever seen. She didn't move, but her eyes filled with tears and her lips parted in a way that stopped his heart—God, to be looked at that way by a girl, just once!—so that he felt as stunned as a jilted lover when a Marine corporal came jostling past him and took her in his arms.

He was weak with envy as he turned toward the subway, and

he tried to make up for it by pulling his crinkled overseas cap down into one eyebrow and hoping that the tension in his face and the hurry in his stride might suggest that he was bound for a welcome as romantic as the Marine's.

But the subway only swallowed him into the dirty, intricate bowels of a city he would never understand, and when he came up into the windswept darkness of Columbus Circle he had to walk a few steps one way and a few steps another, craning his head, before he got his bearings.

New York was his birthplace and he'd spent most of his life in it, but no section or street of it had ever felt like his neighborhood. He had never lived in one house for more than a year. The address now shown on his service record as his home was a walk-up apartment in the West Fifties, on a dark block beyond Eighth Avenue, and as he made his way there he tried to conjure a sense of homecoming among the blown newspapers and the flickering bar signs. He pressed the bell marked "Prentice" and heard the joyous answering bleat of the buzzer that let him in; then he was loping up a warped linoleum stairway through smells of vegetables and garbage and perfume, and then he was staggering in the clutch of his mother's hug.

"Oh, Bobby," she said. The top of her frizzled gray head scarcely came up to his breast-pocket flaps and she was as frail as a sparrow, but the force of her love was so great that he had to brace himself in a kind of boxer's stance to absorb it. "You look wonderful," she said. "Oh, let me look at you." And he allowed himself, uneasily, to be held and inspected at arm's length. "My soldier," she said. "My big, wonderful soldier."

And then came the questions: Had he eaten anything? Was he terribly tired? Was he glad to be home?

"Oh, I've been so happy all day, just knowing you were coming. Old Herman said to me this morning—you know, the ugly little *foreman* I've told you about? At my horrible *job?* I was singing this morning, or kind of humming under my breath, and he said, 'What've *you* got to sing about?' And oh-ho, I looked him right in the eye—this dreadful, smelly little man, you know, in his awful old undershirt, with all of those awful factory noises going on—and I said, 'I've got plenty to sing about.' I said, 'My *son* is coming home tonight on *leave.*'" And she moved away across the room, fragile and awkward in her worn-down heels and her black rayon dress whose side vent was held together with a safety pin, laughing at the memory of her exchange with the foreman. "My *son*," she said again, "is coming home tonight on *leave*."

"Well," he said, "it's not really a leave, you know; it's just a pass."

"A pass; I know. *Oh*, it's so good to see you. Tell you what. How about a hot cup of coffee?—and you sit down and rest. Then I'll get ready and we'll go out for dinner. How would that be?"

While she bustled in and out of her bedroom, still talking, he sipped at the bitter, warmed-over coffee she'd brought him, and strolled around the carpet. The unkempt coziness of the place, full of cigarette ash and sagging, rickety furniture under weak lamps, was very strange after the scrubbed symmetry of the barracks. So was the privacy of it, and the fact that it held, on one wall, a narrow, full-length mirror in which he was surprised to find his own naked-looking face above the brass-buttoned torso of olive drab. He pulled himself dramatically to attention, and then, after glancing away to make sure she was safely in the bedroom, he went through a series of drill turns, whispering the commands to himself. Right face; left face; about face; hand salute; parade rest. In the parade-rest position he discovered that she'd left a smear of lipstick on his uniform.

"There," she said. "Now I'm ready. Do I look all right? Do I look nice enough to go out on a date with a handsome soldier?"

"Fine," he told her. "You look fine." And she did look better, despite a sprinkling of face powder down her bodice. She had managed to close the vent of her dress more securely, and she'd carefully fixed her hair.

When they left the apartment, he noticed how she crouched and squinted to make her way down the stairs—her eyes were getting worse—and out on the street, where she clung to his arm for walking, she seemed very old and slow. At the first intersection she hunched and hurried in fright, gripping his arm tighter, until they were safely on the opposite curb. She had never understood automobiles and always tended to exaggerate their menace. She seemed to feel that any or all of the waiting, throbbing cars might bolt forward against the light with murder in their hearts.

They went to the Childs on Columbus Circle. "Isn't it funny?" she said. "I always used to think Childs restaurants were dreadful, but this really is the only decent place around here—all the others are so horribly expensive—and I think it's kind of nice, don't you?"

They each had a Manhattan to start with, because she insisted it was to be a real celebration; and then, after studying the menu to make sure they could afford it if they held the cost of the dinner down to chicken croquettes, they each had another. He didn't really want the second one—the heavy sweetness of it threatened to make him sick—but he sipped it anyway and tried to relax in his chair.

Her voice by now had become a rich and tireless monologue: ". . . Oh, and guess who I ran into on the bus the other day! Natalie Crawford! Remember the year we lived on Charles Street? And you used to play with the Crawford boys? They're both in the Navy now, and Bill's in the Pacific; just imagine. Remember the winter we were so horribly broke, and Natalie and I had those awful fights about money? Anyway, that's all forgotten now. We had dinner together and had the nicest talk; she wanted to hear all about you. Oh, and *guess* what she told me about the Wilsons! Remember? George and Amy Wilson, that were such good friends of mine that year? And they used to come out to see us later in Larchmont, too; remember? Remember the year we all spent Christmas together and had such a good time? . . ."

It went on and on, while he crumbled his chicken croquette with the side of his fork and made whatever answers she seemed to want, or to need. After a while he stopped listening. His ears took in only the rise and fall of her voice, the elaborate, familiar, endless rhythm of it; but from long experience he was able to say "Oh, yes" and "Of course" in all the right places.

The subjects of her talk didn't matter; he knew what she was really saying. Helpless and gentle, small and tired and anxious to please, she was asking him to agree that her life was not a failure. Did he remember the good times? Did he remember all the nice people they'd known, and all the interestingly different places they'd lived in? And whatever mistakes she might have made, however rudely the world might have treated her, did he know how hard she'd always tried? Did he know how terribly much she loved him? And did he realize—in spite of everything—did he realize how re-markable and how gifted and how brave a woman his mother was?

Oh, yes; oh, yes; of course he did—that was the message of his nods and smiles and mumbled replies. It was the message he'd been giving her as long as he could remember, and for most of that time he had wholly believed it.

Because she *was* remarkable and gifted and brave. How else could anyone explain the story of her life? At the turn of the century, when all the sleeping little towns of Indiana had lain locked in provincial ignorance, and when in that environment a simple dry-goods merchant named Amos Grumbauer had raised six ordinary daughters, wasn't it remarkable that his seventh had somehow developed a passion for art, and for elegance, and for the great and distant world of New York? Without finishing high school, she had become one of the first female students ever enrolled in the Cincinnati Art Academy; and not very many years after that, all alone, she had come to the city of her dreams and found employment as a fashion illustrator, with only occasional help from home. Didn't that prove she was gifted, and didn't it prove she was brave?

Her first great mistake—and she often said afterward that she would never understand what had possessed her—was to marry a man as simple and ordinary as her own Indiana father. Oh, George Prentice might have been handsome in a quiet way; he might even have been a little dashing, with his fine amateur singing voice, his good clothes, and the salesman's expense account that made him welcome at some of the better speakeasies in town. It was undeniable too that a girl of thirty-four wasn't apt to get too many serious proposals; and besides, he was so steady, so devoted, so anxious to protect her and provide for her. But how could she have been so blind to the dullness of the man? How could she have failed to see that he thought of her talent as a charming little hobby and nothing more, and that he could get tears in his eyes over the poetry of Edgar A. Guest, and that his own highest ambition in life—incessantly discussed—was to be promoted to the job of assistant divisional sales manager in some monstrous and wholly unintelligible organization called Amalgamated Tool and Die?

And on top of all that, as if that weren't enough, how could she ever have predicted that as a married man he would disappear for three and four days at a time and come home reeking of gin, with lipstick all over his shirt?

She divorced him three years after the birth of their only child, when she was nearly forty, and set out to become an artist of distinction. It was a confused, desperate, and ever-thwarted career played out against the background of the Great Depression, a hysterical Odyssey that she always said was made bearable only by the "wonderful companionship" of her darling little boy. On a slender alimony which was the very most George Prentice could spare, they

lived at first in Greenwich Village—always in "studio apartments"
that cost more than she could afford. Later, with the help of a man
she had every reason to believe was going to marry her, they moved
out to one of the better Westchester suburbs, "for Bobby's sake."
The man didn't marry her after all—he went back to the wife from
whom he'd never really been divorced—but they stayed on, renting
houses in one town after another, always in trouble with the landlord and the grocer and the coal dealer, never at ease among the
oppressively neat suburban families that surrounded them.

"We're different, Bobby," she would explain, but the explanation
was never necessary. Wherever they lived, he seemed always to be
the only new boy and the only poor boy, the only boy whose
home smelled of mildew and turpentine and cat droppings, with a
wobbling rack of canvases instead of a car in its garage; the only
boy who didn't have a father.

Yet he had loved her romantically, with an almost religious belief
in her gallantry and goodness. If the landlord and the grocer and the
coal dealer and George Prentice were all against her, they would
have to be *his* enemies too: He would serve as her ally and de-
fender against the crass and bullying materialism of the world. He
would gladly have thrown down his life for her in any number of
ways; the trouble was that other, less dramatic kinds of help were
needed. Her paintings were sometimes shown in group exhibitions
and very occasionally sold, for small sums, but these isolated tri-
umphs were all but lost under the mounting pressure of hardship.

"Look, Alice," George Prentice would say on the rare and
dreaded occasions of his visitation rights, plainly forcing his voice to
sound calm and reasonable. "Look: I know it's important to make
sacrifices for the boy—I agree with you there—but this just isn't
realistic. You simply have no business living in a place like this, running up all these bills. The point is, people have to live within their
means, Alice."

"All right. I'll give up painting, then. I'll never ask you for another
cent. I'll move to the *Bronx* and take some wretched little job in
a *department* store. Is that what you want?"

"No, of course that's not what I want. I'm simply asking for a
little cooperation, a little consideration—damn it, Alice, a little sense
of responsibility."

"Responsi*bility*! Oh, don't talk to me about responsibility. . . ."

"Alice, will you please try to keep your voice down? Before you wake the boy?"

Life in the suburbs came abruptly to an end in a welter of lawsuits for unpayable debts, when he was twelve, and they crept shabbily back to the city. And it was three years later, after a succession of increasingly cheap apartments from one of which they were evicted, that Alice Prentice made a final, desperate plea to her former husband. She would never be a burden on him again, she promised, if he would only finance Bobby's enrollment in what she called A Good New England Prep School.

"A *boarding* school? Alice, do you have any idea how much those places cost? Look—let's try to be reasonable. How do you think I'm going to be able to send him to college if I——"

"Oh, you know perfectly well the whole question of college is three years away. *Anything* can happen in three years. I could have a one-man show and make a *fortune* in three years. I could have a one-man show and make a fortune six *months* from now. Oh, I know you've never had any faith in me, but it happens that a great many other people do."

"Well, but Alice, look. Try to control yourself. In the first place——"

"Ha! Control myself. Con*trol* myself. . . ."

The school she chose was not exactly a good one, but it was the only one that offered to take him for half tuition; and the victory of his acceptance filled her with pride.

His first year there—the year of Pearl Harbor—was almost unalloyed in its misery. Missing his mother and ashamed of missing her, wholly out of place with his ineptness at sports, his cheap, mismatched clothes and his total lack of spending money, he felt he could survive only by becoming a minor campus clown. The second year was better—he gained a certain prestige as a campus eccentric and was even beginning to win recognition as a campus intellectual —but in the middle of that second year George Prentice dropped dead in his office.

It was a stunning event. Riding home on the train for the funeral, he couldn't get over the surprise of hearing his mother weep uncontrollably on the telephone. She had sounded as bereaved as a real widow, and he'd almost wanted to say, "What the hell, Mother —you mean we're supposed to *cry* when he dies?"

And he was appalled at her behavior in the funeral parlor. Moaning, she collapsed into the heaped flowers and planted a long and passionate kiss on the dead man's waxen face. Recorded organ music was droning somewhere in the background, and there was a long, solemn line of men from Amalgamated Tool and Die waiting to pay their respects (he had an awful suspicion that her histrionics were being conducted for *their* benefit). And although his first impulse was to get the hell out of there as fast as possible, he lingered at the coffin for a long time after the conclusion of her scene. He stared down into the plain, still face of George Prentice and tried to study every detail of it, to atone for all the times he had never quite looked the man in the eye. He dredged his memory for the slightest trace of real affection for this man (birthday presents? trips to the circus?), and for the faintest glimmer of a time when the man might have known anything but uneasiness and disappointment in the presence of his only child; but it was no use. Turning away from the corpse at last and taking her arm, he looked down at her weeping head with revulsion. It was *her* fault. She had robbed him of a father and robbed his father of a son, and now it was too late.

But he began to wonder, darkly, if it mightn't be his own fault too, even more than hers. He almost felt as if he had killed the man himself with his terrible, inhuman indifference all these years. All he wanted to do just then was to get away from this sobbing, shuddering old woman and go back to school, where he could think things out.

And his father's death brought another, more practical kind of loss: There was no more money. This was something he wasn't fully aware of until he came home the following summer, not long after he'd turned seventeen, to find her in a cheap hotel room for which the rent was already in arrears. She had put all her paintings and whatever was left of her furniture into storage, and the storage payments were in arrears too. For months, with a total lack of success, she had been trying to re-establish herself as a fashion illustrator after a twenty-year absence from the field. Even he could see how stiff and labored and hopelessly unsalable-looking her drawings were, though she explained that it was all a question of making the right contacts; and he'd been with her for less than a day before discovering that she didn't have enough to eat. She had been living for weeks on canned soup and hash.

"Look," he said, only dimly aware of sounding like the ghost of

George Prentice. "This isn't any way for you to live. Hell, *I'll* get some kind of a job."

And he went to work in an automobile-parts warehouse. On the strength of that, they moved into the furnished apartment in the West Fifties, and the "wonderful companionship" entered a strange new phase.

Feeling manly and pleasurably proletarian as he clumped home every night in his work clothes, he saw himself as the hero of some inspiring movie about the struggles of the poor. "Hell, I started out as a warehouseman," he would be able to say for the rest of his life. "Had to quit school and support my mother, after my dad died. Those were pretty tough times."

The trouble was that his mother refused to play her role in the movie. It couldn't be denied that he was supporting her—she often had to meet him outside the warehouse at noon on payday, in fact, in order to be able to buy her lunch—but nobody would ever have guessed it. He kept hoping to come home and find her acting the way he thought she ought to act: a humble widow, gratefully cooking meat and potatoes for her tired son, sitting down with her sewing basket as soon as she'd washed the dishes, darning his socks in the lamplight and perhaps looking up to inquire, shyly, if he wouldn't like to call up some nice girl.

And he was always disappointed. Night after night was given over to her talk about the contacts she was certain to establish soon in the fashion field, and about the fortunes still to be made out of one-man shows, if only she could afford to get her paintings out of storage, while the canned food burned on the stove.

Once, he found her posing for his admiration in a stylish new dress, for which she'd spent more than half the week's grocery money, and when he failed to be enthusiastic about it she explained, as if she were talking to a retarded child, that no one could possibly expect to get ahead in the fashion world wearing last year's clothes.

"Oh, yes. Bobby's fine," he heard her telling someone on the telephone, another time. "He's taken a summer job. Oh, just a little laboring job, in some dreadful warehouse—*you* know the kind of thing boys do in the summertime—but he seems to be enjoying it, and I think the experience will do him a world of good. . . ."

He had assumed, with mixed emotions, that he wouldn't be going back to school for his senior year, but when September came around she told him not to be ridiculous. He *had* to graduate; it would break her heart if he didn't.

"Well, but look: What're you going to do?"

"Dear, I've explained all that. Something's bound to happen soon with this fashion work; you know how hard I'm trying. And then just as *soon* as I can get my paintings out of storage, there's no telling what good things are going to come our way. Don't you see?"

"Well, sure, but I'm not talking about *soon*. I'm talking about *now*. How are you going to pay the rent? How the hell are you going to eat?"

"Oh, I'll always manage; that's not important. 'I'll *borrow* money if I have to. That's nothing to——"

"Who from? And anyway, you can't go on borrowing indefinitely, can you?"

She looked at him incredulously, slowly shaking her head with a world-weary smile, and then she said it: "You sound just like your father."

The argument went on for hours, in ever-rising spirals of unreasoning shrillness, until at last, after hearing one more time and at great length about the valuable contacts that were certain to be hers, he turned on her and said, "Oh, bullshit!"

And she burst into tears. Then, as if shot, she clutched at her heart and collapsed full-length on the floor, splitting an armpit seam of the dress that was supposed to be her means of advancement in the fashion world. She lay face down, quivering all over and making spastic little kicks with her feet, while he stood and watched.

This was a thing he'd often seen her do before. The first time, long ago, had taken place after the landlord in Larchmont had threatened to evict them, and after she'd called George Prentice to plead for the several hundred dollars they would need to settle the debt. "All right!" she had cried into the telephone. "All right! But I'm warning you, I'll kill myself tonight!" And, rising from the slammed-down phone, she had grabbed her breast and fallen to the carpet, and her little boy had tried to put both fists in his mouth to stifle his terror until she roused herself at last and took him, sobbing into her arms. It had happened so many times since then, in various crises, that he knew she wasn't really having a heart attack. All he had to do was wait until she began to feel foolish lying there; before long she turned over and pulled herself up into a tragic sitting position in the nearest chair, hiding her face in her hands.

"Oh, God," she said, with a convulsive shudder. "Oh, God. My *son* calls me 'Bull Shit.'"

"No, now wait a minute. Listen. I didn't *call* you—you don't *call* people—look, it's just an expression. Don't you see? I just said—— Look, I'm sorry. I didn't mean it. I'm sorry."

"Oh, oh, oh, God," she said, rocking from side to side in her chair. "My *son* calls me 'Bull Shit.'"

"No, look. Wait a minute. Please . . ."

In the end, a week before school started, she took a job—not the "wretched little job in a department store" she had so often threatened George Prentice with, but something more wretched even than that: She went to work in a factory that manufactured department-store mannequins.

And the surprising thing was that his senior year turned out to be a kind of success. Through whatever subtle social chemistry it is that turns school outcasts into offbeat school leaders, he became one; and not until the triumphant year was nearly over did he learn that his tuition had gone unpaid for a year and a half.

There were many telephone calls between his mother and the headmaster, during which she probably wept and pleaded and promised, and there were sober talks between the headmaster and himself ("It's a very difficult situation for all of us, Bob") until at last, on the very eve of Commencement Day, the headmaster explained tactfully and with some embarrassment that his diploma would have to be withheld until the debt was paid.

By that time his mother had been fired from the mannequin factory and had gone to work in a small, non-union defense plant that made precision lenses. She described it, to everyone she knew, as "war work."

A month later he was in the Army, with his mother listed as a Class-A Dependent; and now, sitting across from her in the ample cleanliness of Childs, he was letting her words flow past his hearing. With a grim, tender patience, he had begun to watch for the first signs of her drunkenness to show: the thickening and slurring of her speech, the tendency of her upper lip to loosen and bloat, the slowing clumsiness of her gesturing hands.

". . . And then suddenly," she was saying, coming to the climax of a long story about some people she'd recently met, "suddenly his eyes went very big and he said, 'You mean you're Alice Prentice? Alice Prentice the *painter?*'" She had always taken a child's delight in telling anecdotes that allowed her to speak her own name, and those that allowed her to add "the painter" were much the best. "And it turned out they'd been admirers of mine for years. So they asked me in for coffee and we had—oh, we just had the most wonderful time."

He knew he was supposed to join in her pleasure at this, but he abruptly decided he wasn't up to it tonight. "Oh yeah?" he said. "Well, that's interesting. Where'd they heard of you?" And he was fully aware that the question was cruel, but aware too that he had to ask it just that way.

"What? Oh——" Hurt feelings flickered in her face, but she recovered. "Oh, well; friends of theirs had bought a painting from one of my exhibitions years ago, or something of the kind. I don't remember exactly. Anyway, they——"

"Your exhibitions?" He couldn't let it go; he was bearing down on her like a prosecuting attorney. He knew damn well that for all her lifelong talk about one-man shows she'd never had one. (And did they really call it a "one-man show" when the painter was a woman? What kind of nonsense was that?) He knew too that the number of paintings she'd sold from group exhibitions could be counted on pitifully few fingers; most of her sales had been made through a gallery that in truth was primarily a gift shop—and even at that, they had nearly always been bought by friends, or by friends of friends.

"Well, I *think* they said an exhibition," she said impatiently. "It may have been a gallery sale; anyway, that's not important."

He conceded the point, but only to withdraw to a new line of attack: "And how did you say you'd met these people?"

"Through the *Stewarts*, dear; I explained all that."

"Oh, I see. And the Stewarts were probably friends of the other people too, the people who bought the painting. Right?"

"Well, I suppose so, yes. Yes, I suppose that must've been the way it happened." She fell silent for a little while, looking daunted, poking her fork around in the ruins of her chicken croquette. Then, bravely, her voice went to work again and brought the story around to what had apparently been its point from the start. "Anyway, they're awfully nice, and of course I've told them all about you. They're dying to meet you. I told them we might drop by tomorrow after church, if you feel like it. Would you mind doing that, dear? Just to please me? I know you'll like them, and they'll be so disappointed if we don't come."

It was the last thing in the world he wanted to do, but he said yes. And by implication he'd said yes to church, too, which he would also much rather have avoided. He was ready to say yes to anything she wanted now, to atone for the harshness of his questioning. Why had he grilled her like that? She was fifty-five years old and lonely and oppressed; why couldn't he let her have her illusions? That was what her wounded, half-drunken eyes had seemed to be saying throughout his interrogation: Why can't I have my illusions?

Because they're lies, he told her silently in his mind as he champed his jaws and swallowed the cheap food. Everything you say is a lie. You're not Alice Prentice the Painter and you never were, any more than I'm Robert Prentice the Prep-School Graduate. You're a liar and a fake, that's what you are.

He was shocked by the force of his own secret invective but he was carried helplessly along with it, holding his mouth shut tight and allowing his fingers to twist and tear at a raddled paper napkin in his lap.

You're Alice Grumbauer, his soundless voice went on. You're Alice Grumbauer from Plainville, Indiana, and you're ignorant and foolish in spite of all the phony "art" stuff you've been spouting all these years, while my poor slob of a father was breaking his back for us. And maybe he *was* "dull" and "insensitive" and all that, but I wish to God I'd had a chance to know him because, however much of a fool he was, I know damn well he didn't live by lies. And you do. Everything you live by is a lie, and do you want to know what the truth is?

He watched her with murderous distaste as she fumbled with her spoon. They had ordered ice cream, and some of it clung to her lips as she rolled a cold mouthful on her tongue.

Do you want to know what the truth is? The truth is that your fingernails are all broken and black because you're working as a laborer and God knows how we're ever going to get you out of that lens-grinding shop. The truth is that I'm a private in the infantry and I'm probably going to get my *head* blown off. The truth is, I don't really want to be sitting here at all, eating this damn ice cream and letting you talk yourself drunk while all my time runs out. The truth is, I wish I'd taken my pass to Lynchburg today and gone to a whorehouse. *That's* the truth.

But it wasn't, exactly. He knew it wasn't, even while taking deep breaths to fight back the words that wanted so urgently to burst from him. The real, the whole truth was something far more complicated. Because it couldn't be denied that he'd come to New York of his own free will, and even with a certain heartfelt eagerness. He had come for sanctuary in the very comfort of her "lies"—her groundless optimism, her insistent belief that a special providence would always shine on brave Alice Prentice and her Bobby, her conviction, held against all possible odds, that both of them were somehow unique and important and could never die. He had *wanted* to be with her tonight: He hadn't even minded her calling him her "big, wonderful soldier." And as for the whorehouse in Lynchburg, he knew deep down that he couldn't blame his mother for his own lack of guts.

"Isn't this good?" Alice Prentice said of her ice cream.

"M'm," said her son, and they finished their meal in silence.

On their way back to the apartment she kept swaying against him —her grip on his arm at each street crossing was a little spasm of panic—and as soon as they were upstairs she poured herself a hefty drink from the bottle of rye she had probably been working on all afternoon.

"Would you like a drink, dear?"

"No, thanks. I'm fine."

"Your bed's all made up, whenever you're ready. I'm so—tired"— she brushed a loose strand of hair away from her brow—"so tired I think I'll just go to bed now, if you don't mind. You're sure you don't mind?"

"No, of course not. You go ahead."

"All right. And tomorrow we'll have a lovely long Sunday together." She came up close, smelling of food and whisky, and raised her arms to give him a kiss. "*Oh*, it's so good to have you here." She clung to him for a moment, and then, swaying, steadying herself against the wall, she blundered into her bedroom and closed the door, which had to be closed several times before it clicked shut in its warped frame.

Strolling alone with his hands in his pockets, he went over to the black window and looked out. Far down the block, where the lights of a bar and grill spilled out across the sidewalk, a couple of soldiers were standing with their arms around a couple of girls. One of the girls was laughing, making high, suggestive little sounds that floated up the street. Then one of the soldiers shouted something that made them all join in her laughter, and they walked away and were lost in the darkness.

He loosened his collar and tie and sat heavily on his bed, which also served as the living-room couch and which exhaled a fine cloud of dust. From the cluttered coffee table he picked up the only thing in the room that looked expensive and new: his school yearbook. Leafing through its heavy, creamy pages, he found a pleasurable little shock in discovering one familiar face after another, slicked up and posing self-consciously for the school photographer, each looking very young and vulnerable compared to Army faces. And there were the autographs:

"Good luck in the service, Bob. It's been great knowing you.— Dave."

"Bob, I know you'll go far in whatever you do. I'll always value your friendship.—Ken."

By the time he'd finished with the yearbook it was hard to remember that he'd waked before dawn this morning to scrub his cartridge belt for inspection, jostled in the stinking latrine by men who told him to get the lead out. It was hard to remember his nine hours on the bus and the train, and he was only dimly and guiltily aware of the cruel, silent rage that had poisoned his dinner at Childs. The deep, slow, sibilant rhythm of his mother's snoring came from the bedroom now, and he listened to it with a feeling of great tenderness as he undressed and carefully arranged his uniform on a wire hanger. Getting into bed, he found that the sheets were surprisingly fresh and clean: He could picture her scurrying to the laundry with them during her lunch hour, in preparation for his coming—or possibly even going to Macy's and buying new ones.

Tomorrow she would wake him late and gently. They would have some kind of messy, inadequate breakfast together, and then they'd go to church. The Episcopal service, which she'd discovered only in the last few years, after a lifetime of paganism, would make her weep. He could hear her say, "I always cry in church, dear; I can't help it; I don't mean to embarrass you." And then, spiritually restored, they would take a subway or a bus somewhere to visit the people who were supposed to be dying to meet him—the people who'd said, "Alice Prentice the *painter*?" and who would probably turn out to be as mild and bewildered and pathetically pleasant as she herself.

The deadly realities would be there to reclaim them both soon enough, on Monday morning—the infantry and the lens-grinding shop—but in the meantime . . .

In the meantime he could drift off to sleep feeling privileged and safe, cradled in peace. He was home.

MAGAZINES CONSULTED

ANTIOCH REVIEW – 212 Xenia Avenue, Yellow Springs, Ohio 45387

ARARAT – Armenian General Benevolent Union of America, 250 Fifth Avenue, New York, N.Y. 10001

ARIZONA QUARTERLY – University of Arizona, Tucson, Ariz. 85721

ATLANTIC MONTHLY – 8 Arlington Street, Boston, Mass. 02116

AVE MARIA – National Catholic Weekly, Congregation of Holy Cross, Notre Dame, Ind. 46556

CARLETON MISCELLANY – Carleton College, Northfield, Minn. 55057

CAROLINA QUARTERLY – Box 1117, Chapel Hill, N.C. 27515

CHELSEA REVIEW – Box 242, Old Chelsea Station, New York, N.Y. 10011

CHICAGO REVIEW – University of Chicago, Chicago, Ill. 60637

COLORADO QUARTERLY – Hellums 118, University of Colorado, Boulder, Colo. 80304

COMMENTARY – 165 East 56th Street, New York, N.Y. 10022

CONTACT – Box 755, Sausalito, Calif. 94965

COSMOPOLITAN – 1775 Broadway, New York, N.Y. 10019

THE CRITIC – 180 N. Wabash Avenue, Chicago, Ill. 60601

DECEMBER – P. O. Box 274, Western Springs, Ill. 60558

THE DENVER QUARTERLY – Denver, Colo. 80210

ENCOUNTER – 25 Haymarket, London, S.W. 1, England

EPOCH – 159 Goldwin Smith Hall, Cornell University, Ithaca, N.Y. 14850

ESCAPADE – Division Street, Derby, Conn. 06418

ESPRIT – University of Scranton, Scranton, Pa. 18510

ESQUIRE – 488 Madison Avenue, New York, N.Y. 10022

EVERGREEN REVIEW – 64 University Place, New York, N.Y. 10003

FANTASY AND SCIENCE FICTION – 347 E. 53rd Street, New York, N.Y. 10022

FOR NOW – Box 375, Cathedral Station, New York, N.Y. 10025

FORUM – University of Houston, Houston, Tex. 77004

FOUR QUARTERS – La Salle College, Philadelphia, Pa. 19141

THE FREE LANCE – 6005 Grand Avenue, Cleveland, Ohio 44104

GENERATION, THE INTER-ARTS MAGAZINE – University of Michigan, 420 Maynard, Ann Arbor, Mich. 48103

GEORGIA REVIEW – University of Georgia, Athens, Ga. 30601

GOOD HOUSEKEEPING – 959 Eighth Avenue, New York, N.Y. 10019

HARPER'S BAZAAR – 572 Madison Avenue, New York, N.Y. 10022

HARPER'S MAGAZINE – 2 Park Avenue, New York, N.Y. 10016

HUDSON REVIEW – 65 E. 55th Street, New York, N.Y. 10022

IN PUT – 24 Olsen Street, Valley Stream, New York, N.Y. 11580

JOHNS HOPKINS MAGAZINE – Baltimore, Md. 21218

KENYON REVIEW – Kenyon College, Gambier, Ohio 43022

LADIES' HOME JOURNAL – 641 Lexington Avenue, New York, N.Y. 10022

THE LAUREL REVIEW – West Virginia Wesleyan College, Buckhannon, W. Va. 26201

THE LITERARY REVIEW – Fairleigh Dickinson University, Teaneck, N.J. 07666

MADEMOISELLE – 420 Lexington Avenue, New York, N.Y. 10022

THE MASSACHUSETTS REVIEW – University of Massachusetts, Amherst, Mass. 01003

MCCALL'S – 230 Park Avenue, New York, N.Y. 10017

MIDSTREAM – 515 Park Avenue, New York, N.Y. 10022

THE MINNESOTA REVIEW – Box 4068, University Station, Minneapolis, Minn. 55455

THE NEW MEXICO QUARTERLY – University of New Mexico Press, Marron Hall, Albuquerque, N. Mex. 87106

THE NEW YORKER – 25 W. 43rd Street, New York, N.Y. 10036

NIOBE – 202 Columbia Heights, Brooklyn Heights, New York, N.Y. 11201

THE PARIS REVIEW – 25–39, 171 Place, Flushing, N.Y. 11358

PARTISAN REVIEW – Rutgers University, New Brunswick, N.J. 08903

PERSPECTIVE – Washington University Post Office, St. Louis, Mo. 63105

PLAYBOY – 232 E. Ohio Street, Chicago, Ill. 60611

PHYLON – 223 Chestnut Street S.W., Atlanta, Georgia 30314

PRAIRIE SCHOONER – Andrews Hall, University of Nebraska, Lincoln, Nebr. 68508

PRIMIERE – P.O. Box 8008, Mobile, Ala. 36603

QUARTERLY REVIEW OF LITERATURE – Box 287, Bard College, Annandale-on-Hudson, N.Y. 12504

QUARTET – 346 Sylvia Street W., Lafayette, Ind. 47906

RAMPARTS – 1182 Chestnut Street, Menlo Park, Calif. 94027

REDBOOK – 230 Park Avenue, New York, N.Y. 10017

RED CLAY READER – 2221 Westminster Place, Charlotte, N.C. 28207

THE REPORTER – 660 Madison Avenue, New York, N.Y. 10021

SAN FRANCISCO REVIEW – Box 671, San Francisco, Calif. 94101

SATURDAY EVENING POST – 641 Lexington Avenue, New York, N.Y. 10022

SECOND COMING – Box 1776, Beverley Hills, Calif. 90213

SEQUOIA – Box 2167, Stanford University, Stanford, Calif. 94305

SEWANEE REVIEW – University of the South, Sewanee, Tenn. 37375

SHENANDOAH – Box 722, Lexington, Va. 24450

SOUND – P. O. Box 386, Everett, Wash. 98201

SOUTHERN REVIEW – Drawer D, University Station, Baton Rouge, La. 70803

SOUTHWEST REVIEW – Southern Methodist University Press, Dallas, Tex. 75222

STUDIES ON THE LEFT – 260 W. Broadway, New York, N.Y. 10013

TEXAS QUARTERLY – Box 7527, University of Texas, Austin, Tex. 78712

THOTH – Department of English, Syracuse University, Syracuse, N.Y. 13210

TRACE – P. O. Box 1068, Hollywood, Calif. 90028

TRANSATLANTIC REVIEW – Box 3348, Grand Central P.O., New York, N.Y. 10017

TRI-QUARTERLY – University Hall 101, Northwestern University, Evanston, Ill. 60201

THE UNIVERSITY REVIEW – University of Kansas City, 51 Street & Rockhill Road, Kansas City, Mo. 64110

VENTURE (for Junior High) – 910 Witherspoon Bldg., Philadelphia, Pa. 19107

VENTURES – Yale Graduate School, New Haven, Conn. 06520

THE VIRGINIA QUARTERLY REVIEW – University of Virginia, 1 West Range, Charlottesville, Va. 22903

VOGUE – 420 Lexington Avenue, New York, N.Y. 10017

WASHINGTON SQUARE REVIEW – New York University, 737 East Bldg., New York, N.Y. 10003

WESTERN HUMANITIES REVIEW – Bldg. 41, University of Utah, Salt Lake City, Utah 84112

WOMAN'S DAY – 67 West 44th Street, New York, N.Y. 10036

THE YALE REVIEW – 28 Hillhouse Avenue, New Haven, Conn. 06520

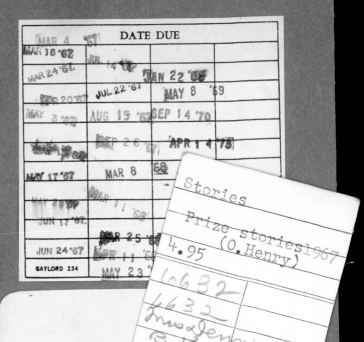